THE
BUTTON MAN

ALSO BY MARK PRYOR

The Bookseller

The Crypt Thief

The Blood Promise

A Hugo Marston Novel

THE
BUTTON MAN
MARK PRYOR

SEVENTH STREET BOOKS®

AN IMPRINT OF PROMETHEUS BOOKS

59 JOHN GLENN DRIVE • AMHERST, NY 14228

www.seventhstreetbooks.com

Published 2014 by Seventh Street Books®, an imprint of Prometheus Books

Cover image © Jim Richardson/Corbis
Cover design by Grace M. Conti-Zilsberger

The characters, organizations, companies, products, and events in this book are fictitious. Any similarities to real persons, living or dead, or organizations or companies, currently or previously existing, or existing product names is coincidental and is not intended by the author.

Inquiries should be addressed to
Seventh Street Books
59 John Glenn Drive
Amherst, New York 14228
VOICE: 716–691–0133
FAX: 716–691–0137
WWW.SEVENTHSTREETBOOKS.COM

18 17 16 15 14   5 4 3 2 1

Library of Congress Cataloging-in-Publication Data

Pryor, Mark, 1967–
    The button man : a Hugo Marston novel / Mark Pryor.
        pages cm.
    ISBN 978-1-61614-994-9 (paperback) — ISBN 978-1-61614-995-6 (ebook)
        1. Americans—France—Paris—Fiction. 2. Motion picture actors and actresses—Fiction. 3. Murder—Investigation—Fiction. I. Title.

PS3616.R976B88 2014
813'.6—dc23

2014012145

Printed in the United States of America

To Nicola,
with all my heart and love because every day you make me laugh,
every day you remind me to be silly, and because . . .
you're English, you are!

CHAPTER ONE

LONDON, ENGLAND, 2008

H ugo turned the corner onto Gable Street, the growl of London's
evening traffic fading away behind him. The winter sun had set
an hour ago and the damp evening settled itself comfortably over the city,
bringing with it one of London's famous fogs, a slow creeper that followed
Hugo from the Whitechapel station, stalking him every step of the way.

By the time he reached the entrance to the alleyway, at the south
end of Gable Street, the fog had swallowed up the first of the terraced
houses behind him. Hugo looked back at the remaining homes for
signs of life; a few windows glowed yellow behind tightly-drawn curtains, but that was all.

He stood at the mouth of the alley, the reason he was here, and
peered into its darkness. Under his feet the gray concrete of the sidewalk gave way to ancient cobblestones, worn smooth by the feet of
man and beast, now shiny with the damp of the evening. Overhead the
night sky was moonless, the stars already snuffed out by the gathering
mist. As Hugo peered into the alley, the blackness seeped across the
cobblestones toward him.

He raised his shoulders and shivered against a chill that was real, or
mostly real. Above his head, a gentle breeze rattled the branches of an

old oak tree that reached over from the cemetery next door, sending a soft shower of rain pattering onto his hat.

He put out a hand and brushed his fingers against the rough brick wall. It was damp and his fingertips came away grimy. Two hundred years of London soot, he thought, and Gable Street had changed very little in that time.

He'd read about this place but had never been here. He'd first heard about it from a colleague in the FBI's behavioral-profiling unit, a man almost as obsessed with unsolved murders as Hugo. And now he was here for the same reason he always visited a crime scene: to make contact with the victim and with the killer. He'd come at dusk on purpose, a time when the senses were keenest. He was no believer in the supernatural, but there had always been something about the death of a day, the hour of the rising of night, that tugged at the part of Hugo that connected most easily with those he hunted.

Or used to hunt. He didn't do that anymore, have cases. He'd solved his last just two days before quitting the bureau for the State Department and now, as head of security for the US Embassy in London, he had duties and responsibilities, employees, and high-level meetings with the CIA. But no cases.

A hundred-year-old murder in the grimy backstreets of London wouldn't be his anyway. A good thing, considering it was all but unsolvable. There was no evidence left, of course, nothing to tag and bag, even to see, so the only connection he could make was through those unnamed senses that fed information to the nerves and the mistier corners of the brain. Pretty much all Hugo could do, with no evidence and no jurisdiction, was stand in the dark alley with the fog slinking around him and hope that he could recreate the fear, generate and experience the creeping sense of menace that lived in darkest London, in the places like this, where evil deeds were committed and where time seemed unable to wipe them away.

He started into the alley, the cobbles hard and smooth beneath the soles of his cowboy boots. The light from Gable Street faded and he stopped to let his eyes adjust to the gloom. A soft, wet smell reached his nostrils: damp earth and something rotting. Vegetable, not animal.

To his right, a twenty-foot brick wall secured the perimeter of a former coal yard, a place now used mostly as a scrap heap for old cars. To his left, another high wall kept vagrants and ne'er-do-wells out of White-chapel Cemetery. He moved forward, his left hand deep in his coat pocket, fingers wrapped around a flashlight, not switched on because he didn't want to spoil the mood. Three-quarters of the way down the alley he stopped, took off his hat, and looked down. Here, on the right side of the alley, is where she'd been found, tucked in the lee of the wall, stretched out with her fingers toward Gable Street, her feet pointing toward the iron gates of the foundry that dead-ended the alley.

Nothing more than a drunk and a prostitute, she'd died in December 1905 at the hands of an unknown killer who, the police had insisted, was not Jack the Ripper. Her head had been sliced open, one or two hard blows crushing her skull, and her throat cut down to the spine. Half-naked and not wearing shoes, the police surgeon found no evidence that she had been sexually assaulted. She'd bled to death on the cobbles, found by a fellow prostitute who'd gone into the alley with a customer and come out in shock. The dead woman was Meg Prescott, her body identified by a woman who sometimes shared her tiny ground-floor room on Dorset Street—a stone's throw away and described by the *Daily Mail* at the time as "the worst street in London." There, the two women spent their days drinking to excess and entertaining men. Or, as the friend told police, they worked as "seamstresses," a polite fiction the police observed back then, at least until things got really nasty. Oddly, when police searched her house the night she was killed, police found the door unlocked and blood on Meg Prescott's bed.

Hugo knelt and put his right hand on the cold stones, finally bringing out the flashlight with the other. He switched it on, the light blanching out the cobbles, showing him nothing. Poor Meg, her death unavenged, her murder forgotten. Not even a part of the many Ripper tours that momentarily chilled the spirits of ghoulish visitors to London. He looked back the way he'd come, the way the killer had fled that winter night.

"I'd have caught you," he said quietly. "Jack or not."

He stood up and cast the light around him. A trickle of water from the afternoon's drizzle ran along the gutter and into a drain, but there was nothing else to see. As he looked down at Meg Prescott's final resting place, another chill settled around his shoulders and he shrugged it off before heading out back toward Gable Street, his foot-falls echoing gently in the narrow confines of the alley.

He turned right, walking alongside the low brick wall topped with iron railing that separated the street from the graveyard. Thirty yards along he reached the entranceway, a tall, double gate that someone had forgotten to close. He paused and put a hand on the cold iron but, as he started to pull it shut, he paused. He wasn't ready to dispel the macabre cloak he'd pulled on, nor to leave the spirit of Meg Prescott entirely. He checked his watch. Not yet six. Plenty of time until his rendezvous at the Coachman pub a mile away. He pushed the gate open and stepped inside. Ahead of him, the path curved away to the left, cutting diago-nally through the churchless cemetery whose gravestones tipped and tilted every way but upright, decades, centuries even, of shifting earth and soggy days, vandals that no graveyard custodian could keep out.

The cemetery was large for central London, the size and shape of a football field, but the closeness of the rising fog and the heavy chill shrank it down, making it more intimate and personal. Hugo paused for a moment. He rested one hand on a moss-covered headstone and noticed the lack of traffic, the absence of construction noise; standing here, London was silent. After a moment, he pressed on and followed the gravel path deeper through the uneven rows of markers, stopping occasionally to try and read the older ones, tracing his fingers over the soft, worn stones and the hard, disfiguring lichen. He was able to deci-pher first or last names, rarely both, and sometimes dates. No catchy epitaphs or sorrowful last words. Just a fading catalog of the dead, filed away in a quiet, tree-lined corner of London, perhaps waiting to be recycled when this patch of land became too valuable and when the descendants of those who lay here had given up all pretense of aftercare. Or, maybe, had left the ranks of the living themselves.

"A good night for ghosts," Hugo said aloud, smiling at an unexpected knot in his stomach. Despite his skepticism for ephemeral bodies, he had to concede that the wraiths of fog that drifted around him, obscuring the lights of the city and trapping the dark, made for a spectral scene of the first order. He stepped up the pace, returning to the path and making for the far side of the graveyard, where he assumed another gate would release him back into London's rush-hour traffic, and a little closer to the pub.

He crested a slight rise and saw the gates in front of him, twenty yards away and the twins of those that had let him in. He breathed a sigh of relief and tried to guess which major street would be closest, but stopped short when he saw a movement to his right.

He peered into the dark but saw nothing except the last rows of markers and, beyond them, a line of oak trees as old and twisted as the stones. The fog shifted as a slight breeze rattled the upper branches of the oaks, and he saw movement again, conspicuous not because of how much it moved, but because of the way it moved. A long, narrow object dangling in the middle branches, a gentle sway, back and forth.

Hugo dug his hands deeper into his coat pockets, feeling the reassuring weight of his flashlight. He moved forward, his jaw clenched. The wind rose again, and a few last leaves floated past his face as the branches above clattered more loudly. He lost sight of the object for a second, but as he drew nearer he heard the faint creak of a rope above him. He looked up, his gaze trapped by a silhouette that slowly rotated in front of him, a figure that swayed in the breeze. Like a kaleidoscope image, the black limbs of the oak sank into the background and the clear outline of a human form took shape, a human being hanging from a rope that looped around its neck.

He quick-drew his flashlight and the beam arrowed up, a weak light in the thick, pressing, cemetery dark. As he watched, the body rotated toward him and Hugo steeled himself to see the dead man's face, to see the sunken pits of his eyes and the sagging look that Death painted on all His victims. But as it turned toward him, the body remained faceless, the beam of Hugo's flashlight ending in a blank and empty pool where the face should have been. Hugo looked harder, not understanding what he was seeing until a momentary shift in the wind gave him a clearer view of the light-colored cloth covering the dead man's head.

CHAPTER TWO

Hugo removed his hat, an automatic display of respect. He looked around quickly, though not for anything or anyone in particular, then stepped closer to the dangling figure. For a split second he contemplated grabbing the legs, lifting the body high in case its owner wasn't yet dead, in case there was a chance that breath and life might yet be restored. He resisted the urge and instead pressed his fingers against bare skin by the ankle, and the cold skin told him that the artery he was looking for no longer pulsed. In truth, Hugo had known from the figure's stillness that Death had come and gone, His heart cold and without remorse, caring only that this empty shell, whoever it was, remained in His graveyard as lifeless as its other residents. The indignity of how this person had died would be addressed later, the sacred rites of the living imposed on this corpse by family and friends. For now, though, nothing could be disturbed, because for Hugo the only thing more sacred than death was a crime scene.

A fresh spatter of rain fell about him, and he started to worry about preserving evidence. His mind took him away from the macabre scene, switching off his emotional senses and firing up his physical ones, letting him rely on careful observation to detach him from the horror of a human being hanging from a tree and to put him into the protective zone in which he'd lived as an FBI agent. He looked around, eyes scanning the ground, not sure what to look for other than something that shouldn't be there. But the ground gave nothing away, dusted with dead leaves, littered with broken twigs and the occasional branch. He couldn't even see his own footprints in the damp earth, but he knew which way he'd come and moved slowly backward in that direction. He stopped ten yards away, took another look at the dangling figure, and pulled out his cell phone. Slowly and calmly, he identified himself to the emergency operator and explained what he'd found. As he spoke, the wind rose again, turning the body slowly and setting the limbs of the oak trees chattering with excitement.

He followed an elderly couple into the pub, holding the door for them as they wiped their feet on the mat outside. As he waited, a patient smile on his face, he looked into the room for the man who had brought him to London six months ago, Ambassador John Delaney Cooper. He saw him, perched at a small table beside the fireplace talking with the landlord, Al Grafton. The old publican knelt by the hearth, striking matches at scrunched-up balls of faintly damp newspaper, which he swore were harder to get going but burned hotter once lit. The room already glowed golden from its yellow lamps, and Hugo felt the warmth drift over to meet him.

The elderly woman finally finished wiping her feet and reached for her husband's arm, giving Hugo an apologetic smile and a nod of thanks. Inside the room they stopped again, this time to help each other out of their coats, but they stood to one side of the door, letting Hugo pass.

Hugo approached his boss. "Mr. Ambassador," he said, offering a hand.

"I've told you before, it's John," the seated man corrected. It was their routine; Cooper was "Mr. Ambassador" at the embassy, but insisted on "John" after hours. A willowy figure, Cooper had large, sad eyes and a drooping mustache to match, though his personality was far from forlorn. In fact, before they met, Hugo had been warned of a playboy diplomat, and there was no doubt that Ambassador Cooper had a penchant for life's pleasures. These included an ever-roving eye and frequent, late-night visits to the ambassadorial residence from a string of different ladies, providing endless gossip to his staff. Informal in dress and manner, his preference was for backstreet pubs over white-linen restaurants, and Hugo had found him more of a harmless epicurean than a cavalier libertine. Good company on cold nights like this.

"Beer?" Cooper asked.

"I'll get it. You need a refill?"

"You know I do. I have a tab running, stick 'em on that."

"Yes sir, Mr. Ambassador," Hugo smiled.

He dropped his hat and coat on the third chair at the table and headed for the bar. They came here once a week, sometimes more, for the booze, the food, and the two pretty barmaids. Cooper's generous tips had been instantly welcome, and the Americans were soon on first-name terms with Lucy and Jen. President George W. Bush was on the television behind the bar, near the end of his second presidency and looking tired, Hugo thought. Politics touched his own job often enough, and Hugo couldn't fathom the pressures heaped on the world's most powerful man.

"Hi, Hugo. The usual?" Jen asked, barely looking up.

"Please." Hugo looked around as he waited. Ambassador Cooper stretched back languidly in his seat, feet stretched toward the fire. Al, father to Lucy, had managed to get it going and the flames were devouring the last of the newspaper and kindling, crackling and popping the way a young fire should. The other fifteen or so tables were filling slowly, city types grabbing a quick pint before heading home and early diners who knew that the cottage pie would be gone by eight, maybe before. In the far corner of the room a man sat by himself, broad-shouldered and watchful, a newspaper and a glass of water on the table in front of him. Hugo caught his eye and nodded. The man nodded back, folded his newspaper, and stood. Hugo waited as he brought his glass to the bar.

"Sorry to keep you waiting, Bart," Hugo said to the man. "Got held up, I'll tell you about it tomorrow."

"No problem, sir."

"Stay and have a drink with us?"

"Not tonight, sir." Bart winked. "Getting a babysitter for Amy and taking a date to the theater."

"Get going, then." Hugo was delighted to hear that his colleague, and friend, was going on a date. Denum had been raising his daughter, Amy, alone since his wife had been killed in the same car crash that took Hugo's wife, Ellie. Since then, Denum had focused all his attention on his daughter, wrapping her in cotton wool and letting no other woman near him or his precious girl. Hugo smiled. "Glad to hear it. Have fun, and have her call me if she's upset about you being late.

"I will. Good night, sir."

"Good night." He turned to the bar as Jen appeared with the drinks.

"Here you go, luv," she said. "John's tab?"

"That's the one. Thanks."

Cooper sat up as Hugo arrived with the jugs of beer. He nodded toward the door that Bart had just closed behind him. "If I have to have a bodyguard everywhere I go, could you at least find one who'll sit and have a beer with me?"

"Sure," said Hugo, sitting opposite his boss and with his back to the wall. "Course, if I saw him do that I'd have to fire him."

"Not if I fired you first."

"True. So I need to tell you why I was late."

"Don't worry about it." Cooper held up a silencing hand. "You'll want to hear about a little task I have for you."

"Right, you said on the phone you had something new and interesting for me to do."

"Yes." Cooper stooped to his beer, taking the top inch off it with a practiced slurp. He sat back and wiped his mustache with the back of his hand. "Good stuff. A little high profile, this endeavor, which is why I want you on it. Personally."

Hugo raised an eyebrow. "Not sure I like the sound of that."

"Me neither, frankly. But I have a boss, too, and she's paying attention for once."

"OK." Hugo watched Cooper over the rim of his beer glass.

"That little accident that made the front pages," Cooper said.

"Accident?"

"Yes, the one involving Dayton Harper and his lovely wife."

"Ginny Ferro. What does that have to do with us?" The accident Cooper was talking about involved two of Hollywood's up-and-coming movie stars. Two days previously, while shooting a movie in Hertfordshire, they'd disappeared from the set in Harper's convertible Jag. The newspaper stories were sparse, but the headlines had screamed to the world that they'd run down a local farmer and sped away, leaving him to bleed to death in a ditch beside a winding country lane. An eyewitness and a damaged hood had led the police to Harper and Ferro, who quickly confessed and, from jail, threw themselves on the mercy of the British public.

"That's what I wondered," Cooper frowned. "Only it seems that our Dayton Harper was born as Dayton Horowitz, the son of a certain Jasper Horowitz."

"The guy who owns half of Texas, most of its oil, and almost all of its water rights."

"You know him?"

"Of him. As does everyone who grew up in Texas. And you either love him or hate him."

"Which is it for you?"

Hugo smiled into his pint. "No comment."

"Not that it matters. Jasper Horowitz is also a huge supporter of my boss's boss. Not that the secretary of state or the prez have put any pressure on me directly, of course."

"Oh, no, of course not. But if you know what's good for you, you'll pitch in and do your bit, right?"

"Right. Which is where you come in."

Hugo sat back and looked at his boss. "Wait. Don't tell me . . ."

"I'm afraid so. Harper is getting out of jail tomorrow morning, and I need you to look after him."

"For how long?"

"As long as it takes. Though I don't know what 'it' means in this situation." Cooper sipped his beer. "As you might know, and if you don't you'll soon learn, a large part of your job will be babysitting."

"That's fine, I don't mind."

"I appreciate that. A movie star could be interesting, if a little high maintenance."

"Better an actor than a politician," Hugo said with a smile.

"Oh, you'll get one of those sooner or later, don't you worry."

"I'll manage. So the tabloids have people pretty riled up about this accident, huh?"

"Putting it mildly." Cooper grimaced. "He's lucky they don't have the death penalty here."

"Maybe." A thought struck Hugo. "Doesn't he have bodyguards of his own? He can certainly afford them."

"Probably. But the last set didn't keep him out of trouble. And even if he does have them, and they manage to stick with him, the last thing we need is half a dozen freelance American bodyguards beating up outraged members of the British public." Cooper drained his glass and licked his lips. "He's a US citizen accused of a serious crime and in potential danger of vigilante justice. Movie star or otherwise, he deserves our protection."

"Fair enough." Hugo smiled to show there were no hard feelings. "But I'd be happier sticking close to his wife."

Cooper chuckled. "You and the rest of the male world." He cleared his throat and looked around the pub. "And that's where this gets a little delicate."

"How so?"

"She's already been released. This morning. Kind of an administrative cock-up, actually. Her bail was paid and she was supposed to be held until tomorrow, when she and her hubby would go home with us. With you."

"So what happened?"

"We're not too sure. That's the delicate part. Apparently some flunky looked at her paperwork, opened her cell door, and handed her a bus pass into London. No doubt she's hiding in a beauty salon or a coffee shop somewhere. Getting a good haircut, with any luck."

"I see," Hugo nodded. "And you don't want hubby to know she's on her own."

"Correct. If he finds out, his father finds out . . ."

"Your boss finds out."

Cooper shrugged. "That's the gist of it. Plus, the more people who know, the more likely the media find out. Talk about vigilante justice." He shuddered, then picked up his empty glass. "Still, that's tomorrow's business." He looked at this watch and then toward the bar. "Cottage pie should still be available. My treat."

Hugo stood and collected their glasses. "I'll order and get refills."

❈

The secret, Al had told them a few months back, was to use lamb, not mutton, and let it soak in red wine for a few hours. Warm red wine, apparently. And lots of garlic in the mashed potatoes that topped the stewy pie. "Thank the bloody Frogs for that tidbit," he'd laughed. Hugo did thank them, and Al, every time he ate this dish.

As they tucked in, Hugo said, "We may need to move off the beer and onto something stronger."

"Fine with me, but why?"

"I found a body in a cemetery." He started his story, skipping over his trip to the alley for the time being and telling Cooper about the graveyard next to it, his walk through the fog-shrouded path, and the body hanging at the end of a rope in the far oaks.

Cooper listened, his mouth opening wider with each detail. "Jesus. No wonder you were late. And here I was, all concerned with my own problems."

"I've seen that stuff before, John, it's OK."

"I suppose you have, but still." He shook his head. "So, who was he?"

"No idea. I left as soon as they let me, and I didn't see the crime-scene people find any identification. They left the hood in place, so they wouldn't disturb any forensic evidence."

"A hood, Jesus. You think suicide, or not?"

"Hard to say, but I doubt it." Hugo frowned. "The hood, the location . . . an unusual one if it is."

"What were you doing out there?"

"Well, the cemetery is near Gable Street." Hugo grinned sheepishly. Cooper knew about his little obsession.

"Hugo, I admire your investigative spirit. Really. But a hundred historians and amateur crime buffs have gone over every inch of every corpse in London from that period. If she was a Ripper victim, someone would be saying so. Someone other than you."

"You forget, I'm not an amateur."

"No, you're not. You're a stubborn son of a bitch." He speared a cube of lamb. "What was the one thing all known Ripper victims had in common?"

"You mean cuts to their abdomen."

"Your girl didn't have any."

"I know. And I know how badly the other victims were mutilated, while Meg Prescott wasn't."

"There you go."

"Jack might have been disturbed, run off by a passer-by."

"In a dead-end alley?" Cooper shook his head. "And what about the timing?"

"Almost seventeen years after the others, I know. But serial killers do go dormant, you know, they go to jail or get sick or go somewhere else. Or they control the urge, or maybe even evolve so they don't get caught, to the degree that their crimes aren't even discovered. They become masters of their art."

"It's art now, is it?"

Hugo smiled. "You know what I mean. It's possible that Meg Prescott was a late victim and that others killed in the years before her simply weren't found, or all that killing in 1888 had frightened him into inaction for a few years until he couldn't stop himself. Those are possible, John, you have to admit."

"You sound like a lawyer, Hugo. I'll admit those things are pos-

sible, and that you're the expert. They just don't seem very plausible."
He sipped his beer. "Look, I get it. It's an unsolved murder, which bugs
the crap out of you. But I don't get why this is so personal for you.
And Hugo, the fact is, you're on your own. There's not going to be any
new evidence to back up your position, and the existing evidence isn't
enough to prove you right."

"Or wrong." Hugo sat back and rested his hands on his stomach.
He'd run the pie off tomorrow, if it wasn't raining. "I know, you're right.
But let me keep hitting my head against that brick wall until it shakes
loose, won't you?"

Cooper held his hands up in surrender. "It's your head." Cooper
looked into his almost-empty glass. "As you said, time for something a
little stronger."

"Good idea," Hugo said. "My treat."

"Thanks. I'll have what you're having." Cooper's cell phone buzzed
on the table and, with a discreet burp, he picked it up and answered.
His eyes swung up to Hugo, who guessed the subject was Dayton
Harper. He listened for a full minute before speaking. "I see," Cooper
said. "Thank you for letting me know, Superintendent." He hung up
and looked at Hugo. "You'd better make those doubles."

"Oh yes? Something happen with Harper?"

"Not Harper, his wife."

"They found her?" Hugo asked.

"No," Cooper said. His eyes rested on Hugo for a moment.
"They didn't find her, Hugo, you did. Two hours ago, hanging in the
graveyard."

CHAPTER THREE

They moved Dayton Harper in the night, finding him awake and cowering on his bunk. His only knowledge of prison came from the silver screen, watching and a little acting, and he believed in the tales of crooked guards opening prison doors for blood-thirsty inmates, and had small faith in the reality of the heavy metal and thick glass that kept him in and others out.

They took him down the long, narrow corridor normally reserved for guards moving between the men's and women's sections of the Whitechapel jail. There, in a cell with the door open, he changed into civilian clothes before walking in lockstep with his guards to an elevator that took them down to the basement parking lot. One of the guards held the car door open for him, the other shook his hand, and Dayton Harper climbed into the back seat of the waiting, unmarked police car. Fifteen minutes later he was at the Hammersmith Police Station, taken in through the rear entrance and locked, for his own safety, in a cream-colored cell with a cup of tea and a packet of biscuits. He was not surprised, and was somehow comforted, by the curious eyes that peered in at him every few minutes. Comforted, especially, by the soft brown eyes that bore mascara and lingered a little longer than the others.

Just before ten in the morning he woke up to the sound of keys in the lock. A red-headed policeman, as large as any linebacker, stepped into the cell and handed him a brown paper bag. "Your things, sir. If you'd sign for them."

Harper took the clipboard and pen from the man and signed.

"Thank you, sir. Now, if you'd please follow me."

They left the cells and walked past several uniformed officers who stared, two of them women constables who shifted uneasily from foot to foot, trying not to smile at the movie star. At the back door, the large policeman stopped. They stood there for a moment and then his radio crackled, the word *Clear* being the only one Harper could understand. The constable unlocked the door and stood aside. "That black one's your car, sir. No media anywhere, and it stopped raining for you."

Harper stepped into the wet street and turned to shake the policeman's hand, but the door clicked shut in his face. He threw a look up at the sky, a solid gray that hung low over the city, and started toward the black SUV that idled by the curb. He smiled when he saw the Cadillac insignia. He went to the rear door, but before he could open it, the front window rolled down.

"Sit in the front, please," said the driver. "I'm your nanny, not your chauffeur."

Harper had been following orders like a conscripted private for two days and reacted automatically, pulling open the front passenger door and climbing in. The driver, a solidly-built, brown-haired man, looked at him. "How'd the Brits treat you?" the man asked.

"Fine. Fine, I guess." The man had the kind of face his wife and costar, Ginny, would go for. Strong jaw, intelligent brown eyes, and a fatherly quality that he, Harper, with his delicate features, would never possess. "Sorry, who are you?"

The man reached into his coat and pulled out a black wallet. He flipped it open and Harper inspected the bronze badge. "US Embassy security," he read aloud. "Are you arresting me now?"

"Nope. Like I said, I'm your au pair."

"Why do I need one of those?"

The man put the car into gear and started to pull away from the curb. "Do you drink?"

"What does that have to do with anything?"

"I'll explain why you need me when we get to the embassy. And, if you drink, you might want to start early today."

Harper looked out of the window. No city, he thought, ever looked so drab and depressing as London on a rainy day. Maybe because it had so many of them, day after day, year after year, that the color had just been washed from the buildings and its people. "You didn't tell me your name."

"Oh, right," said the man, looking over and smiling, though Harper couldn't tell if it was sincere. "Where are my manners? I'm Hugo Marston."

A light drizzle started the wipers of the Cadillac automatically as Hugo turned the car onto Upper Brook Street from Park Lane. He'd taken a roundabout route, partly for security reasons—but mostly because he wasn't entirely looking forward to sharing his apartment with a pampered movie star charged with vehicular homicide. Or whatever the British equivalent was.

Policy at the US Embassy in London, as he saw it, forced him to live on campus. He'd been given a three-bedroom apartment in the embassy complex, fully furnished by its previous occupant and partially refurnished by his wife, Christine. The chintz-to-leather ratio now tilted the wrong way, but Hugo hadn't said anything—challenge enough to get Christine to London in the first place. He hoped, vainly he suspected, that an emotional investment in delicate chairs and blown-glass vases would persuade her to use the place as more than a staging point for shopping expeditions. But with her family money and friends in Dallas, where she was now, his hopes weren't high.

Inside the compound, Hugo waved his passkey and waited as the grill slid up to allow them into the underground parking lot. Harper, as best Hugo could tell, was in a daze, registering events and sights with some delay. He'd asked a question about Hyde Park several minutes after they'd turned away from Park Lane, which bordered the green space. Now, the actor shook his head and looked over as Hugo pulled into his parking spot. "Is this the US Embassy?" he asked.

"Yep," Hugo said.

"We should go to my hotel," Harper protested mildly. "My stuff is all there. I have a room booked for the whole shoot."

"Not anymore." Hugo opened his door and climbed out. He bent down and looked at the blank face of the actor. "You're staying with me now. Your stuff is already here." He closed the door and waited for Harper to unbuckle himself and get out of the car. "Elevator's this way, follow me."

Harper trailed a few steps behind, clutching his paper bag to his chest. He looked at Hugo as the lift bumped them slowly up to the fourth floor. "Is Ginny here? She already got bail, right?"

"Yes," Hugo said. "She already got bail."

"She's here already?"

"No." Mercifully the lift stopped and the doors opened into the marbled foyer of Hugo's apartment. In front of them the enormous living room, bright even on dull days thanks to the ceiling-high, bullet-proof windows that overlooked Grosvenor Gardens.

"Nice place," Harper said, his voice distant.

"Thanks. Kitchen and my bedroom off to the left. Your room is off the living room, first door on the right. Shares a bathroom with the third bedroom, which I use as a study."

"Right. Thanks." Harper walked to the windows and looked out, then turned and put his paper bag on the coffee table that Christine had bought from an antiques shop in Camden. He walked to a pure-white armchair and turned to Hugo. "Where's Ginny?"

Hugo had done this before. Many times. Too many times. For a while it had gotten easier, but not any more, not now. It had been years since he'd looked someone in the eye and told them the worst news a person could hear. He poured a shot of brandy into a tumbler and walked over to Harper, putting the drink in his hand and steering him into the chair.

"There's no easy way to say this," Hugo began, his voice softening for the first time since they'd met. "I'm very sorry, but Ginny is dead."

"What?" Harper's eyes widened. "No, she's not. She can't be."

"I'm sorry, she is."

"But she was just . . . in jail, she was in protective custody, right? Like I was."

"Yes, she was but—"

"So nothing could happen to her, that's why . . ." His voice trailed off. "That's not right. It can't be."

"It didn't happen in jail," Hugo said gently. "It happened after she was released."

"Happened? What happened? Didn't she come here?"

"No. That was the plan, but . . ." Hugo spread his hands. "Someone screwed up. They just let her go without telling us."

Harper looked up at Hugo, his eyes wet, his face still showing confusion and disbelief. "What . . . what happened?"

Hugo sat in the chair opposite him. "We're not sure exactly, not yet. But she was found in a graveyard." Hugo took a deep breath. "She was hanging from a tree."

Harper's hand flew to his mouth, the brandy glass falling with a thunk onto the rug. "Oh no, no." He started to shake his head, eyes fixed on Hugo. "She did it . . . herself?"

"We don't know yet, but it's possible."

Harper rose to his feet and Hugo saw that his knees were shaking. The actor walked slowly to the large windows where streaks of rain blurred the view, and Hugo watched as Harper put his forehead against the glass. A moment later his shoulders started to shake, and he sank to his knees. He banged a weak fist against the window and then wrapped his arms around himself, mumbling his wife's name over and over. Hugo watched, helpless, as Harper rolled onto his side and curled himself into a ball on Christine's polished hardwood floor, his body wracked with the desperate sobs of a small child.

CHAPTER FOUR

The doctor had come and gone, and Hugo sat watching cricket highlights as a sedated Harper slept in the spare room. Occasionally Hugo flicked through the channels for a good movie, but there was something about the game of cricket that entertained him. The slow pace was hypnotic, like a ballet at half-speed, and he enjoyed the challenge of figuring out the rules without looking them up.

During the game's lunch break, Hugo channel surfed again, pausing on the national news when he heard a familiar name. A once-infamous murderer called Sean Bywater had been found dead in a halfway house in Liverpool. A burgeoning serial killer, Bywater had been caught after three murders, but his "signature"—carving his initials on the victim's back and his surgically clean use of a chisel to kill—had made it to the FBI training grounds at Quantico, Virginia, decades later. Hugo had himself tried to get access to Bywater to interview him, but the man had rebuffed every approach. Hugo hadn't been surprised because after the killer's sentence, he'd lapsed into silence, which he broke only a few times, mostly while stabbing other inmates.

At the time of his trial, Bywater had been the poster boy for the reinstatement of the death penalty: his crimes had been committed in 1965, just weeks after abolition. According to today's news account, and a little ironically, Hugo thought, just two weeks after being released he'd hanged himself in the halfway house, ill-health and forty years of institutionalization too much for even a serial killer to deal with. He'd left behind no money, no friends, no family, and not even a note; just the word *SORRY* chiseled into the wall of his tiny room. A nice touch, considering his former MO, Hugo thought. The newsreader concluded the story by noting that another infamous killer, the former model June Michelle Stanton, was due to be released in three days into the care of her twin sister and her daughter, who'd been just two years old at the time her mother was sentenced to forty years for killing a policeman during a botched robbery. He switched back to the cricket match before the news story ended—not the kind of thing Harper needed to be seeing, should he wake up and wander in.

An hour later, at two o'clock, Harper was still in his room when the phone rang. Hugo answered to hear the ambassador's voice.

"All safe and secure, Hugo?"

"Sleeping like a baby."

"Good. I would have called before, but you know how it is."

"No, but I'll take your word for it."

"Good enough." The ambassador chuckled. "What's he like?"

"He's like one of those wedding cake decorations, but with bright, blue eyes. About the same height, actually."

"Be nice Hugo. How did he take the news?"

"The way you'd expect a married man to react when you tell him his wife was found hanging from a tree."

"Poor bastard."

"Yes." Hugo cleared his throat. "So, without meaning to sound callous and just out of curiosity, how long do I have to babysit this poor guy?"

"I'm not sure. We're hoping for a quick resolution to his criminal case. But I'm sure you understand, Hugo, his wife's death has complicated things."

"Another investigation to get through."

"Right. And the media will go ape shit when they hear about her death."

"Have you thought about shipping him back to the United States for a while, then having him come back to face his charges?"

Ambassador Cooper hummed down the phone. "That may not be a bad idea, though the Brits would have to be persuaded."

"Isn't that what you do for a living?" Hugo smiled.

"So they tell me. In the meantime, you're having a visitor this afternoon."

"Oh?"

"Your local member of parliament. Or, more precisely, the MP for the Whitechapel area, where you found her body. Graham Stopford-Pendrith."

"What does he want?"

"He's former MI5, quite a big shot in the House of Commons. He's a lord, with the plummy accent, British Army mustache, and tweeds, but he prefers to operate as an elected official and not because his daddy gave him a title."

"Very noble."

"Yes. Anyway, he's been pro-America for a long time and could be helpful. So be nice to him."

"Sure, but I still don't understand," said Hugo. "Why exactly is he coming?"

"Because he wants to be seen doing something, investigating the death of that poor farmer and, when the news gets out, Ginny Ferro's death."

"Politics, in other words."

"You could put it that way, though I think his interest is genuine."

"Making nice with MPs, am I now doing your job for you, Mr. Ambassador?"

"I'll get the next shepherd's pie."

"That'll do, I suppose," Hugo said. "When he gets here I'll make him a nice cup of tea."

"I've known him for a couple of years. You might start with something stronger."

Hugo returned to the television and watched as a giant West Indian raced up to bowl at a man encased in protective padding. The ball dug into the ground and kicked up at the batsman's head, his arms and bat flying as he threw himself out of harm's way. Hugo waited for the batsman to charge the bowler and throw punches, but other than some gentle applause from the crowd, nothing happened. Hugo heard a noise behind him and turned.

"You got anything to eat?" Harper stood in the doorway to his bedroom, his famously perfect brown hair sticking up every which way, as if it were trying to escape not just its reputation, but Harper's head altogether.

"Sure. Cold pizza in the fridge. I think I've got eggs, bread, and cereal, if you prefer. Help yourself."

"Thanks." Harper walked through the living room and into the kitchen. After a few cupboard doors had slammed shut, he reappeared with a plate and two slices of pizza. He stood behind Hugo, looking at photos on a side table. "You married?"

"Yes."

"Where is she?"

"Dallas." Hugo put the television remote down, having settled on golf.

"Oh. She doesn't live with you?"

"Yes, she does. Some of the time."

"None of my business, huh? Fair enough." Harper moved from the table and sat down. He stretched his legs out and took a large bite of pizza, watching Hugo as he chewed. "I still can't believe this." He shook his head. "What happens now?"

"Well, we lay low while the Brits do a thorough investigation. Then whatever they turn up, we deal with it."

"Deal with it? Why can't we go back to America and deal with it from there?"

Hugo wasn't sure if he was serious, or if the sedative had screwed up his thinking. "You understand that you're still charged with a serious crime, right?"

Harper sat forward, his elbows on his knees, and ran a hand through his hair. His bright, blue eyes looked up at Hugo. "This is fucking crazy. It was an accident. A fucking farmer got in the way, by accident, and I accidentally hit him." He spread his hands wide. "Accident. A fucking accident."

"I don't think you get to decide that," said Hugo. "And his name was Quincy Drinker. Be nice if you could use that instead of calling him 'the farmer.'"

"It was a fucking accident," Harper repeated. "And then my wife commits suicide. My wife, goddammit! What the fuck else do they want from me?"

Hugo sat back. "Maybe an apology would be a good start."

"I did that already," Harper said. "About fifty fucking times. And I am sorry that farmer . . . Mr. Drinker is dead. Jesus. It's not like I'm a fucking serial killer or anything."

You show about as much remorse as one, Hugo thought. His wife's body barely cold and he's worried about his own neck. "There's an MP coming over in an hour or so. You should get cleaned up and put on your friendly, I-love-Brits face. You know," Hugo said, standing, "act nice. I hear you can act."

Harper stood, too, and his blue eyes flashed with passing indignation. "You 'hear' I can act? Funny." He patted his pocket. "It's a craft for me, you know. Right here I carry a notebook to write down little moments, thoughts, that I can use for my characters. Writers do it, but I don't know any other actor who does. Don't tell me you've never seen one of my movies."

"Sure, I've seen one. Something about a murder in Rome."

"*Seven Hills.*"

"Sounds right. I don't really remember your performance, sorry." Hugo smiled, unable to resist. "Now, the female lead, her I remember. Phenomenal."

"Yeah, she was good," Harper muttered. He sank back into the chair. "I met Ginny on the set of that movie. That Italian chick had the tits and ass, sure, but Ginny was class. Did you know she was born here, in England?"

"I didn't know that. And you're from Texas, my home state."

"Born in Utah, though my family is all from Texas. Ski trip for my father while my mom had me in the nearby hospital, somewhere outside Park City."

"When did Ginny move to the States?"

"When she was fifteen. Came from a good English family, well-bred, you know. She lost her accent, but never her class." He shook his head again. "The opposite to everyone else I ever met in Hollywood. All image. Nothing there; it's all about image."

"I can imagine," Hugo said dryly.

"No, you can't." Harper shook his head, earnest, as if explaining something truly important. "The prissy prima-donna actresses who spend their days ordering people to bring them purified water and organic grapes, then spend their nights snorting coke and chugging gin. There are directors, ones you would know, who hire a succession of pretty assistants, each one younger than the last, each one looking more and more frightened than the one before her. And those action heroes, flexing their muscles on screen for the ladies and then experimenting with their understudies when the lights go off."

"Gay leads? I thought we were past caring about that."

"You may be, but not the powerful people who rule my world, especially not for the male leads." Harper looked at Hugo with amusement. "You really think they'd hire a gay actor to play Spiderman or James Bond? No chance, because every time he kissed the girl the audience would be chuckling. Image is everything, absolutely everything. Know who makes more money in Hollywood than anyone else? The image consultants. You think politicians know how to spin things, you should see those guys at work."

"I had no idea," Hugo said truthfully.

"Those guys make millions," Harper said, with a rueful smile. "But then they're also the only ones in Hollywood who really work for their money. Trust me, it's all about the image."

"And you? I suppose you're a beacon of morality and goodness."

"Me? No. That's the thing. Everyone on the planet has something they don't want the world to know about. I'm no different." He gave Hugo a sharp look, then smiled. "And no, I'm not gay, if that's what you're wondering."

Hugo shrugged. "Wouldn't mind if you were."

"No. Me and Ginny, we're for real." Harper's voice fell off. "Were for real. Jesus, I can't believe she's gone."

"I know. I'm sorry." Hugo felt a twinge of guilt for needling him. Harper's self-absorbed behavior didn't justify Hugo's own insensitivity, and he needed to remember that even actors had feelings.

"Can I see her? I feel like it's not real, like I need to see her to believe it. And to say . . . good-bye."

"I don't know," Hugo said. "I honestly don't know, but I can ask."

Both men looked up as the phone rang. Hugo picked it up and nodded as the security guard told him that a Graham Stopford-Pendrith was there to see him.

"Sure," said Hugo. "He's early, but send him right up."

Hugo went to the television and turned it off.

"Who is it?" Harper asked.

"Our visitor."

"Who?" Harper stood, visibly nervous. "The police?"

"No. You're on US soil, remember. The cops aren't going to just come and take you away." Not yet, he wanted to say.

The elevator doors opened and a head appeared around the door, led by a red and pocked nose and the handlebar mustache Cooper had mentioned. "Hullo. Graham Stopford-Pendrith."

"Come in, my lord," Hugo said, moving forward and hoping he'd used the right form of address.

Stopford-Pendrith stepped through the door, a hand extended. "None of that 'lord' nonsense, old boy. I go by Pendrith."

"You're a lord? A real one?" Harper moved forward, hands working his hair back into place. "Dayton Harper, nice to meet you."

"Pleasure's all mine, old chap." Pendrith said, pumping his hand. "Never met a movie star before, jolly exciting."

"You've seen my movies?" Harper shot a sideways look at Hugo.

"Lord no, can't stand the cinema. Wait, I did see one, something about hoodlums in Chicago. You played . . ."

"Johnny Moretti. A button man."

"A what?" Pendrith asked.

"Low-ranking hood," Harper explained. "I was a Mafia soldier. Started off low down and worked my way up. Ended up sleeping with the boss's wife, which got me killed at the end."

"Right, if you say so. Generally don't watch movies, all that public chewing and sticky floors, it's downright uncivilized. Even so, a movie star. Marvelous." He finally let go of Harper's hand and moved over to Hugo. "Heard a lot about you, sir. Delighted."

The men shook hands and Hugo steered him to the couch. "Cup of tea?"

"I think something a little stronger to mark the occasion, eh what? What do you have?"

"A decent Macallan."

"Splendid." Pendrith turned back to Harper, and the smile on his face melted. "Good heavens, Harper, I am a fool. Please, accept my condolences. I am frightfully sorry, so caught up with meeting you that I . . . forgot myself. Terribly sorry, old boy. Suicide. Unimaginable." He shook his head slowly, then looked over at Hugo. "Just a couple of rocks, Marston, if you don't mind. Don't like to pollute the good stuff too much."

"Yes, sir," Hugo said. "Dayton?"

"No, thanks, I'm fine. Wait, you got any beer?"

"Fridge," Hugo said. Harper got up to help himself, and Hugo's hand hovered on the bottle, wondering whether he should. Might as well join the party, he thought.

Pendrith mumbled his thanks as Hugo handed him his drink. "Bloody rotten do," he said, shaking his head again. "How's he holding up?"

"Hard to tell," Hugo said truthfully. "People deal with this kind of thing differently."

"I gather you have some experience with the seamier side of life."

Hugo smiled. He couldn't help but enjoy the Brit's mastery of understatement. "Yeah, I've seen my share."

"More than, I'm sure," Pendrith said. He stood and held up his glass as Harper came back into the room with an open bottle of beer in his hand. "To your good lady, Mr. Harper. May she rest in peace."

It was actually quite touching, Hugo thought. Pendrith's obvious sincerity and Harper's surprise at the Englishman's words. He raised his glass.

"Right, shall we talk shop?" Pendrith said, settling himself back on the couch. Hugo sat in his chair, Harper to his left. "Bit of a horror what happened up in Hertfordshire," he went on.

"Yeah. I really am very sorry about what happened," Harper said, looking into his beer. "Sorry for Mr. Drinker and his family." He looked up at Pendrith. "But it was an accident."

"Yes, of course. No doubt. Thing is, the whole business of not stopping to help, not calling the police, not upping and taking responsibility." He compressed his lips. "Rather smacked of the movie-star arrogance, you see. People are a little bit riled up by the whole thing."

"That farmer—"

"That's the other thing," Pendrith interrupted. "It wasn't just some old farmer. Chap was the only son of a rather important landowner."

"Does that make a difference to anything?" asked Hugo.

"I'd like to say no, but honesty forbids. Fellow has pull and doesn't want this incident to go quietly into yonder night, so to speak."

"Meaning?" Hugo asked.

"That's rather what we need to hash out."

Harper looked over at Pendrith. "I want to go home," he said, his voice sharp. "I want to take Ginny and go home."

Hugo saw the pained look in Pendrith's eyes. "Yes, I'm sure you do, old boy. A few hurdles to that one, I'm afraid."

"Hurdles?" Harper looked between them. "What are you talking about?"

"Thing is, rather need you to stick around for a bit."

"What are you talking about?" Harper said again. "Why can't I just pay a big fine, get put on probation, and go home?"

"Well," Pendrith frowned at his scotch. "See now, there's been a bit of a spanner in the works."

"What the hell does that mean?" Harper said.

"Look," Pendrith began, "I'm not sure how to tell you this but you can't go anywhere for a while. Weeks, probably." He cleared his throat and looked up at Harper. "This is a murder investigation now."

"Murder?" said Hugo and Harper together.

"It was a fucking accident!" Harper was on his feet. "Fine, I was drunk, I admit it. Two beers, maybe three. Fuck it: four. But Jesus Christ, can't you people understand? It was a goddamn accident. Now you're saying I murdered that farmer?"

Pendrith was staring at Harper, eyes wide and unmoving. If Harper didn't get it, Hugo did, and he put a hand on Harper's sleeve, pulling him gently back into his seat. "No, he's not."

"Yeah, he is. He just fucking said it. Murder, for fuck's sake."

"No, Dayton. He's saying someone murdered your wife."

CHAPTER FIVE

Harper looked back and forth between them. The silence was broken by the phone ringing in the study, but Hugo ignored it.

"I thought you said suicide?" Harper said to Hugo. The actor wandered over to the large windows and stared into the gray world outside.

"I don't think anyone can be sure at this stage," Hugo said gently. He turned to Pendrith, who was recharging his glass. "Why are you saying murder?"

The Englishman looked at Harper and then back at Hugo, as if to say, should we do this in front of him? Hugo walked past the actor, sunk deep into his own world, and stood by Pendrith, who murmured, "Thing is, we're not sure. All a bit odd, but given everything together, the chaps at Scotland Yard think it best to pursue it as a murder."

"What things?" Hugo asked.

"Odd place to hang yourself, for one. Then the lack of note or any kind of message." Pendrith leaned forward, his voice a whisper. "And she had a hood over her face."

Hugo inclined his head. *So, I was right about that.*

"Silk. A bag. Bloody strange, if you ask me," Pendrith said. "The whole business." His mustache twitched with concern, only calmed by a steady draught of whisky.

So, I'm stuck with him for a while, Hugo thought, immediately chiding himself for being uncharitable. He looked at Harper, who stood staring into space, a megastar to millions but a hollow-eyed waif today, the superhero sucked into oblivion, leaving behind a fragile shell.

Harper caught him looking. "Am I going back to jail?" he asked.

"You're on American soil now, old chap," said Pendrith. "To be honest, I suggest you stay here." He furrowed his brow. "Why would you think you're going back to jail?"

"Aren't you accusing me of killing her?"

Hugo and Pendrith exchanged looks. "You were in jail when she died," Hugo said. "Do you know something about what happened?"

The blank look on Harper's face gave the answer long before the actor shook his head. "God no. Who would do this?" he mumbled. "Why?"

"And how, that's what I want to know," said Pendrith. "Doesn't seem very likely to me, frankly. Murder by hanging? Hardly likely."

Hugo silently agreed. He'd never seen it, and he'd seen more murders than any other cop or medical examiner he'd ever met. And, as one of the FBI's roving behavioral scientists, he'd been all over America to the most bizarre crimes scenes imaginable. No hangings, not one. "So what happens now?" he asked Pendrith.

"'Fraid I have to ask for his passport. Scotland Yard chappies wanted to come in here, meet the fellow, you know, do it themselves. Told them to keep their autograph books at home, I'll collect it and spare the poor fellow more harassment."

Hugo nodded. "Thanks." He'd known someone would come for Harper's passport and had kept it apart from his other belongings for that very reason. "They really think murder?"

They both turned as Harper got up and walked slowly past them toward the spare bedroom, his head down. When he reached the doorway he stopped and looked back at them. Hugo hadn't realized how pale the man looked, how the strong features had been borne down by the weight of events, aging him ten years. Harper ran a hand over his face and shook his head slowly. The ghost of a smile appeared.

"It's like a movie, isn't it?"

Then he went into his room and shut the door, not waiting for an answer.

"Poor bugger," Pendrith said, a finger stroking his mustache. "Listen, you going to be chaperoning him while he's here?"

"Looks like it," Hugo said with a grimace. "My boss thinks so, I guess that's what matters."

"Come now, he's Dayton Harper, a bloody movie star. Jolly exciting, I should say. Probably pop back for a visit or two myself, if it's all the same to you."

"Sure. Have him stay with you, if you like," Hugo offered hopefully.

"Love to, old thing, but like I said, best he stays on American soil. The mood's a little unpredictable right now."

"Whose mood? Public or the police?"

"Yes, well, insightful question, actually." He wrapped his fingers around his glass. "You asked before, whether they really think it's murder. I'm not sure they do."

"What are you saying?" Hugo loved England and the English, but had never felt that he understood them. It was as if they moved through life determined to keep their true motivations and thoughts hidden, revealed only when absolutely necessary, and maybe not even then. That was more true of the upper classes, people like Pendrith, brought up to believe that blunt honesty was a crude and unnecessary affront to civilized society. Every member of the ruling class had been raised to act like a spy; polite, friendly even, but with a hidden agenda you didn't discover until you'd been stripped, skewered, and roasted.

"Unlikely scenario for murder, as I said before," Pendrith was saying. "Did you know her sister was killed by a drunk driver?"

"Ginny Ferro's?"

"Yes. I gather the family went haywire after she was killed. Mum blamed Dad, Dad blamed Mum, and little Ginny caught in the middle. Or rather, left in the middle and ignored. Point is, family destroyed by the whole thing."

"You know a lot about the family dynamic," Hugo said, an eyebrow raised.

Pendrith smiled. "It's not only the FBI who do their homework, you know."

Ah, yes. Former MI5. "Fair enough," Hugo said. "So why tell Harper it's murder if you don't think it is?"

Pendrith looked surprised. "Better than suicide, isn't it?"

"Is it?"

"Buggered if I know."

Hugo put his glass down. "There's something you're not telling me."

"What makes you say that?"

"You're talking in circles. You're contradicting yourself, trying to figure out how I feel about . . . something."

"I am?"

"Yes. I'd be grateful if you'd tell me what's going on."

"No idea what you're talking about, old boy."

Which is why you won't look at me, Hugo thought. And then something else occurred to him. "Jesus, it's not me you're playing with, is it?"

Pendrith said nothing, but a smile shaded his lips.

"It's not me at all, is it?" Hugo repeated. "It's him. Suicide, then murder. No one does that."

"Does what, old boy?"

"Lets a man think that his wife committed suicide, and then tell him she was murdered."

"Not me who changed the schematics. Thank the coroner for that."

"No, Pendrith, when you got here you said 'suicide,' knowing full well it wasn't. Or might not be. You're MI5. You know what meaning those words carry and you don't use them unless you're sure. Or unless you're very unsure."

"Now who's talking in circles?" Pendrith turned back to his whisky.

"It's not a question of what you think happened, is it? It's a question of what he thinks happened. Why?"

"Cooper was right, you are a clever fellow." Pendrith shot a look at Harper's closed door. "Look. I don't know if she was murdered or committed suicide. But her death is as high-profile a tragedy as you get and if he knows something, anything, I'd like to find out. I'm not always as subtle as I should be, but then I was trained in this shit a few hundred years ago."

"Hey, I get it," Hugo said, holding up his hands. "You like to get your facts straight, I'm just not sure toying with a grieving man's head is the best way to go."

"Yes, well, like I said. A hundred years ago." Pendrith glanced up. "And I really do like the chap, admire him. His wife, too."

"Yes," Hugo smiled, "I did notice the crush you have on him."

"What?" Pendrith colored. "What absolute nonsense. Crush indeed, never heard such guff."

"Sure, OK." Hugo turned away to stop himself from laughing. A moment later, they both looked over as Harper's door opened. He stopped in the doorway and looked at them, and Hugo noticed that he'd changed clothes and brushed his hair into perfection. "You guys think we could get out of here? Feeling kind of cooped up."

"'Out of here' where?" Hugo asked.

"Wherever. Tour of London or something. I just need to be doing something, looking at something other than these walls." He smiled. "I'm not real good at sitting still, you'll find that out about me pretty quick."

"Well," Hugo said, "we need to stay on US soil, so we could take a stroll around the embassy grounds."

Harper gestured to the rain-streaked windows. "Yeah, sounds awesome. We can't take a drive around town?"

"No," said Hugo. "Not a good idea."

Pendrith cleared his throat. "Oh, come now, Marston. A wee drive in our fair city can't hurt. Maybe a spin through Chelsea, where I live. You have diplomatic plates on your car, yes?"

"Yes," Hugo said. The idea of an evening inside with a grieving and bipolar Harper was even less appealing than a rainy drive around London. But the embassy was a safe zone.

"Well then. And I'll come along, too, be your tour guide. No harm in that, eh?" Pendrith was talking to Harper now, and the actor held up two thumbs and disappeared into his room. Pendrith looked back at Hugo. "What? Oh, for heaven's sake, don't start that again. I'm just trying to help. International comity, and all that."

"Yes, of course," said Hugo, chewing back a smile. "You know, I have a pen and paper if you want to go ahead and get his autograph before we leave."

"Hush, man," Pendrith snorted, "you're being ridiculous."

Hugo drove the Cadillac with Pendrith sitting next to him; Harper had insisted on sitting in the back seat. "I move around a lot, want to see everything," he'd said. They drove in silence down Saint Audrey Street toward Piccadilly, shuffling along in the traffic, the only sounds the brush of the windshield wipers and the occasional, heavy tick of the car's turn signals. Hugo always wondered how the English stayed sane in this weather, the endless rain and drizzle and the sun setting before four o'clock in the depths of winter. Once he'd tried to shake the blues by using a tanning bed, like the Scandinavians do, but he spent the rest of that day catching whiffs of burned pork, so he didn't do that again.

A car honked at them as he swung onto Hertford Street, toward Park Lane and Hyde Park Corner, one of the thousands of undersized cars that in America would have been laughed off the road but that here, Hugo had to concede, were far more sensible than the hunk of metal he had to drive. He braked hard as the car hopped in front of them, red brake lights flashing. Sensible, but crushable, he couldn't help thinking.

"Bloody fool," Pendrith muttered. "There's no one in front of him, why's he braking?"

Hugo felt a cold hand clutch his stomach as the doors to the little car swung open. He checked the rear view mirror but a flat-nosed van was inches from his bumper, giving him no room to reverse. He looked back at the two men, now out of the car, both wearing long overcoats and hats.

"Get down, both of you," he snapped, pulling his embassy-issue pistol. A patter of rain blurred the windshield, but Hugo saw a black object in the right hand of one of the men, the car's passenger. Hugo's mind screamed *Gun!* and his whole body tensed as the man raised it up.

Hugo reached for the door latch and threw the door open, instinctively hitting the button to lower the window to clear his view. In two seconds he was crouching behind the open door shouting at the men to stand still, his eyes blinking away the rain. A bright flash, then another from the passenger, and immediately Hugo knew he'd made a mistake. He swore under his breath and quickly tucked the gun back into his shoulder holster.

"Is that Dayton Harper in the car?" the car's driver said. "Have him step out. We're the press. We just have a few questions."

"You're blocking traffic," Hugo said.

"And you're waving a gun in a public place, arsehole," the photographer snapped.

"Shut up, Gary, he's just doing his job," the driver said. He held up both hands, the peacemaker. "I'm Phil Larson, *Daily Express*. You his bodyguard?"

"Nice to meet you, Phil," Hugo said. "Sorry we can't stay and chat."

"So when did he get out of jail?"

"Call our press office, they'll answer all your questions."

"Whose press office? And no they won't, mate. You know that. If I want information the last place I go is someone's bloody press office. Come on, do me a favor, give me something. Where are you taking him?"

"What makes you think he's in the car?"

"A tip and some surveillance."

"Tip from whom?" Hugo didn't much care, but he wanted to keep the reporter and photographer where they were until he figured a way out of this. A horn sounded from behind the Cadillac and the photographer shifted on his feet.

"Can't say, you know that," Larson said.

"Course not," said Hugo. "But no harm in asking. Look, why don't you leave me your card, and we can talk later."

"Now's better." Larson's tone was polite, gentle even, but he wasn't budging. To Hugo's left, the photographer started forward, apparently tired of the civility, intent on doing his job whether Hugo liked it or not. As he approached the passenger side of the car, Pendrith stepped out.

The photographer stopped and looked at Larson, the sight of an MP in the company of an American security officer and a recently released movie star too much to take in. But not for long. His camera leapt to his face and Hugo heard the shutter whirring, the *click-click* as Pendrith was captured for the public, standing beside a shiny black Cadillac.

Another door opened behind Hugo, and he looked over his shoulder to see Harper slipping out of the car. Hugo turned back to Larson, exasperated that the situation was going in completely the wrong direction.

In front of Hugo, the photographer let his camera fall to his side and Larson started forward, pointing. Hugo swiveled to see the rear passenger door still open and no sign of Harper.

Pendrith strode to the back of the car and received a chorus of honks from frustrated drivers, and his calls to Harper were lost in the din. Hugo ran to join him and was immediately flanked by the journalists.

"What the hell's going on?" Larson turned to Hugo. "He just ran off. Dayton Harper just ran off."

"No shit." Hugo was already on his way back to the driver's seat, closing Harper's door and shouting at Pendrith to get in. Hugo glanced at his mirrors, looking for a tiny break in traffic. When he didn't see one, he squealed into a U-turn anyway, clipping the reporter's rear bumper and setting off an angry chorus from the cars on the other side of Hertford Street. He ignored them, eyes scanning for Harper. "What the hell is he playing at?"

"There!" Pendrith pointed through the windshield, and Hugo saw him jogging thirty yards ahead, apparently trying to keep a moving van between him and them. Harper turned and looked over his shoulder, hair flat and face glistening in the drizzle, and he quickened his step. Hugo feathered the steering wheel and whisked the car past a cyclist.

"Careful man, these are my constituents," Pendrith said.

"Feel free to get out any time you like," Hugo replied. "I'll take full responsibility. In the meantime, hold on tight." He yanked the wheel to the right and the tires squealed as he followed Harper onto Down Street.

"I say, stop!" Pendrith grabbed the dash. "Lord, man, this is a one-way street."

Hugo clenched his teeth. "I'm only going one way." He hit the horn to let Harper know he wasn't giving up and to push the oncoming Mini over the curb and onto the narrow sidewalk. "When I get my hands on that little shit . . ." *If I get my hands on him*, he thought. *If I don't, Cooper will be the one doing the throttling.*

Harper was thirty yards ahead still, the iron railings that fronted the redbrick homes keeping him from jinking left or right. Hugo looked forward and saw trees the other side of a main road. "What's ahead?"

"That's Piccadilly. And Green Park is the other side of it."

"A park? Shit."

They were right behind Harper now, Hugo could see his hair flopping as he ran. Ten yards from the intersection with Piccadilly, Hugo slowed, then stamped on the brake as a blue truck loomed on the right. But Harper barely paused, flitting between the back of the truck and a pair of motorcyclists who swerved in unison to miss him. He hopped the metal barrier that divided the road, and Hugo and Pendrith could do nothing but watch as he jogged across the street and disappeared into the trees.

CHAPTER SIX

The Cadillac swept along Constitution Hill, the rolling grounds of Buckingham Palace Gardens visible through the trees on their right. But the beauty of the carefully tended green space went ignored as Pendrith and Hugo stared into the gloom for a glimpse of Dayton Harper.

As they drew near the marble Victoria Memorial, Hugo swung into a gentle U-turn to head back the way they'd come. As he straightened up, they passed a policeman on a bicycle flagging down a red Mini for the exact same maneuver. Hugo had forgotten U-turns were illegal in England. He looked over at Pendrith and grimaced, then watched with concern as the Englishman pulled out his phone.

"Who are you calling?" Hugo asked.

"You're not going to like it, but I think we need to get the police involved." Pendrith held up a hand, "It's not ideal, I know, but what else can we do?"

"Wait just a minute." Hugo swerved to the side of the road and stopped. He stared at Pendrith. "About twenty seconds after you call the cops, the press will know that Dayton Harper, movie icon and farmer-killer, is wandering the streets of London. Every human being north of the equator will be out looking for him, and what do you think they'll do when they find him?"

"I have no idea, old boy. Not been in this situation before."

"Me neither, but a mob has three options: kill him, hide him, or turn him over to the authorities. You willing to gamble on them picking number three?"

"And your suggestion," Pendrith said quietly, "would be to drive around London until we find him? How long do you think it'll be before someone out there spots him and recognizes him?"

"That's the truth." Hugo sank back into his seat. "We need to find him in the next hour. After that we'll call in the cavalry."

"Agreed." Pendrith rubbed his chin. "Those bloody reporters."

Hugo had momentarily forgotten the reason Harper was able to run off—the journalists, who had witnessed firsthand Harper's flight. "Let's find them first."

"Drop me off where we last saw them," Pendrith said. "I'll tackle those buggers while you look for Harper. If I don't find them, I have some sway with their boss. Maybe I can hold the story up for a little while."

"Good. Write your phone number down, and take mine." Hugo rattled off his number as he pulled back into traffic. "I'll start with the assumption he's headed somewhere familiar. Maybe his hotel."

"I believe he took rooms at the Ritz."

"That's right," said Hugo. "But how did you know that?"

"Homework, old boy," Pendrith said with a slight smile. "Always do your homework."

❋

Hugo drove slowly along Piccadilly, scanning the rain-soaked sidewalk for Harper, touching his brakes every now and again as pedestrians ducked across the road in front of him, scurrying toward the raised islands of safety between the waves of smog-chugging cars and buses. The blank faces of those on foot matched the featureless sky, and Hugo wondered briefly if the sun would ever shine again. Rain in Texas was a respite, a welcome and occasional relief from the ever-present threat of drought, a threat realized virtually every summer as the plains and hill country surrounding Austin baked, day after day, under a merciless sun.

But not here. In England, especially in London, it seemed as though a heavy sky and constant drizzle were part of the scenery, landmarks as permanent and gray as Parliament or Saint Paul's Cathedral. He longed to escape, just for a weekend, and was convinced that his normally positive mood—his optimistic view of the world, even—had been slowly but surely worn down, eroded away by the relentless drizzle and perpetually overcast skies.

Soon the Ritz London Hotel loomed to his left, and not for the first time Hugo wondered why one of London's most famous hotels had been built to resemble a French chateau. Not that he minded: the intricate stone architecture of Paris had always been more appealing to him than London's mishmash of occasional beauty wedged alongside postwar mediocrity.

He pulled to the curb just before reaching a marked bus stop, hoping that his car wouldn't be crushed or towed. As he climbed out, a white-gloved and uniformed employee swept toward him.

"Are you a guest, sir? I'm afraid the authorities don't allow cars . . ."

Hugo pointed to the diplomatic plates on the front of the Cadillac and brushed past him with a smile. He didn't like to abuse the privilege, but this was an emergency.

He trotted up the steps and nodded his thanks at the old man holding the door open for him. Three guests were waiting for service at the reception desk so he headed straight for the concierge, where two smartly dressed employees, a man and a woman, stood looking at computer screens and talking quietly.

"Yes, sir," said the young man. He had tired, hungover eyes and a wedge of black hair thick with gel. A gold name tag identified him as Caleb. His female colleague was rail thin and very pale, with large, almond-shaped green eyes that spoke of Asian heritage, currently ringed with black eyeliner. Thick black hair was tied up and pulled behind her head. A Goth in her spare time? Hugo wondered. If so, she was a Goth named Merlyn, according to her tag.

Hugo looked around to buy himself some time. He realized he hadn't planned what to say, how to figure out whether Harper had been here, without causing a stir. He looked back at the expectant faces and smiled.

"I work for the United States Embassy," he said, slipping his credentials from his pocket and displaying them discreetly on the counter. "I'd like to know if Dayton Harper has a room here still."

"Dayton Harper?" Caleb said. He swapped looks with his colleague. "He's not been here for days. A week. I thought he was in some kind of trouble."

"You could say that," Hugo smiled. "I just need to know whether he has a room here still."

Caleb glanced at Hugo's badge and then his computer. "I don't think I'm supposed to . . ."

"I understand," Hugo said. "Celebrities and all, you need to respect their privacy."

"Yes, sir, that's exactly it," Caleb said, clearly relieved.

"Which is why it would be much easier for you to tell me whether or not he has a room still, you know, to save the four armed policemen waiting outside from striding through here and accosting your supervisor."

"Armed . . . ?"

The English weren't used to guns, Hugo knew, even in the hands of law enforcement, so the prospect of putting his boss in the firing line had rattled the kid.

"On the other hand," Hugo said gently, "a simple yes or no could save everyone a lot of trouble, don't you think?"

"He checked out two days ago," Merlyn said, looking up from her computer. "Says here his reservation for the next two weeks was canceled, as well."

Hugo nodded. "That's all I needed to know, thanks." He started to go, then turned back. "Wait. Does it say who checked him out and canceled the reservation?"

Merlyn looked down at the computer. "No, sorry." She looked at him for a moment as she spoke, and Hugo had a feeling that he'd not quite asked the right question.

Hugo thanked them again and started back across the reception area, deep in thought and impervious to the glistening finery around him. In truth, he'd never much liked these luxurious hotels. Not only were they ludicrously expensive, but he'd always felt there to be an odd dynamic between most staff and customers, the former trying to impress with the poshness of the premises, the latter eager to show they were wealthy enough to belong. These kinds of hotels were havens for snobbery and inverse snobbery, and Hugo imagined both guests and employees walking around with their noses so high in the air the luxury around them was sniffed but not seen.

"Excuse me, sir?" The voice behind him was low but firm and he turned to see Merlyn trailing behind him.

"Yes?" he said.

She inclined her head and he followed her toward the exit, stopping beside a marble column, as if she wasn't supposed to be talking to him.

"Can you tell me if he's OK?" she said.

"Harper?" A Goth and a groupie, Hugo thought. Great.

"He's a nice guy and what happened," she shrugged and looked away. "Seems like people are being extra hard on him because he's so famous."

"Do you know him?" Hugo asked.

"A little." She looked up at him. "That's why I stopped you. If you're from the embassy, you're here to help him, right?"

"Yes, that's right."

"OK. Well, I don't know what's going on with him or anything else, but he does have a room. He and his wife."

"So he didn't check out?"

"Oh, he did. Or someone did. From here."

"Meaning?"

"Meaning he has a room at another hotel. A couple of streets away. He and his wife use it as a getaway I guess. They seem really nice and in love, so I suppose they want to be able to sneak away without anyone finding out."

"How do you know this?" Hugo asked.

She hesitated, but not for long. "I work at that hotel, too. A six-hour shift here, then one there. It's decent money and I need it."

Hugo felt his pulse quicken. "What's the name of the hotel?"

"The Cork Hotel. Not even a mile from here, on Cork Street."

"Never heard of it."

"It's a boutique hotel," she said. "Used to be a pub and has a butcher's shop next door. Has fifteen rooms, and a reputation for being quiet and discreet."

"What do you mean 'discreet'?"

She had given him that lingering look again and now she winked. "Thick walls."

"OK, thanks."

She nodded. "You are . . . you really are trying to help him, aren't you?"

"Yes," Hugo said. "I really am. Which is why I need to get over there right now."

Merlyn looked over her shoulder, then back at Hugo. "Wait here, I won't be a sec."

"I have to—"

"You won't get anywhere over there without me," she called over her shoulder as she strode toward Caleb. "Discreet, remember?"

"Right," Hugo muttered. "Discreet."

She followed him out to the car and climbed into the front seat.

"So you didn't make fun of my name," she said.

"I didn't know I was supposed to."

"You're about the first person who didn't."

He looked over as he buckled up. "I assume there's a story behind it. Your dad was a wizard?"

"I was born Hailey," she said. "When I was ten my parents had a baby boy and called him Merlyn. I think they were high when they named him, and probably when they conceived him. Anyway, he died when he was five. I changed my name so he'd always be around."

"I'm sorry to hear he died, but that's very sweet of you."

"I used to hate the name. Made fun of my parents for giving it to him. But now, every time I hear it, I smile." She shrugged and touched the wood dash of the car. "Anyway, nice wheels. You Yanks always get the biggest and best, huh?"

Hugo suppressed a smile. "Where to?" he asked.

"Cork Street is one-way, so probably best to go down Albemarle Street and around." She pointed. "That one."

Hugo checked the mirrors and pulled out, the tires under the heavy vehicle screeching on the damp road as he accelerated across the intersection into Albemarle Street.

"Go all the way to the end, then follow the road to the right into Old Bond Street."

Hugo grunted, his eyes scanning the sidewalk for careless pedestrians as he zipped along the narrow road, scanning also for Harper. Just in case. He fought the car around a tight corner bringing them into Old Bond Street, slowing as he caught sight of a small, slim figure closing the door of a red phone booth, swearing under his breath when he saw the man was older and bald. Merlyn pointed and he turned left into Burlington Gardens for one short block, then left again onto Cork Street.

"There's an alley on the right," she said. "Park in there. It's a dead end so it won't matter if you block it." Hugo looked over and a smile twitched on her face. "You probably have diplomatic plates, don't you?"

"I probably do," Hugo said, slowing and easing into a side street that was barely wider than his car. "This good?" he asked.

"Yep. We can go in through the service entrance."

Out of the car, they walked twenty yards farther down the alley, then Merlyn stopped at a pair of innocuous, green metal doors. A waist-high trash can next to them tinged the air with the odor of rotting food, wearing its circular lid at a jaunty angle like a drunkard unable to hang onto his cap. She waved a keycard over a pad on the wall and the right-hand door clicked. She tugged it open and they walked into what Hugo saw was a storage bay, its tile floor damp from a recent mopping. Crates of fruit and vegetables lined the walls, and ahead a curtain of thick plastic strips hung between them and what he assumed was the kitchen.

"Follow me," Merlyn said. She pushed her way through the plastic curtain and strode past two men in white smocks, a tubby older man with white hair, and a scrawny kid who looked more like an apprentice than a chef. Hugo was right about it being a kitchen, a compact one, with an eight-burner stove to his right, several refrigerators and a sink on the left wall. "Hey guys, don't mind us," she said with a wave.

The two men gave Hugo barely a glance before going back to work, the chef chopping and his helper dropping dirty pans into a tank-sized sink brimming with bubbles.

They passed from the kitchen into a narrow hallway, the tiles replaced by flagstones, the walls beside him white stone. They paused at an archway; to their left, a reception area continued the stone motif. He could see several arches, all adorned with tortured angels or grotesque demons. It reminded Hugo of a church crypt or the cellar in an old monastery. He half expected to see spider webs on the ceilings and rats scuttling across the flagstone floor, but the place was immaculate and the ornate wooden reception desk, almost black, so perhaps teak, looked sturdy and new.

"Hang on, I'll get a key," Merlyn said.

Hugo waited by the archway and watched as Merlyn walked over to the reception desk, looking around as if she were surprised to see it unattended. She circled the end of the desk and typed something into a computer. Then she took a blank key card and swiped it through a machine, punched a couple more buttons on the computer, and started out from behind the desk.

She stopped in her tracks and Hugo heard a woman's voice, deep and scratchy.

"Hey hun, what are you doing here so early?"

A short, round woman with tight red curls waddled into view, bumping Merlyn out of the way with a playful hip as she rounded the reception counter. She waved a stack of cash at her employee and winked before stashing it below the counter. Merlyn shot Hugo a look and turned the key card over and over in her hands.

"Hi Rose, what's up?"

Rose stopped in front of the computer and frowned, then looked at Merlyn. Then she saw Hugo and looked back and forth between the two. "Everything OK, hun?" she asked.

"Sure," Merlyn said. "Dandy."

"So who's the gentleman? Checking in?"

Hugo stepped forward and gave Merlyn a look. Once again, the choice of lying or being up front.

"My name is Hugo Marston," he said. "Merlyn is helping me with a matter that is both urgent and sensitive."

"Oh yes?" Rose lifted an eyebrow. She turned to Merlyn. "What is so urgent and sensitive in my hotel that I can't be told?"

"Rose, it's OK, trust me," Merlyn said.

"Trust you about what, missy? If that's one of my keys, I need to know what's going on." She put her hands on her hips, and Hugo saw they were at an impasse.

"One of your guests is in a lot of trouble," he said.

"Meaning?"

"Meaning we need to find him," Hugo said. "And fast."

"Who?"

Hugo looked at Merlyn and realized he was seeking confirmation about the trustworthiness of a stranger from an almost-stranger. But when Merlyn nodded for him to go ahead, he knew he had little choice.

"Dayton Harper."

"Well, now I know you're lying," Rose said. "He's in jail."

"No, he's not," Hugo said. "He was released today to my custody and he's disappeared."

"You lost him?" Rose smiled slightly. "And who might you be?"

"I work for the US State Department."

Rose turned to Merlyn. "And how do you know him, my dear?"

"He came into the Ritz looking for Mr. Harper," Merlyn said.

"And you believed every word he said, I suppose?"

Hugo reached for his badge and stepped forward. "She did. And you should, too. As I said, I'm Hugo Marston and I'm looking for

Dayton Harper. Merlyn told me he had a room here. I need to know if he's been back."

"Why?" Rose asked, unmoving. The eyebrow went up again. "National security, I suppose?"

"Not really," Hugo said. He put away his badge and looked her in the eye. "But his security is very much in question."

"Like I said, I heard he was in jail."

"And like I said, he's not."

"Then he's probably at a spa or holed up with that hot little wife of his."

"No," said Hugo, deciding to take a risk. He'd wasted enough time and needed to find Harper above all else. "His wife is dead, and I plan to make sure he doesn't end up the same way."

"Dead?" Doubt swept across the woman's face and she shifted nearer to the cash register as her eyes flicked over to Merlyn. Hugo looked at her, too, and saw that the blood had drained from her face, her pale lips mouthing a silent question: Dead?

When Hugo glanced back at Rose, she was eyeing the stairs. Harper clearly had a room here, still, but why did she move away from him to the register like that?

"Where did you get that cash?" Hugo asked.

"None of your business," she bristled. But again, the flick of the eyes toward the stairs.

Hugo started forward, eyes now on Merlyn. "You have his key and room number?"

"Yes," she said, doubt in her voice for the first time. "Rose, we should—"

"He's here," said Hugo. "Now. Let's go, hurry."

Rose sailed out from behind the counter, blocking their way up the stairs. "No you don't, you have no right."

Hugo, a foot taller and just as broad, put a firm hand on her shoulder and shunted her to the side. "We can talk about rights later."

He started up the wooden stairs, taking them two at a time. He glanced over his shoulder and saw Merlyn ignore Rose's glare and follow him. The staircase curved up and to the right, breaking at a landing before continuing to curl up to the second floor. Hugo paused to let Merlyn catch up and show him the way. She ghosted past him and looked quickly left and right, down each corridor where Hugo could see doors recessed into more stone.

"This way." She headed to the left and Hugo followed, suddenly aware of the sound of his feet on the wooden floor. Cowboy boots scored high on comfort but less high for stealth, something he'd not needed to worry about for several years. Merlyn slowed and nodded toward a door. Harper's room. She handed him the key and stepped back. Instinctively he pressed his elbow to his side, feeling the reassuring weight of his holster and SIG Sauer P229. He had no plans to use it but, like the long, slow breaths he took to calm himself before breaching a door, a reminder that he had a weapon calmed him in the final seconds before action.

He stepped close to the door and listened for two, three, four seconds. No sound. He moved the card toward the electronic lock but froze at a sound behind him, at the far end of the other corridor. He looked back and saw a heavy metal door swinging shut.

"Where does that door go?" His voice was low, urgent. And before Merlyn answered, he saw the small, rectangular signs, like Hansel and Gretel's cookie crumbs.

Exit signs to the fire escape.

"That's him." Hugo pressed the room key into her hand. "Stay here."

Hugo sprinted down the hallway, not caring about the noise. He passed several rooms, the doors set back under stone archways. *He must have heard us coming and been lurking in one of the doorways.*

Hugo hit the door at a full run, his ears ringing as it crashed into the wall as it flew open. He took the steps two and three at a time, touching the wall and metal rail to keep himself upright, slipping once as his boots lost traction. As he righted himself, he heard the bang of another door below.

He was there in less than ten seconds, barging through and finding himself in an alley, the mirror image of the one he'd left his car in. He looked right toward the dead end and saw no movement, then left to Cork Street, but saw only the flitter of traffic as cars passed the end of the narrow alley in the fading day, their headlights casting explosions of light on the wall as they went by.

Hugo ran toward Cork Street, anger and disappointment mixing in his chest and he fought to stay focused. At the entrance to the alleyway he stopped again and looked up and down the street. Small stores lined both sides to the left and right, and he saw just three pedestrians, none of whom was Harper.

Why the hell was he running? And to where?

Hugo pulled out his cell phone and dialed Pendrith's number. The Englishman answered on the second ring.

"Pendrith here."

"This is Marston. I found him but he's back on the run."

"Where?"

"Cork Street, he was staying at a hotel here."

"I thought he was at the Ritz?"

"He was. He got a second room so I came to check it out, to see if he was here. He was, but he heard me coming and split."

"The little bugger. Does he think this is a movie or something?"

"No idea what he thinks," said Hugo honestly. "But we have to catch up with him, or at least figure out where he's going."

"I'm on my way."

"What about the media?"

Pendrith laughed. "Don't worry about them. There's no greater keeper of England's moral code than a tabloid reporter, until he commits a moral indiscretion of his own. Then he becomes quite the secret keeper. For now, anyway."

"OK, good work," said Hugo. "I'm going to check out Harper's room; he came back here for a reason and I don't think he was carrying anything when he hightailed it. Maybe he left something behind that will help us find him."

"Wait for me, will you old chap? You're a little out of your jurisdiction."

"Maybe," said Hugo with a smile, before closing his phone.

He started along Cork Street to the front of the hotel, pulling up in surprise as a police car nosed into the curb by the entrance, its blue light flashing. Two uniformed constables strode into the hotel, pulling caps onto their heads as they went. Hugo moved forward, cautiously now, but the hotel's front door had closed behind the officers so he couldn't see in. He assumed Rose had called them, and the last thing he wanted was a manhunt for him launched by London police.

He pushed the wood-and-glass door open and stepped into the lobby. Merlyn sat morosely on the stairs, and Rose was gesticulating angrily as she shouted at her and the officers. They all turned and looked at Hugo as he closed the door behind him and moved farther into the room.

"That's him," Rose said, a quivering finger pointing at Hugo. "Be careful, he's got a gun."

CHAPTER SEVEN

The policemen moved away from Rose and toward Hugo, approaching him from each side, encircling him as best they could.

"Sir, keep your hands where I can see them." The cop on the right had three stripes on his arm and moved like a cat, cold gray eyes on Hugo.

"I'm US Embassy security," Hugo said. "I have a weapon and a permit for it." He stood still and slowly raised his arms away from his body to show he was no threat. The policemen didn't slow, used to stories from suspects, trusting only their procedures and training.

The sergeant stopped just over an arm's length from Hugo. "Where are your credentials, sir?"

"Inside my coat pocket. Right side."

"Please take them out with your fingertips. Slowly, please, sir."

Always with the politeness, Hugo thought, and wanted to say. But he did as the man asked, letting his wallet fall open as he drew it out. As the sergeant took it, the other officer casually reached in and slipped Hugo's gun from its holster, then stepped away, his eyes still on Hugo, waiting for instructions from his superior officer. Hugo was impressed and guessed that both men had been in the military. They had that calm confidence about them, an efficient way of moving, and coolness that said, "This is nothing, pal, and you pose no threat at all."

Hugo heard the door behind him open, and a rush of cool air

rustled his jacket. He wanted to look around but didn't dare move. He relaxed, though, when he heard the familiar voice of Pendrith.

"What the bloody hell is going on here? Leave this man alone."

Pendrith carried with him an air of authority and, being a member of parliament, of vague familiarity. Enough to make the uniformed officers hesitate for a second.

"Sir? May I ask who you—" started the policeman holding Hugo's gun.

"Lord Stopford-Pendrith?" The sergeant spoke, and for the first time Hugo saw uncertainty on his face. "Sir, do you know this American?"

"I do, and we're working together. We need to search one of the rooms here and we need to do it now."

"Not likely," said Rose, advancing on the men. "This is my hotel and I'm not about to let some nosey Yank wave his gun around and bully me and my guests. They expect privacy and discretion when they come here, and unless a judge tells me otherwise, that's what they will get."

"Do you have a warrant, sir?" the sergeant said.

"No," said Hugo, "we have exigent circumstances. The room we need to search belongs to a man who may be in serious danger. He's missing and if we don't find him soon, he may be worse than missing." Hugo knew that in the United States, cops could do what the hell they liked if they could show "exigent circumstances," but he had no idea if the same rule applied here or not. Judging by the glances they were shooting each other, the cops weren't sure either—or weren't sure whether American exigent circumstances qualified.

Pendrith caught Hugo's eye and winked, then took charge. "Sergeant, do you know what the actor Dayton Harper looks like?"

"Yes," said the sergeant. "Yes, of course. Isn't he in jail?"

"No, he's not," said Pendrith. "He's on the loose and very close to here. I'd like you and your colleague to hop back in your car and look for him. Ever widening circles, with this hotel as the fulcrum. He was here ten minutes ago and is on foot."

"He's in danger?" asked the sergeant. "You want me to call it in, get a bunch of squad cars here?"

"No. For his own safety, we need this kept quiet. And I do mean quiet, I would consider it a personal favor, Sergeant . . ."

"Axelrod, sir. David Axelrod." The officer nodded toward his companion. "Constable Miles Standish. We'll get right on it, sir. And don't worry about discretion—this doesn't go beyond us."

"Thank you." Pendrith was scribbling in a notepad he'd pulled from his jacket pocket. He ripped the page out and handed it to Axelrod. "My cell number. Call every ten minutes, and sooner if you find him."

"Very good. You want us to watch him or detain him, sir?"

Hugo spoke up. "If he's somewhere you can watch, and be sure he's not getting away, do that." Hugo looked at Pendrith. "I want to know what he's up to."

"Me too," said Pendrith. He turned to the policemen. "Right, chaps, get to it. And you can rest assured your cooperation will be noted."

The officers both nodded and headed for the door. When they'd gone, Hugo turned to Merlyn. "Got the key?"

"What key?" Rose said, still fuming. "You can chase that nice young man all over London for all I care, but you damn well leave my hotel alone."

Hugo was about to give her a tongue lashing when Pendrith spoke up. "Certainly, madam, please forgive our intrusion."

Hugo couldn't believe his ears and turned to stare at the Englishman, who gave the barest of nods. The two moved toward the door and, behind them, Rose started in on Merlyn.

"As for you, you can get the hell out of my hotel, too. Sneaking around like a little spy, how dare you? And give me that damn key back, right now."

They were at the door, and Pendrith put a hand on Hugo's shoulder to stop him. The Englishman turned and spoke, his voice strong enough to freeze Rose in her tracks.

"Be sure to keep that key available for the authorities," he said. "I imagine they will be here within thirty minutes or so."

"Who will be here?" Rose frowned, unsure if she was being tricked again. "Don't you be threatening me, just because you're a politician."

"Not at all, my good lady. I'm sure you have nothing to fear from an environmental-health team, no matter how thorough they are." Pendrith rubbed his chin. "Of course, they may ask you to evacuate the hotel for a day or two. Depends on the type of hazard they are looking for. But that gives us plenty of time to get the search warrant that you keep insisting we get."

"You wouldn't . . ." Rose began, but stopped. Her face told Hugo she'd realized that he probably would. Her shoulders sagged and she shook her head. "Fine, go ahead. Search his room, what do I care? He's long gone, and by the looks of you two, he won't be coming back."

Hugo didn't wait for her to change her mind, striding past her and taking the key card from Merlyn's outstretched hand. He heard Pendrith on the wooden stairs behind him and kept going until he reached the door to Harper's room, where he turned to see Pendrith panting slightly.

"Ready?"

"Yes," Pendrith said. "But why do I get the feeling we need a crime-scene team with us?"

"Let's hope not. But be careful what you touch, just in case. The way things have gone so far, I'd rather be safe than sorry."

"In which case we should wait for a crime-scene unit and a search warrant."

Hugo smiled. "Not *that* safe." He looked over Pendrith's shoulder and saw Merlyn and Rose standing at the top of the stairs, watching. "Ladies, please stay out here. I don't want your fingerprints getting on what might turn out to be evidence."

Hugo slid the card into the reader and watched as the little light changed from red to green with a soft *click*. He pushed the door open and stepped inside.

The room was smaller than he'd expected, sparingly furnished in the style of the hotel. The bed was a four-poster in dark wood with a silk canopy. It sat on a heavy cream carpet that covered the whole floor. The walls were unadorned, an off-white stone that was almost yellow, and thick beams crossed the ceiling. A pair of wrought-iron sconces were bolted to the beams, adding to the gothic look, though Hugo noted that they held energy-efficient bulbs. A stone archway with an engraved keystone capped an iron-studded wooden door that, Hugo assumed, led to the bathroom.

He took in as much as he could before walking into the room, noting that the bed was made and the room was tidy, but definitely occupied. A pair of shoes sat neatly under the main window opposite him, and from where he stood he could see that the open closet to his left was filled with clothes, mostly black. Men's and women's, as far as he could tell without touching anything.

He moved farther into the room and, in the far corner, he saw a small desk and a laptop computer. He stepped toward it as Pendrith spoke behind him.

"I'll check the bathroom, make sure there are no bodies in the tub." Hugo knew the Englishman was joking, but if there were bodies in there, Pendrith was welcome to find them.

Hugo slid the lever on the front edge of the laptop, but it wouldn't open. He applied a little more force and managed to get it open but frowned when he saw the keypad. It had been beaten with a blunt instrument, and when Hugo looked down to his left he saw the murder weapon, a retro-style phone, black, heavy, and very broken. An empty can of Coke lay on the desk beside the computer and, by brushing his fingers over the brutalized keypad, Hugo could tell it had been emptied over the laptop. *Beaten and drowned*, he thought. Hugo tipped the computer back and saw that the hard drive was still in place. That was the thing about computers. If you didn't know anything about them, how they worked or what information they stored, they'd get you every time. If Harper had been trying to destroy evidence of a crime, or some other secret, he'd managed only a temporary destruction. Hugo was pretty sure a forensic computer scientist would laugh at broken keys and a sticky motherboard.

On the other hand, Hugo was no computer scientist and had hoped to find something that would locate Harper now, so even a temporary hurdle like this was a victory for the man on the lam.

"Got something?" Pendrith asked, looking over his shoulder.

"Busted computer," Hugo said. "Fixable but no use to us right now."

"He didn't take the hard drive out?"

"Apparently doesn't know much about computers."

"Even so, the Coke seems to have done the trick. What a bugger."

"Anything in the bathroom?"

"Nothing that tells me where our runaway is headed."

They separated and started searching the bedroom, Hugo stooping to look under the bed, where he spotted a suitcase. He reached under and pulled it out, then heaved it onto the bed and flipped up the lid.

The case was light and now Hugo saw why. It was empty except for half a dozen silk scarves, all black. Besides those, the suitcase contained just one large, clear plastic bag and a roll of Saran Wrap.

"What do you make of this?" Hugo said to Pendrith, who had emptied out the closet and stood there frowning at a pile of clothes on the floor.

"What do you have there, old boy?" He walked over and stood by the bed, looking into the case. "A magician's kit?"

"I don't see any doves or a white rabbit, do you?" Hugo said dryly.

"No," Pendrith guffawed. "But our man Harper is pretty good at the old disappearing trick."

Hugo nodded, committed the items in the case to memory, and closed the lid. As he did, a small rectangle of paper fluttered out of the lining and landed on the bedspread.

"What's that, a business card?" asked Pendrith.

"Looks like it." Hugo picked up the card by the edges and inspected both sides. All it contained was, on one side, the words *Braxton* and *Weston*, and a phone number. The type was heavy and the card itself flimsy. A cheap business card with little information, but it was all they had. Hugo pulled out his cell phone and dialed the main number to the security offices at the embassy. The phone was answered by one of the duty officers, Jeremy Sylestine. Hugo asked him to run the names and phone number and see what came up.

"It's not a working number, sir, and never was from what I can see.

The prefix is for . . . Hertfordshire. And in Hertfordshire, I'm showing a Braxton Hall, in the village of Weston. That what you're looking for?"

"No idea," Hugo said. He turned to Pendrith. "Weston village, in Hertfordshire, ever heard of it?"

"Yes, as a matter of fact, I know it quite well," Pendrith said. "They have a couple of first-class pheasant shoots up there; I go two or three times a year. More if I can. What's the specific address?"

"Braxton Hall. No street number, or even street name apparently. Just a postal code."

"Don't know it," Pendrith frowned.

Hugo thanked Sylestine and closed his phone. "Great, a vague address and no information about the people who live there."

"Call the number," Pendrith suggested.

"And say what? That a movie star is on the run in London and we found your card in his suitcase, can you please tell us what is going on?"

"You have a better suggestion?"

"Maybe." Hugo thought for a moment. "Hertfordshire. Isn't that where he was filming a movie?"

"Yes," said Pendrith. "But I can't imagine it was in Weston. Or any-where around there."

Hugo sat in one of the armchairs and flipped open his cell phone again. "Well, we're at a dead end so I need to let my boss know what's going on."

"The ambassador?"

"Yes."

"Be happy to make the call for you, old chap, I'm guessing he won't be too happy, and I'd be glad to soften the blow."

Hugo shook his head and dialed the ambassador's secretary. He'd screwed up by letting Harper run off, and he was perfectly willing to tell his boss that. As long as Ambassador Cooper let him fix the problem, that was all Hugo wanted. As the phone rang, Pendrith started for the door.

"I'm going to talk to the lady of the house, see if she can be a little more helpful." He eyed the phone in Hugo's hand. "Give the old boy my regards. And good luck."

They set off almost immediately, heading north along Holloway Road and making for the A1, which would take them due north out of London and into Hertfordshire. Pendrith assured Hugo that with light traffic, they would be there in an hour, maybe less. They made good time out of central London, spearheading the first wave of rush hour, leading the charge of Jags, Porsches, and Mercs of those who didn't need permission to leave work early and did so every day to make it to their country homes in the counties surrounding the capital. Not for them the cramped or overpriced London flats, not for them swallowing the fumes of the buses and the flaccid sedans of the middle classes.

As they cleared the last stop-and-go traffic in northern London and hit the A1 proper, Hugo drifted into the left lane to let a speeding taxi go by. That's fine, he thought, let the fast cars exercise their muscles and sweep the road ahead for hungry cops. He tucked the Cadillac four car lengths behind a Range Rover that'd had its right blinker on for two miles already, set the cruise control at seventy miles per hour, and watched his mirrors out of habit rather than necessity. Once he thought he saw a car he recognized, but not being able to place it, he put it down to healthy paranoia.

One thing Hugo did like about England was the suddenness with which its cities seemed to end. One minute you would be neck deep in traffic, crawling past kebab shops and pet stores, and the next minute the road would start to flex and bend, sweeping you through the greenest of countryside. It was as if these ancient English towns and cities had dug themselves into the land over the centuries, too afraid or respectful of the countryside to spread their grimy fingers into the fields and woods.

And so, twenty minutes after turning the Cadillac's key in the heart of London, Hugo and Pendrith found themselves flying through the countryside, the concrete and glass of the boroughs replaced by freshly plowed fields of brown knitted together by the winding strands of green hedgerow that divided up the landscape around them.

As they passed Welwyn Garden City, Hugo gave Pendrith instructions on how to program the car's GPS, and soon they were on automatic pilot. Hugo signaled to exit on the northern end of Stevenage,
but Pendrith tutted at the GPS and told Hugo to take the Letchworth
exit.

"I shoot pheasants up this way, remember? Know the route better
than that bloody instrument."

Two minutes after leaving the highway, Hugo turned left up
Lannock Hill, the kind of narrow, steep, and hedge-lined road that
explained England's smaller cars. The Cadillac roared with irritation,
and Hugo clenched the wheel, hoping no other vehicle would crest
the hill and start down toward him. Other than the lumbering tractors
and once-a-day buses that populated these roads, Hugo figured he'd be
bigger and heavier than anything else he'd meet.

They made it to the top unmolested, and Hugo eased off the power
to direct the car through several bends. Then the road straightened and
the hedges backed off, giving them a view of green pastures to the left
and right.

"Weston is just a couple of miles ahead," Pendrith said. "Interesting
place, too."

"That so?" asked Hugo.

"It's got one of those wonderful legends, from hundreds of years
ago. Chap named Jack O'Legs lived in the fourteenth century; they say
he was a giant."

"A giant."

"Indeed. He used to rob wealthy travelers and local merchants
alike back on that road we just took, that hill. Then he'd give money or
food to the poor, after taking his share."

"The original Robin Hood?"

"Right," said Pendrith. "Except things turned out a little badly
for our man Jack. He was captured by a co-op of bakers who were fed
up with him stealing their food. If I remember the story right, they
blinded him with hot pokers and were about to kill him when he asked
to be allowed to shoot one last arrow from his mighty bow and then

be buried wherever it landed. He fired his arrow and it traveled several miles in the air until it hit the roof of Weston Church and bounced into the graveyard."

"How convenient."

"Quiet, man. If you don't believe me, you can see it for yourself."

"Meaning?" Hugo shot him a quizzical look.

"Meaning his grave is still there."

"Are you serious? He actually has a grave at the church? After six hundred years?"

"This is England, old boy. We build things to last, including churches and burial plots. You Yanks might learn a thing or two from us."

"So how big is this grave, if old Jack was a giant?"

"Well, there are two stones marking the head and foot, and I was told they are fourteen feet apart."

Hugo smiled. "I like that story. No one has ever dug him up to check?"

"Good Lord no!" Hugo heard real outrage in the man's voice. "That would be sacrilege."

"After six hundred years, I don't think he'd mind."

"It's a churchyard, for heaven's sake." Pendrith leaned forward and looked at the GPS screen. "Looks like the place we're headed for is just the other side of Weston."

They slowed as the road narrowed, houses appearing out of nowhere on either side, white and red-brick row houses that looked as though they'd settled into the earth. Heeding the voice on the GPS, Hugo turned left past a tiny store that doubled as the post office, then paused at a four-way stop. The car growled as he pressed the accelerator and they drove up behind a tractor rumbling along the main street. To their left he saw a wide triangle that was the village green, immaculately kept and with a pond in its center. Three weeping-willow trees leaned over the hollow, dangling their branches into the water as if trawling for fish, or testing the temperature. To their right was a high brick wall that ran for several hundred yards.

"What's behind there?" Hugo asked.

"Not what, but who," Pendrith replied. "That's Dunsmore Hall. The family owns the hall, as well as Dunsmore Manor, Weston Lodge, and the vicarage."

"Like their privacy?"

"Don't we all? Very nice people, as it happens. They've been in the village since the days of old Jack O'Legs himself. Probably the ones who helped bury him," Pendrith smiled. "Super people now, though, very active in the community."

"And very active," Hugo guessed, "in the pheasant shooting business?"

Pendrith harrumphed. "Around here it's a tradition, not a business. And they happen to be excellent hosts."

A minute later the land to their right rose and the houses on both sides gave way to hedgerows and thickening woods.

"That was it?" asked Hugo.

"That was Weston," Pendrith agreed. "If we'd gone straight instead of past the post office, we'd have seen more. The cricket field, a couple of pubs. Up that road is the church."

Hugo looked ahead and to the right, where Pendrith was pointing. A narrow lane rose away from the road, running parallel with it for fifty yards before cutting right into some trees. The church, and Jack's famous grave, was out of sight from the road.

They drove on, and the road narrowed and darkened as stands of oak and birch rose up on both sides. The trees fell away after a mile, but the sense of darkness and closeness remained because the road itself sat low between high banks topped with thick hedges. Every hundred yards or so a lay-by had been cut into the earth to allow cars to pass each other.

A mile outside Weston, with nothing but muddy brown fields on either side of them, the polite voice from the GPS instructed Hugo to take the next left. He slowed, eyes searching for the entrance to a road. There it was, a lane slicing through the hedgerow to meet them. He glanced at Pendrith, who just shrugged. May as well go in.

The Cadillac fit through the narrow opening to the lane, but only just. The lane itself was straight as an arrow and may once have been tarmac but was now more gravel than anything.

"Looks like an old Roman road," Pendrith said. "They crisscross the countryside out here, all of them straight as can be. My father used to tell me that they were straight so the Britons couldn't hide around the corners and ambush Roman soldiers. No idea if it's true or not."

Silver birch trees lined the road like sentries, their branches forming a canopy over the car, wrapping them further in darkness. The car rocked and bumped over the potholes, and the tires spat gravel at the grass embankment, but after a hundred yards Hugo saw no end to the lane.

"There!" Pendrith was pointing ahead and to the right, to a footpath leading away from the road into a spinney. At the entrance to the path, Hugo could make out the dark silhouette of a man. He was standing with one foot on the stump of a long-dead elm, a shotgun held loosely at his waist but aimed directly at them. Hugo stopped the car twenty yards short of the man, who wore a green Barbour jacket and whose face was obscured by a cap pulled low over his eyes.

"This car bulletproof?" Pendrith asked.

"His shotgun won't do much more than scratch the paint, so we should be fine," Hugo said. "Until you get out, of course."

"Me?" asked Pendrith, not moving.

"Sure." Hugo reached down and unbuckled Pendrith's seatbelt. "He's one of you, judging by the jacket and the gun. Why don't you go talk to him?"

"I can think of one good reason," said Pendrith. "What if he doesn't like trespassers?"

"He probably doesn't. But I can guarantee that he dislikes trespassing Americans more."

"Can't say I blame him," Pendrith muttered, opening the door. He looked back at Hugo. "Do me a favor, will you old boy?"

"Sure."

"If he shoots me, crush the bastard with your big American car."

CHAPTER EIGHT

An orange streetlight flickered on as the red Mini pulled into the parking lot of the Rising Moon public house in Weston. A gigantic SUV took up two spaces near the door of the pub, which looked more like a thatched cottage than an inn.

The man parked his Mini on the opposite side of the lot and switched off the engine, then sat and listened as it ticked quietly into silence. The driver's door creaked when he finally opened it, and the whole car rocked when he slammed it closed, necessary because of the old hinges and a prang or two over the years that had reshaped the frame. It was an old car, but the man was fond of it, trusted it. Sometimes old was simply better. Old meant reliable—and even when this old car wasn't reliable, it was fixable.

It wasn't much for country driving any more, though, the tired old wheels and almost-bald tires had spun a little too much when he'd started down the muddy country lane. Luckily, he'd had the sense to pull over and proceed on foot. Smart move: that lane was dead straight and they'd have seen him coming, dim light or no. As it was, he'd been able to put himself within sight and sound of Pendrith's conversation with the man with the gun—the farmer who owned the land, the man assumed.

The old MP hadn't gotten far out of the car before the gun swung toward his groin, making even the surreptitious watcher pause and wince. He'd then heard Pendrith call out, introduce himself. The armed man didn't respond. Then Pendrith told him they were looking for someone, that it was urgent, a matter of national and international interest. That had been enough to get the man to shift his foot off the stump, though the gun never wavered. A question about Braxton Hall got no response but made the man wonder if that's what lay at the end of the lane. Even when Pendrith told the farmer the name of their quarry, the only response he got was a shake of the head.

Poor old Pendrith had finally shrugged and turned back to the car, and the watcher had scurried back to his Mini, his heart in his mouth as the wheels slipped a few times before dragging him backward out of the lane. He'd waited in a lay-by for the Escalade to come out, then made a few calls to try and find out about the farmer and his property. He lost the Cadillac for a few minutes but figured they'd be heading for the one pub with rooms to rent, and he'd been right. After all, this was his territory, had been all his life. Which is why he thought it odd he didn't know about any Braxton Hall.

The man wondered if it might be time to present himself to the American. He checked his right overcoat pocket for his notebook and pen, his left for his wallet, then started toward the front door of the pub. A bell jingled as he pushed it open, and two men on barstools, locals from their dress, glanced his way, looked him up and down, then went back to their beers. He went to the bar and hoisted his small frame up onto a barstool, sure to leave one between the locals and himself. After all, it wasn't them he was here for.

The man ordered a half-pint of bitter from the publican, a stocky man in his sixties with the nose of a drinker and the breath of a smoker. Judging by the placard and licenses behind the bar, his name was Jim Booher. His half-pint arrived quickly and the man sipped at it, trying not to pull a face. He turned to look at the only other occupants of the room.

He'd know Stopford-Pendrith anywhere. It was his job to know, after all. And the tall guy was, by the process of elimination, the American. The driver of the Cadillac. The parker of the Cadillac.

The man wanted to go over and talk to them now, but he bided his time. The American and the politician each had a pint of amber liquid and a shot of something darker on the table in front of them. They'll be friendlier, thought the man, once those drinks sit a little lower in the glass.

He took another sip of his beer and looked up at the publican.

"Are you serving food tonight?" the man asked.

The publican nodded. "Like I told those blokes in the corner. My wife usually does the cooking but she's ill. All I have is some day-old stew in the fridge—it's bloody good nosh if you like stew. I'm reheating some for them now."

"Well," said the man. "If it's good enough for them, it's good enough for me."

Hugo looked up as a short, thin man walked into the pub and headed for the bar. He looked to be in his sixties, roughly the same age as Pendrith but without the MP's ruddy glow of good health. The man wore wire-rimmed glasses, and, as Hugo watched, he took them off, polished them with a handkerchief, then poked them back onto his nose with a bony finger.

Not a regular, thought Hugo, judging by the city-style trench coat, the mud on his business shoes, and the way the local boys checked him over and then ignored him. Hugo leaned forward but could see only half of the poorly lit parking lot through the window and couldn't see the man's car at all. He told himself to relax and enjoy his evening in the pub with a few good drinks and an entertaining politician. Pendrith had been complaining about his colleagues in Parliament for about twenty minutes, though it was plain to Hugo the old man loved the cut and thrust of being an MP.

"But try and get them to work on anything that matters, good bloody luck," Pendrith was saying. "Terrified the damn press will criticize or ridicule them. Bloody oafs get into power and then are too afraid to exercise it."

"So what matters, then?" Hugo asked. "When people say that, they usually have something specific in mind."

"Absolutely. Piece of legislation I've been working on for a while. Probably anathema to you as a Yank, especially as a Texan, where they're all for the chop."

"The chop?"

"Execution, dear boy." Pendrith waved a hand. "Used to be all for it, but I think we've moved on a bit, as tempting a solution as it may be. Civilization moves us to save lives, not end them, if you ask me. I know you don't chop people's heads off, don't worry. But you do zap them, poke them with a needle, or some damn thing. Well, that's one way to go about it, but the liberals and do-gooders here put an end to wringing necks back in the sixties. Now we have jails stuffed full of pensioners. Everyone is looking around trying to save money, get the government to spend less, and all the while we're stacking old people in jail cells and giving them food, medical care, and free nappies, I dare say."

"And your solution?"

"Well," Pendrith said, talking into his beer, "they won't let us shoot them, so I say we cut them loose."

"What do you mean? Just let them out?"

"Yes. Why not? Send them home to their families, let them pay for their food and housing. State will probably be stuck with their medical care anyway, but we could probably close down a few prisons if we let all the old people go."

"I can see why you're having trouble getting support for this," Hugo said.

"Well I bloody can't." Pendrith fumed in silence as the publican arrived with a tray laden with food and drink.

"Your beers, gents, but I can't remember who ordered what so sort yourselves out." He deposited two pint glasses, two bowls of stew, and a basket of French bread on the table. When their host had gone, Pendrith started up again.

"What is that, pale ale? Frightful stuff, watered down dishwater."

"Each to his own."

"Anyway, where was I? Ah yes, what's the harm in letting elderly convicts out? What's the downside?"

"For one thing," Hugo said, "assuming these people are no longer dangerous and assuming they've been in prison a few decades, what makes you think they will know how to survive on the outside?"

"Survive?" Pendrith looked at him, wide-eyed. "I don't give a hoot whether they survive or not! This isn't some molly-coddling idea to let poor old Joe the Strangler spend his last years on a beach in Clacton-on-Sea. This is a way to save a boatload of money for the government. The only people it could possibly impact negatively are those released and, frankly, I don't see why we should worry too much about them."

"I saw the news this morning," Hugo nodded. "Do you know who Sean Bywater is?"

"Name's familiar," Pendrith said. "What of him?"

"A murderer, famous in my line of work, just killed himself after being released. The report basically said he had nothing to live for on the outside."

"Yes? Good riddance, if you ask me."

"Maybe. I'm sure many would agree, but do you even think these people will have families to take them in after decades in prison?"

"Look," said Pendrith, leaning forward. "My point is merely that the spineless weasels in power right now are so afraid of looking soft on crime, they can't see this for what it is. It's tough on crime, for Chrissakes. It takes a bunch of decrepit no-goods, makes them fend for themselves, and saves the government a bundle in the process. And yet all they see, because all the reporters will say, is that we're letting a bunch of murderers into the community."

Pendrith shook his head and stabbed his stew with a spoon, stirring it and releasing a plume of steam. They ate in silence for a few minutes, Hugo quickly concluding that the two-day-old stew was, as the publican had suggested, still very edible. He wasn't so sure about the bread, whose brittle crust and chewy interior suggested a vintage very similar to that of the meat. But he ate hungrily and found the room-temperature beer to be a fine accompaniment.

"Speaking of murder," Hugo said. "How would I get ahold of information about an old case? Information that only the police have."

"How old?"

"Late 1800s."

"Ripper stuff? Most of that is in a museum, I think."

"No, actually it's not Ripper. Not officially, anyway. A little after, in 1905."

"I think I can help you." Pendrith pulled a pen from his jacket pocket and wrote a name and a number on a paper napkin. "Chap's an archivist, worked at Somerset House and Scotland Yard. Loves all that true-crime stuff. Mention my name and he'll get you what you need, though it may cost you a bottle of claret."

Hugo thanked him and tucked the napkin into his pocket.

As they were wiping their bowls with the last of the bread, a movement at the bar caught Hugo's eye. The man who'd been sitting by himself was walking toward them, a smile on his face and a full pint of beer in each hand.

"Gentlemen," the man said. "Do you mind if I join you for a minute or two? I come bearing gifts." He set the beers down on the crowded table, pints of bitter for both men. He offered his hand to them. "My name is Harry Walton. I'm a freelance reporter. Been putting together a piece about the little accident that two of your countrymen had up this way. I saw your big car outside, heard your accent, and I know Lord Stopford-Pendrith from television. So I'm putting two and two together and wondering why you are in Hertfordshire but not particularly close to the scene of the accident."

"You have a lot of assumptions in there, Mr. Walton."

"Assumptions and research."

Hugo sat back. "By research I assume you mean following us. Am I right in thinking you drive a red Mini?"

"Very impressive," Walton said.

"Red Mini?" Pendrith looked back and forth between the two men. "What the bloody hell does that have to do with anything?" He leaned toward Hugo. "And how did you know he has one?"

"He was following us in London," Hugo said. "Got a ticket for an illegal U-turn, if I remember right. Then I saw him again on the A1 earlier but didn't make the connection."

"Following us?" Pendrith puffed. "What the devil . . . ?"

"Let's just say we were headed in the same direction." Walton smiled innocently. "Anyway, I don't know if you know my name, but lately I've been doing more celebrity stuff. It's crap, most of it, but pays well and isn't too taxing for freelancers like me. And while you'd think we have to hunt around and nibble away at the privacy of our wonderful celebrities, most of them are media whores and love attention."

"I'm sure they do," said Hugo. "I also assume there is something specific we can do for you?"

Walton leaned back as the publican arrived with a tray and began loading it with their empty beer glasses and stew bowls. When the rotund man had gone, Walton cleared his throat. "As you can see I'm no spring chicken, though I could chase you all over Christendom if I wanted. Lately, though, I've been finding that the direct approach works best, saves everyone time and effort." He grinned. "After all, if you tell me to get lost I can still follow you all over Christendom, right?"

"The hell you can," said Pendrith.

"Anyway, that's not something I want to do," Walton said. "I'm here thanks to some well-placed sources who told me that a pair of very famous American guests were being let out of jail and put in the care and custody of the US Embassy."

"And I don't suppose you'd care to reveal the identity of those well-placed sources?" Hugo asked.

"Funny thing," Walton said. "Lord Pendrith here was the one who helped strengthen our press-shield laws so I don't have to. Nice irony, don't you think?"

"Very nice," said Hugo. "You were about to tell us what you wanted."

"Same thing you do, I expect," said Walton. "I want to find and have a chat with our friend Harper. Maybe a little interview before you whisk him away into the bosom of the American embassy."

"And what would you be seeking in return?" asked Hugo.

"I won't say anything about you having lost him. Seems like that would set off a bit of a frenzy, don't you think?"

"No can do, old boy," said Pendrith. "Assuming you got your info from a couple of London reporters I know, then I shall further assume you'd appreciate that I already made that deal with them. So you can follow us all you like, write what you like, and pretty much go to hell."

Walton sat back and stroked his chin, his head cocked as he stared at Pendrith. "Here's the way I see it. By telling me about your little escapade in central London, they broke their promise to keep mum. Which means you owe them nothing. And, of course, they won't know you have a deal with me because I wouldn't be stupid enough to tell them." He turned to face Hugo. "I will also assume that finding your lost charge is priority number one and that double-crossing a couple of London hacks wouldn't be of great concern to the American ambassador. Am I right?"

"You are quite right about that, Mr. Walton." Hugo leaned toward him, a thin smile on his face. "I can also assure you that the ambassador wouldn't object in the slightest to a small red car being accidentally crushed by a large American one in the parking lot of a quiet English pub. He would be mildly upset if someone was in that small red car, but he'd get over it when he found out it was a journalist."

"Mr. Marston, are you threatening me?"

"Yes," Hugo said. "Very much so. I don't like blackmail, Mr. Walton. Not one little bit, and in my experience the blackmailer almost always ends up getting squished, either by his supposed victim or by the law. Sometimes both."

"Well then." Walton rubbed his hands together and sat back. "If you will excuse me, I have a story to write. I'm not completely up to speed on the whole Internet thing, but my guess is that if you are here, you think Dayton Harper is. And that means anyone who reads my story will think so, too, putting about two thousand people into this village by daybreak. How will you get on, Mr. Marston, with two thousand people following your every move?"

As Walton stood, Hugo fought the urge to grab him by the neck and throttle him. He and Pendrith sat and watched as Walton stopped to pay his tab at the bar, then walked slowly out of the pub without looking back.

"Should dash out and slash the bugger's tires," said Pendrith. "And possibly his bloody throat."

"Tempting," said Hugo, "but would make for bad press."

"Talking of which, I'm not sure he's wrong."

"About what?"

"About us being better off having him around than a thousand screaming Harper fans coming up from London and another thousand locals baying for his blood. All in this little village."

"The shit is blackmailing us, Pendrith. I don't take kindly to that."

"I know, I know, and neither do I." He stood. "Look, you don't have to worry about constituents, but you damn well do need to worry about Harper. If that little twerp Walton makes this public right now, it's not going to end well for either of us."

"Where are you going?"

"To recruit that bastard to help us."

"I don't want his help." Hugo drained his whisky glass and stood, reaching for his wallet. He threw three ten-pound notes onto the table, and both men moved quickly after Walton, shrugging on their coats and nodding to the publican on their way past the bar. "Be right back," Hugo told the man.

A gust of wind tipped Hugo's hat as they pushed open the door and started across the parking lot. He hurriedly buttoned his coat against the cold and briefly wondered if he'd ever get used to the combination of perpetual damp and slicing winds that seemed to take turns battering his body and souring his mood. He could see Walton putting his key into the door of the Mini, and he looked over at his own vehicle. He could squash the little rat with barely a dent to the Cadillac, and the world would have lost nothing more than an old, red Mini and one aging, blood-sucking journalist.

CHAPTER NINE

The pub had three guest rooms, all on the third floor and all variations on the same theme: small. Each had a bare wooden floor that creaked underfoot and a single bed tucked under a sloped ceiling that threatened to give its guest a firm kiss atop his head if he tried to sit up in bed. There was no television and no telephone anywhere upstairs, as far as they could tell. And the only other furniture in Hugo's room was a battered wardrobe that wouldn't open and that leaned against a slightly sturdier oak dresser like an aging couple waiting for a bus that wouldn't come, the tired and frail old man using his short, plump wife for support. Narrow but clean windows gave views over the parking lot or the beer garden out back. When checking out the rooms, Hugo had let Pendrith choose first and, for his kindness, the American had wound up with a view of the parking lot.

The door to each room opened into a foyer that was larger than all three rooms put together and furnished with two chintz-covered armchairs and a cloth sofa that smelled faintly of beer—and rather less faintly of mildew. The shared bathroom was also accessed from this seating area, and Walton got the bedroom beside that.

After assuring their host that these rooms would be fine for the night, they took a key to the front door from him. They waited until he descended the stairs past his own living quarters back to the bar, mumbling all the way about having to run a pub and take care of a sick woman at the same time.

Hugo and Pendrith took an armchair each, Walton noticing the smell too late to avoid the sofa. He sat down and wrinkled his nose, and Hugo suppressed a smile.

"I meant to say," Walton began. "I'm a big fan of things American; I know sometimes English people can be a little snobby."

"I've not noticed," Hugo said, "but I'm glad you like us."

"You've probably heard it before, but without you people the world of movies would be in a poor state."

"Some say it is in a poor state because of the Yanks," Pendrith chimed in.

"Nonsense," Walton said. "The best movies come from there. My favorites are the old cowboy movies, and their modern version, the gangster movies."

"We do good work with those," Hugo said.

"I've always been fascinated by those living on the wild side, maybe because I write about them sometimes. But not the bad guys, the ones in the black hats or doling out favors while smoking fat cigars. No, I'm more interested in why the people lower down in the pecking order do what they do. The ones who ride behind the villain and rob the train with him. The man who does the don's bidding, shaking down businessmen and whacking rivals."

"The button man," said Hugo.

"Right," Walton nodded. "The button man. So, how do you like our little village, Mr. Marston? Off the record, so to speak."

"I've not seen much of it. Why do you ask?"

"No reason. You have your movies, we have our history, and I'm always amused by the stock Americans put in the past, how impressed they are that our cottages and pubs are older than their entire nation."

"You think they shouldn't be impressed?"

"Oh, no, quite the opposite. I think England would be a better place if its citizenry looked a little more to the past than the future. Have you heard the tale of Jack O'Legs, for example?"

"As a matter of fact, yes."

"A wonderful, cautionary tale." Walton rubbed his chin. "I have always thought, though, that he was actually executed at the church itself. I mean, it makes sense to do the deed where the hole is located, right?"

"Never really thought about it," said Hugo.

"Right then," interrupted Pendrith. "I suggest now is a jolly good time to start worrying about the future, specifically of our young friend on the lam. What's our plan?"

"I'm not entirely sure," Hugo said. "Do you guys have any bright ideas?" He nodded toward Walton's shoes. "I assume from the state of those, and the fresh mud splattered all over the underside of your car, that you followed us into the lane?"

Walton smirked. "Regular Sherlock Holmes, aren't you?"

"Hardly," said Hugo. "If I were, I'd have known you were following us." He sat back and looked directly at Walton. "So what do you know about Braxton Hall?"

"Not a damn thing," the reporter said. "I grew up around here, got my first newspaper job on the *Hitchin Gazette*, but I've never heard of the place."

Pendrith cleared his throat. "We're assuming that because of its name, Braxton *Hall*, it must be old. Maybe not. All these villages have been yuppified over the last ten years, people moving in from the city and commuting every day. People with money. Perfectly possible some banker or lawyer bought a few acres and built himself a mansion."

"True," Walton said. "Enough construction going on, dozens of bedroom communities, you could easily build a house in the woods or the middle of a hundred-acre field and no one would pay much attention."

Pendrith looked around them, as if for something he'd lost, then got up and went into his room, mumbling to himself. The other two watched him go.

"Why's he in on this?" Walton asked.

"Seems like that's a question for him." Hugo eyed the journalist. "So what happens if we find Harper and he doesn't want to give you an interview? You've risked blowing an exclusive for nothing."

"Some risks are worth taking, Mr. Marston." Walton shrugged. "If I can break the story of him escaping and get an interview to boot, I'll be on every news program for a week. I'm too old to be chasing starlets and their drunken husbands, I want them to know who I am, to come find me for a change."

"You been doing this for a long time?"

"Not this exactly, no. Crime is my main interest, my first beat, you might say. I like to lighten it up with some celebrity stalking now and again." He grinned. "And you'd be amazed how often the two subjects intersect."

They looked around as Pendrith came back into the room, locked his bedroom door with a frown on his face. "A pub and not a drop to drink in there. Bloody disgrace." He sat back in his chair, then turned to Walton. "Be a good fellow, run down and grab a bottle of something strong and three glasses. My tab."

"You serious?" Walton asked, wide-eyed.

"Lord yes," Pendrith said. "Didn't have time to pack a toothbrush, let alone stock up on other essentials. No point drying out too much up here, especially if we're going to sort out some kind of plan of action. After all, we're not savages."

Walton stood, uncertain at first, then started down the steps. Halfway, he turned as if to say something but apparently decided better of it and soon disappeared from view. Pendrith looked at Hugo.

"So what are we going to do?" he said.

"Braxton Hall is the only lead we have," Hugo said. "And because we're not officially welcome, our options are limited."

"Are you, by any chance, suggesting a stealth visit?"

"Not if you've got a better idea."

"No, old boy, I don't. But I don't think we want our weaselly friend with us when we go, do you?"

"You think he'll insist on coming?"

"Let's not find out."

They grabbed their jackets from their rooms, Pendrith again locking his with a wry smile at Hugo, and met back in the sitting room.

Hugo closed the door to his room, too, then went into the bathroom, turned on the cold tap, and left it running as he closed the door behind him. He nodded to Pendrith and the two men trotted quietly down the stairs. At the second floor landing, Hugo spotted a bathroom that, he assumed, belonged to the owner and his wife. The door stood open and he couldn't see movement elsewhere in the apartment, so he beckoned for Pendrith to follow him. They stepped into the little room and closed the door most of the way, Hugo watching for Walton through a small opening. He knew they wouldn't have much time, maybe a minute or two before Walton figured out they were gone.

The journalist trudged by a few seconds later, carrying a bottle of Bell's whisky and three glass tumblers. Behind Hugo, Pendrith sighed at the quality of the booze Walton had procured and Hugo silenced him with a nudge. As Walton's feet disappeared up the final flight to their rooms, Hugo stepped into the hallway and the two men moved quickly down the stairs to the bar.

The pub had filled since they'd gone upstairs, a group of rowdy young men eyeing a larger group of even more rowdy young women, slightly older and dressed for a bachelorette night, Hugo thought. They waved at the harried publican on the way past, but he was too busy to care what they were doing. Hugo glanced back as they went out the front door and saw no sign of Walton, just the red-faced landlord balancing a bottle of white wine and too many glasses on a small tray.

Hugo winced at the beep of the Cadillac when he unlocked it, and they climbed quickly inside. The doors closed with a gentle *whump*, and in three seconds they were out of the parking lot.

"He might guess where we're going and follow," Pendrith said.

"He might. But he also knows he might get an ass full of buckshot if he goes back down that lane. Assuming his Mini will even make it down there."

"Any particular reason that we won't be in for some lead shot ourselves?"

"Yes, actually."

"Care to share?" Pendrith said.

"Let's assume you are right about Braxton Hall being fairly new. How did the builders get in there? It wasn't down that Roman road, I'm pretty sure of that."

"Another entrance," Pendrith nodded. "But how do we find it?"

"Easy," Hugo said, patting his GPS monitor. "This thing."

"Well, it didn't find it before."

"That's because it figures out the most direct route, depending on where you are coming from. So from London, that lane was the most direct route. All we have to do is circle around the village and come in from the opposite direction. Then this lovely lady will bring us in."

"I say," Pendrith said. "How clever."

"Yep," said Hugo. "But first we have to go low-tech. There should be a map in the glove compartment—can you steer us to the back side of Weston?"

"No need for a map, old boy. We just need to head for the best pheasant shoot in the Home Counties, and you can bet your last, grubby American dollar I can get us that far, at least."

CHAPTER TEN

They came at the place from the north this time. As Hugo had predicted, once they were on Baldock Road the GPS system locked onto the postal code and guided them in, the softness of the woman's voice contrasting with the urgency felt by her lost subjects, as if the narration for a nature film had somehow been dubbed onto a Hitchcock thriller.

The last turn she had them make was onto an obviously new road, signposted as Braxton Lane.

"Should have guessed that," said Pendrith.

The road ran straight like the Roman road but low between two fields, bursts of occasional hedgerow on either side. It was wide, certainly wide enough for construction vehicles, though Hugo noticed that grassy banks had started to grow into the road, which told him it wasn't overly used or maintained. They saw no sign of houses or other connecting roads, as if Braxton Lane was really an extended driveway to the hall. After a mile, the road rose to become level with the land around and then curved gently to the left before ending in front of a high, barred gate that was the only break that they could see in a fifteen-foot brick wall apparently circling the property. Hugo turned the car parallel to the gate and doused the headlights.

"Secure," said Pendrith. "Lot of bricks."

"Surprised?" Hugo scanned the darkness for a way into the place but from the car saw none.

"Hardly. Don't see men with guns, though, so that's an improvement." Pendrith opened his door. "Shall we?"

They stood at the front gate and Hugo inspected a metal panel containing a keypad and a screen. He bent down and scooped up a handful of mud, then smeared it over the top of the screen where he suspected a camera would be. He looked at Pendrith and shrugged. "Just in case. See any other cameras?"

"Nope, but out here they're more likely to have dogs. Though if they did, we should be hearing them by now."

"True. They wouldn't be the first people to rely on a big gate and a brick wall."

They stood at the gate and looked toward the house, a hulking silhouette at the top of a low rise directly in front of them, maybe a hundred yards from the gate. It was an Edwardian-style mansion of at least a dozen bedrooms, judging by the long line of windows on the top floor.

"So, how do we get in?" Pendrith asked.

Hugo glanced over at him. "You're the James Bond—I figured you'd know."

"He was MI6—I'm MI5."

"The branch that needs keys."

"Apparently. FBI got any tricks?"

"No, that'd be CIA. The only thing I can think of . . ." Hugo rummaged in his pocket and pulled out the business card they'd found in Harper's suitcase.

"You're going to call them and ask for the code?" Pendrith asked, incredulous.

"Hopefully won't have to." He held the card so he could see it in the moonlight, then tapped the last four digits of the phone number on the keypad. For a second, nothing happened, then the gates jerked once and began to sweep inward toward the house.

"Nicely done," Pendrith said, as they climbed back into the Cadillac.

"Well, it seemed like they were taking half-assed security measures, with no guards, cameras, or dogs, and look at the size of the place."

"Meaning?"

Hugo left the headlights off but turned the running lights on as he steered between the brick pillars and started slowly up the driveway. "Meaning they probably have a lot of people coming and going, so they need a code that's easy to remember or easy to distribute. Which is why it came back as not a real phone number."

"Right, because it isn't one. And no dogs because they don't need wild beasts attacking their guests," Pendrith said. "I get it."

"Right. On the other hand, chances are the opening of the gate has alerted someone to our arrival." He hit the brakes and turned off the running lights. "Out, quick."

"What the . . . ?"

But Hugo was at his door, pulling him out. "You're driving."

"What are you doing?"

"I'm going to hide behind you, or in a bush somewhere, then check the place out. When you find someone to talk to, be up front about what we're doing here, but if you get turned away, just head back down Braxton Lane half a mile and wait. I'll call or just show up. And if I'm not out by morning, call the cops."

"Wait, we haven't discussed—"

"No time for planning. And I have to be the one to do this—wouldn't be good for an MP to be caught sneaking about in the dark. Now get going."

Hugo trotted behind the car as Pendrith drove slowly up the gravel driveway to the front door. Forty yards out, a waist-high privet hedge popped up on his right and he angled off behind it, following it away from the drive but parallel to the house.

The hedge went on for thirty yards and ended at a pagoda, giving Hugo an opening to get to the front of the house. He walked through the structure, running his fingers across several beams. New wood.

He started across the lawn, wrapped in darkness now but exposed should security lights come on. Within seconds he was close enough to see inside some of the lower windows and, directly ahead of him, he was able to look in on a library. Beside it, to his left, looked to be a long hallway, and to the right was a dining room. He stopped to take in that room, and it told him something about how the house was being used: it contained one long table rather than a bunch of them, so it wasn't a hotel or commercial property.

He looked up before moving on but couldn't see into any of the upstairs rooms, the windows were opaque rectangles that glowed yellow behind pulled curtains.

Still hidden in the dark, Hugo checked to his left and saw Pendrith in front of the main entrance talking to a portly and uncommonly short man who, even though he stood on the third or fourth step, was still eye level with the MP.

Hugo dropped to one knee and watched for a moment. The men's faces were in shadow and their voices too low for him to make out any words, but from the short man's gestures it seemed clear he wasn't going to let the stranger in. The only question was whether Pendrith was getting any useful information, which Hugo also doubted.

Hugo had seen no other entrance to the house, so he moved to his right, glancing over his shoulder to measure Pendrith's progress. As Hugo reached the corner of the house, he looked back and saw the MP climbing back into the Cadillac. *I thought not.* Hugo looked along the side of the house and saw a patio, empty of people and furniture. He moved on, staying close to the house, passing several windows that had curtains pulled, blocking his view. He assumed they looked into the dining room, and, when he reached the patio, he saw light spilling through two closed French doors. He stepped away from the wall and peered into the room. He was right, the dining room. Two people in white jackets moved about the long table, setting out plates and silverware. Servants? Hugo wondered. In this day and age?

He skirted the patio, staying out of the weak light that fell out of the dining room. At the far corner of the house, he stopped and looked along the backside of the house. The grass made way for gravel, and a dozen cars were parked in a tidy line. A stone outbuilding sat on the other side of the parking area, but Hugo couldn't see a door or a window to the place.

He took out his cell phone, waited for a moment, and when he saw no movement, he dialed Pendrith.

"It's Hugo. No luck?"

"None. Rude bugger, too, wouldn't say who he was or give me any information at all."

"He has his rights, Pendrith."

"You Americans and your rights. Come to think of it, he has the right to shoot you, too."

Hugo couldn't help but smile. "Good point. What can you tell me?"

"Not much. He's short, fat, and smokes good cigars. But he'd not been drinking, which is odd."

"It is?"

"Of course. This time of night, to be smoking cigars without a glass of something, very odd. Also, he's from the north. Yorkshire or Lancashire, I can never tell the difference."

"OK, that it?"

"'Fraid so, old boy. Where are you?"

"Coming to the back of the house. Looking at a gravel parking lot and a barn of some sort."

"And your plan?"

"I was hoping to find a way in."

"And then?"

"Not too sure," Hugo had to admit.

"Sounds like a great plan."

"Thanks, I'll call you if I find anything. Where are you?"

"In a lay-by about fifty yards from the gate. I'll stay here as long as I can."

Hugo closed his phone and watched for another moment before starting across the gravel. He made it ten yards before, from the far side of the house, a growing pool of light signaled an arriving car. He looked around for a place to hide and, seeing none, darted into the shadows, pressing himself against the wall of the house. A few seconds later, a small car crunched into the parking area. A city car, one of those two-seaters that he'd only ever seen in London. A Smart Car, he thought it was called. He moved slowly back the way he'd come, back pressed to the stone, and as he reached the corner he saw the driver get out of the little car and walk toward the house. A security light flicked on, momentarily blinding him and causing the driver, a woman, to shield her eyes. Hugo squinted but couldn't make out her face, and seconds later she was gone.

This was his chance. He trotted toward the entrance she'd used, no longer worried about triggering the security lights, which stayed on as he moved. He got to the door a split second before it closed, and he saw that it would have self-locked. Whoever she was, she had a key.

Inside, he found himself in a small foyer. The floor was marble and the walls painted a rich red. Ahead, one of a pair of glazed double doors stood open, giving Hugo a view of a dimly lit hallway that led to and past the dining room. To his right, a wide staircase led upward, the lower steps watched over by a wooden owl perched on, and carved into, the end of the banister.

Hugo hesitated. He didn't want to bump into the woman, and, while he couldn't tell which way she had gone, he assumed a new arrival wouldn't head straight upstairs; she'd be more likely to announce her arrival to whomever lived there. Or ran the place. Or whatever.

Hugo started up the stairs. He crossed a landing, eyes trained on the next flight, listening for any sound. He took the steps two at a time, and at the top of the next set he stopped and looked around. He was in a small seating area, furnished with a plush velvet sofa and two ornate bergère chairs. Behind the sofa was a bookcase, and even a cursory glance told Hugo, an amateur book collector, that it contained some expensive volumes. Ahead, a long and wide hallway opened up in front of him, and he could see on both sides high double doors, as if he'd reached the finest suites at a top hotel. An Oriental-style rug ran down the middle of the wooden-floored hallway, and delicate tables filled the spaces between the doors.

Hugo stood there, deciding on his next move. There was something amiss, he thought, something odd that he couldn't quite put his finger on. And then he realized how quiet it was. For all the cars in the parking lot, the woman who'd just come in, the servants downstairs preparing for a meal, there was no sound up here at all. The only thing he could think to do was listen at a few doors, though the idea made him feel more like a voyeur than a cop. *That's what happens when you don't have a plan*, he thought.

He started forward, his feet silent on the rug, his ears pricked for sound, and just as he reached the first set of double doors to his left, one flew open and a figure stepped out. They stood face-to-face for several seconds before Hugo was able to speak.

"What the hell are you doing here?" he said.

The diminutive figure shrugged. "I'm guessing the same thing as you."

CHAPTER ELEVEN

She had let her hair down and changed clothes, putting on jeans and a cashmere sweater—which seemed odd because she must have hurried up here.

"Let's sit over there," she said, indicating the velvet sofa at the top of the stairs. She turned to make sure the door to her room was closed properly, and Hugo tried not to notice how well her jeans fit. He'd been wrong about her being rail thin.

They headed to the seating area at the top of the stairs, walking in silence, and when they sat Hugo was surprised to see anger on her face.

"Did you find him?" she asked.

"Not yet. From your question, I'm guessing you didn't either."

She didn't answer, just looked at him with her watchful green eyes.

Hugo took a breath to ease his frustration. "Merlyn, I need to know what's going on. I need to find him before he gets himself in trouble."

"What kind of trouble? What aren't you telling me?"

"Plenty, I'm afraid. And I'm not understanding what you think you are protecting him from."

"You, I suppose."

Hugo sat back. "OK, let's do some information sharing. I'll start. I want to find Dayton Harper because I'm supposed to be looking after him until his criminal charges here are resolved. I'm worried because his wife is dead, and he's in a fragile state of mind. And because I have no idea where he is or what he's doing. Your turn."

"What do you want me to tell you?"

"You said you don't know where he is, and I believe you. But I want to know about your relationship with Ferro and Dayton, how well you knew them."

She nodded. "That all?"

"No. I want to know what this place is."

"OK." She chewed her lip for a second. "You remember what I said about the Cork Hotel? The word I used?"

Hugo thought for a second. "Yes, you said it was 'discreet.'"

"Right. Same goes here, but more so. This is a private residence that is used for certain . . . groups to enjoy. To rent out."

"Groups?"

"Yes. I'm sorry but I can't be much more specific than that." She watched him for a moment. "Have you heard of the Viles, or the Society of Janus?"

"No, can't say I have," said Hugo.

"Didn't think so." She shrugged. "Google them, you'll see what kind of people I'm talking about. Good people who share particular interests. All sorts."

"This isn't helping me much, Merlyn. Why would he come here?"

"Same reason everyone comes here. For privacy and yet to share with others, to feel accepted, and to have some fun."

"Fun? Jesus, Merlyn, his wife just died, how the hell could he—"

"No, Hugo, calm down. I didn't mean it that way. Before she died, that's why he came. Why they came."

"Then tell me, was he here today?"

She sat back, moving her body away from his in what Hugo recognized as a subconscious effort to hide something.

"Whatever you're not telling me, Merlyn, that's fine. But I need to know if he was here today, I need to know that."

"No," she said. "I haven't seen him."

Hugo didn't believe her, or at least wasn't convinced. She was hiding something and he needed to find out what it was. "You know, you never asked me how Ginny died."

"Didn't have the chance. If I had, would you have told me?"

"Probably not, but I will now. She was found hanging in a grave-yard in central London. I found her."

Merlyn's mouth dropped open. "Hanging? A graveyard? Oh, Jesus, I didn't know." Her head sank into her hands and then she sat up and hugged herself. "That's . . . unbelievable."

"Yes, it is." Hugo filled her in on the details, then added: "If she was murdered, which is possible, whoever killed her might be looking for Harper."

She held his eye for a moment, then stood. "Come with me."

It was behind the stone barn, a neatly manicured cemetery enclosed by an intentionally ramshackle wall, carefully constructed to replicate the kind of churchyard found in any English village. Or Hollywood ghost story. Overhead, the night sky played along, its watchful stars peeping down at them through spectral wisps of black cloud, and a cold breeze crept up behind them to brush Hugo's cheek.

Merlyn pushed open the wooden gate that, of course, creaked, and they walked along a gravel path between randomly placed headstones and concrete crosses. Ahead, right in the center, was a mausoleum.

"I assume there aren't actually people under all these stones," Hugo said.

"No, of course not. See that," she pointed to the mausoleum, "it leads down to a special chamber."

"And all this is for?"

"Play acting," she said. "Not just sex, I know what you're thinking. People hear the word *fantasy* and just assume it's about sex, and it's not. Not always. Sometimes it's just being someone else, being someone you can't be in your regular life."

"And being someone else is good?"

"We're all hiding things, Hugo. For the longest time, gay people had to hide it, but they're not the only ones. People are into spanking, bondage, infantilism." She shrugged. "You name it, people are into it.

And even though everything's consensual, the vanilla world doesn't understand and, usually, doesn't want to. Here people can truly be themselves, that other self the world doesn't approve of. And experiment, learn more about themselves."

"Push boundaries, try new things," Hugo said, nodding.

Merlyn stopped and looked up at him, a twinkle in her eye. "So you do understand. A little, anyway."

"I'm trying," Hugo said. But before he could ask another question, his phone buzzed in his pocket. He ignored it for a second but then pictured Pendrith sitting in a dark lay-by. He fished it out and looked at the screen. He'd missed a call from his wife, Christine.

"You get lots of missed messages out here," Merlyn said. "Reception's not great in the countryside, right here anyway. And they block cell coverage in the house. A privacy thing."

Hugo nodded and decided to call Chris back later. He smiled at the thought. *Sorry darling, I'm busy talking to a pretty, young girl about adult role playing in a fake cemetery.* He tucked the phone back in his pocket and looked at Merlyn. "I think you were going to tell me about Dayton Harper."

"Yeah, OK. He and Ginny, they are . . . were experimenting. Their thing was autoerotic asphyxiation. Did you know that in Victorian London they used to have what were called Hanged Men's Clubs? Basically, prostitutes would provide strangling services in a safe environment. Safe as it gets, anyway."

"Apparently there's a great deal I don't know," Hugo said, frowning.

She touched his arm. "That's OK. But look around, what do you see?"

"I see this case going in the wrong direction, getting more and more complicated. You're saying that it's a possibility that Ginny Ferro died accidentally in that graveyard? What do you call it, breath play?"

"Yes."

"I thought that was something just men engaged in. That's what you always read about . . ."

"Hugo, for heaven's sake. Why would just men be into it? It's not just sexist, it makes no sense."

"Fine, OK. But you're saying this might be playtime gone wrong?"

"No idea," Merlyn said. "I really don't. And it doesn't seem very likely she'd be playing there and then, I just thought you should see this." She sighed and looked around. "I like this place. It's peaceful. And safe."

"I can see that," said Hugo. "So how did you, and they, get hooked into all this?"

"Well, I saw Ginny and Dayton at the Ritz, obviously, and then again at the Cork. They recognized me, we got talking, and one thing led to another."

"Dayton asked you to join them," Hugo concluded.

"Dayton?" Merlyn laughed. "No, no. I would say he's the more vanilla of the two."

"Vanilla?"

"Yeah," said Merlyn. "You know. Like you."

"Thanks. So what's your . . ." he searched for the right term, "interest?"

"Mine?" She arched an eyebrow. "That's none of your business."

It was Hugo's turn to laugh. "Fair enough." He checked his watch. "OK, time for me to get out of here, I have a missing movie star to find." He started to walk back the direction they'd come, but Merlyn wasn't following. He stopped. "Everything OK?"

"I want to come with you."

"Sorry. Stay the night here, drive back to London, whatever you want, and I'll call you when I find him. I promise. But you can't come."

"I can't drive home, either."

"You have a car, don't you?"

"No, actually I don't." She looked at the ground, then back up at Hugo. "Not anymore."

Hugo stared at her as the pieces fell into place. "Oh, no, Merlyn, you didn't."

"I'm sorry, Hugo."

"Jesus, Merlyn . . ." He shook his head. "The truth, please."

"He was in the room. That's why I brought you out here. Anyway, we didn't really get a chance to talk. He saw you follow me in, he was watching through the window. I'm sorry, I didn't know what all this was about and I trusted him. I wanted to help him. I really thought that's what I was doing, helping him."

"You gave him the keys to your car."

"Yes. He came by taxi."

Speeding taxi, Hugo thought. *Dammit.* "Do you know where he's going?" Hugo asked.

She nodded. "The farm where that man was killed. He wants to apologize in person. He really does feel bad, you know."

"No doubt. Do you know where it is?"

"Yes, I helped him find it on a map. It's easy enough," she said, "although he seems horrible with directions, so he'll probably get lost on the way. Anyway, maybe it'll give us time to catch him?" she said, hopefully.

"Maybe." Hugo pictured an angry father, a farmer carrying a rifle and a grudge, faced by the man who'd killed his only son. "Then let's hope he gets lost," Hugo said. "Just a little."

Reluctantly, he let Merlyn come along. She'd pointed out, validly, that if Harper saw Hugo or Pendrith he'd disappear again, whereas if he saw her first, well, maybe she could talk to him, make him see sense.

They took the same route to the front gate that Hugo had taken before, across the lawn and through the pagoda. Not because they needed to—Merlyn knew the short, fat man who ran the place—but just because Hugo didn't want any more holdups. According to Merlyn, the farm where the accident happened was just outside Bishop's Stortford, which wasn't that far as the crow flew, but Harper had a head start and they weren't crows.

Worse, Merlyn had no idea what Harper's plans were after his apology, assuming he survived it.

At the gate, Hugo called Pendrith, leaving a message that they were on the way. Then he punched the code into the pad and, when the gate swung open, they started down the road. Merlyn walked close to him, closer than she needed to, and after a minute Hugo thought maybe she wanted to talk.

"So tell me about the Cork Hotel."

"What do you want to know?"

"Well, is it like that place, Braxton Hall? You kept talking about discretion, so I figured maybe it's the same deal there."

"No," she said, "not really. I mean, they are big on discretion, that's their thing. But it's not a place like Braxton Hall, not really."

"I just wondered," Hugo said, "what with all the stone archways and iron grills everywhere."

"Kinda dungeon-like, huh?" she said. "Maybe that's why I like it so much." Her voice dropped. "Guess I'm done working there. Rose was pretty angry."

"I noticed," Hugo said. "Can't blame her—we did bust in there and surprise her. Maybe I can help smooth things out with her when we get back."

"Yeah, sure," Merlyn said, her voice thick with sarcasm. "She just loves you."

Hugo smiled, and a quick glance told him that Merlyn was smiling, too. He pulled out his cell phone and dialed Pendrith again, but still there was no answer. They walked on in silence, and five minutes later they reached the lay-by. They stopped in unison beside the high bank, and Hugo looked into the dark, at first wondering if the black shadows around him were playing tricks.

Neither his car nor Pendrith were there.

CHAPTER TWELVE

It took Harry Walton less than a minute to run out of patience and bang on Pendrith's bedroom door at the pub. A growing sense of alarm made him stare at the closed bathroom door as he waited for a response. Not getting one, he marched over and called out.

"Pendrith? Marston?" He waited at the door but again got no reply. "Who's in there?"

He guessed what they'd done and barged into Marston's room without bothering to knock. He went straight to the window and looked out in time to see the Cadillac backing out of its space. He clenched his jaw in anger. Partly at himself, but mostly at them. They'd had a deal. They had a damned deal. Typical of an American and a politician to back out of a fucking deal, those pricks.

But he knew where they were going. There was only one place they could be headed and he'd damn well see them there.

Unless they'd taken his keys.

He stalked to his room, ready to scream with rage, but found his keys where he'd left them, in the top drawer of the dresser. He grabbed them and patted his pocket to make sure he had his wallet. Everything else he'd need was already in his car, so he ran down the stairs and through the bar, ignoring the startled look of the publican.

The Cadillac was gone by the time he got into the parking lot, and he almost expected to hear the angry hoots of local traffic as they were forced off the narrow lane by the monstrous American machine.

Walton unlocked his car and then paused, wondering exactly how he was going to fix this. Part of him—most of him right now—wanted to call his news editor and break the story, slather it all over the front pages. He'd be in time for the early editions and by midmorning there would be a mob of pitchfork-wielding farmers scouring the fields and woods for the movie star. And, depending on how he wrote the story, chasing the arrogant American and his lapdog, Pendrith. Walton smiled, imagining the three of them on the back of a hay cart, arms pinned to their sides with rope snatched from someone's barn, a horse whinnying as it was led under a sturdy oak limb. At the Weston Church, for example. He knew of an old oak that would do just fine. Justice the old-fashioned way, as it should be, some thought.

But he had higher goals in mind. At least, higher from his perspective. A story printed tomorrow would be nothing more than wrapping for fish and chips by the weekend, because the reality was that Dayton Harper and Hugo Marston would slink back to their embassy and be whisked off to America, safe and sound. There'd be no justice.

So he'd wait and get his story. He'd give that conniving pair one more chance to live up to their bargain, and it galled him because he knew he didn't have much choice. Did they know that? Did they know that this was his big opportunity? Journalists were being let go all around him, and he was past switching careers if his services were no longer required. No, he'd seen that before.

He sat in his Mini, one hand on the steering wheel, the other clutching his keys, his breath coming and going in little puffs before his eyes, gentle clouds of warmth on a cold night. He sat there and thought about his father, a man who'd been feared and respected, at the top of his profession. Too proud or stubborn or some damn thing to realize what was coming. He'd not just lost his job, but the whole damn profession had gone down the tubes and then, as now, it was happening all around. Technology hadn't been the culprit then, but Walton wasn't about to be caught short like his old man. Out of work and sitting in his chair at home, a bottle in one hand and a glass he never bothered using in the other. It only took him six months to do it, and they found him one morning in his underwear, lying by his armchair, the empty bottle under him, his skin yellow and burnished with fist-sized bruises that made young Harry, who six months previously had wanted to be just like his dad, think the old man had been beaten to death in the night.

He had, sort of. Beaten by time. Beaten relentlessly from the inside by the contents of a few hundred bottles of cheap whisky.

But Harry still had a shot to get it right. If only the old man were around to see.

The red Mini left the parking lot of the pub with a squeal of tires. The anger had returned, and Harry Walton wanted to catch the American tank before it got too far ahead. But a nail, just one little piece of metal, put paid to his chase after half a mile when the car pitched to the right and Walton had to fight with the steering wheel as he brought the car into a lay-by to see what was what.

He changed the tire quickly, despite the dark, his movements efficient, precise, and fueled by anger and desperation. Old cars, even small ones, had real spares in them, not like those stupid little donut wheels they put in the new cars. No, Walton was down for a few minutes but he wasn't out. No chance of catching up, but he knew where they were going, so he'd meet them there.

He wondered for a moment what they'd do if they ran into the man with the gun again. He didn't understand what they might have in mind should that happen. But that was their problem, and maybe it'd be enough to slow them and let him catch up.

A flat tire for him, and a man with a gun for them. Sounded fair.

But when he pulled into the muddy lane, he saw no car and no man. Walton drove slowly, suddenly aware that he'd used up his spare, knowing that the flint stones or debris from a thousand years of traffic along the track could slice into the old rubber tires and leave him stranded.

That's when Mr. Shotgun will appear, he thought. That'd be just my luck.

Ahead of him, trees danced in and out of the shadows caused by his headlights, and the darkness away from the beams seemed complete. The flickering branches, reaching out and then pulling back, made him want to blast through this creepy place, but he fought the urge. Care was essential, he knew. In all things.

And ghosts weren't real.

A flash of light right in front of him made Walton stamp on the brake, and the little car skidded just a little before stopping. Someone, a car, was pointed directly at him, someone who had only just turned his headlights on.

That damned Mr. Shotgun, Walton just knew it. Probably sitting on the verge in a clapped-out old Land Rover just waiting for someone to shoot.

Then the lights angled away for a moment and Walton realized that the vehicle had driven off the track to let him pass. Or lure him closer.

He put the car in gear and started forward, inching toward the lights, unsure how much passing room there was, if there was any at all. But then they were nose to nose, like lovers, brushing past with care, his car rocking over the potholes even at this speed. It wasn't a Land Rover at all, and when his window drew level with that of the other driver he felt obliged to look over, compelled to see and, for politeness's sake, to acknowledge the other man.

But Harry Walton didn't wave, and nor did the other driver. The face, so familiar yet so stark and pale, those famous eyes burning forward as if the man could will himself down the lane by staring through the windshield. Even the hair seemed familiar, like a bedraggled puppy coming inside on a rainy day.

Harry Walton's mouth fell open, just a little, before he put his foot on the brake pedal and stopped beside Mr. Dayton Harper, sometime movie star, sometime fugitive, and whose life story would now become the sole possession of Harry Walton, the freelance reporter who was about to become a very famous journalist indeed.

CHAPTER THIRTEEN

For the first time in a very long while, Hugo was at a complete loss. He was standing in the pitch black with an almost-stranger, in a place he didn't know, with no car.

He knew the main road that led to the town of Baldock was about a mile away, a slow and not very safe walk on this road by night, but he didn't know what else to do. If Pendrith had gone in search of food, a bathroom, even a bottle of something, he'd come back this way.

They started walking, their footfalls the only sound on the mud-spackled road. They had traveled less than a hundred yards when twin headlights cut through the dark, dazzling them. Hugo put out an arm and grabbed Merlyn, pressing their bodies into the bank to avoid being hit. When the vehicle was thirty yards away, the nose dipped and the engine calmed, as if the driver had seen them. Seconds later, Hugo realized it was Pendrith in the Cadillac.

"Frightfully sorry," Pendrith said, through an open window. "Tried phoning but the call wouldn't go through. Dashed around the back wondering if maybe you'd headed out that way, but saw the blighter with the gun again and had to turn back."

"Glad you did," said Hugo. "Now hop out and let me drive. And say hello to our passenger."

Pendrith turned in the driver's seat and looked over Hugo's shoulder. "I say, what the bloody hell is she doing here?"

"I'll tell you on the way." Hugo went around and opened the driver's side door and waited as Pendrith slid out. With everyone buckled in, Hugo sped to the lay-by and executed a quick three-point turn. "Now then, Merlyn," he said. "Where to?"

✲

She'd called it a farm, but that was too rustic a word. It was a manor house, redbrick in the symmetrical Georgian style with five large, rectangular windows across the top floor and dormer windows, once for the servants' quarters, Hugo assumed, set into the roof. Thick ivy clambering up the brick walls, and the cracks that made way for the clinging green tendrils, suggested that there were no servants now, nor had there been for some time. The ends of the house were capped with tall chimney stacks, and at least one of them still worked, judging by the smell of wood smoke in the air.

Hugo knocked on the door, and after ten seconds of silence the visitors swapped glances. Hugo looked past them and saw no cars, no signs that the house was occupied. Just the chimney smoke.

"Wait here," Hugo said, "I'll check around the back."

Merlyn started to say something, then changed her mind. She waited with Pendrith as Hugo moved off to his right, peering into each window that he passed. So far, all had been dark. He reached the front right corner of the house and looked into the night, able to make out a lawn stretching away into the darkness as it reached around to the back of the house. He stood there for a moment, then made his way back to the front door and, without saying anything, turned the handle.

"You sure that's a good idea?" Pendrith said.

"Nope," Hugo said. "But I don't have any others."

The door opened silently, and Hugo stepped into the house. Pendrith followed him, and Merlyn stood in the doorway, eyes wide and worried.

"Police!" Hugo called. "Anyone home?"

Pendrith looked at him sideways. "'Police'?" he whispered.

Hugo turned and flashed a quick smile. "You'd rather I announced us as burglars?"

They moved into the hallway. To the right, a staircase curved up to a landing and then on to the second floor. On their left, a door stood open and Hugo stepped through it into an untidy study. In front of him sat a large wooden desk, littered with pens and glass paperweights. Sagging cardboard boxes lined the wall on the left, and opposite them, stacks of yellowing papers spilled across a leather couch that had also seen better days.

He joined the other two and led them past the staircase into a large room that took up the back half of the house and, in daylight, looked out over the back garden. The left half of the high-ceilinged space was used as a dining room and was dominated by an oversized table covered in a cloth that had once been white, a dozen chairs tucked tidily under its skirt. Former generations of the Drinker family gazed at each other across the table, grim and formal in their gilt frames. On the right side was the sitting room, populated by cloth couches and a scattering of armchairs, an even mixture of cracked leather and faded floral prints. Here, the pasty-faced relatives made way for various bucolic scenes, a few in heavy oil and a handful of smaller and more cheerful watercolors. One of the large windows had been converted into French doors, and he guessed that a patio lay just outside.

The room smelled musty, dusty even, and Hugo saw that the walk-in fireplace glowed orange. He listened but heard no one, no sounds at all. And yet he felt sure they weren't the only ones here. He started to his left, to head through the dining room toward where he thought the kitchen would be, when a sudden thump from upstairs stopped them. A weak cry filtered through the ceiling and they heard another thump, then silence.

Hugo pushed past Pendrith and Merlyn, heading back toward the stairs. He grabbed the banister and started up, taking them two at a time and drawing his gun as he ran. He paused at the top and looked both ways. He saw no one but the sound came again, from his left, so he went that way, slower now, more careful. He heard Pendrith behind him and hoped the Englishman had had the sense to make Merlyn wait at the bottom of the stairs.

The hallway was wide and dim, and on each side there were two closed doors leading to bedrooms or bathrooms, Hugo assumed. From one of them, on his left, light was leaking out from under the door. He looked down the hallway, but the others seemed to be dark. He stood to one side of the door and motioned for Pendrith to stop where he was, ten feet away. Hugo rapped on the door with the butt of his gun.

"Anyone in there?" he called. "Police here."

From inside the room they heard another cry, and Hugo recognized the sound of a man in pain. He reached down and tried the handle, and it turned in his hand. Still to one side, he pushed the door open and light spilled out into the hall. Hugo moved into the doorway, gun raised, and found himself in a large bedroom.

Directly opposite him, propped up with his back against a wooden dresser, sat a man clutching his stomach. Blood coated the man's left hand, and his right held an object that Hugo couldn't immediately recognize. His legs stuck straight out toward the door, and his eyes rolled slowly up as Hugo moved closer. They had the glazed look Hugo had seen a handful of times before when he was with the FBI, a look that spoke of a man in deep physical shock, a whisper away from death.

Hugo turned when he heard Pendrith speak behind him. "I'll call for an ambulance."

"Good," said Hugo. "Tell them to hurry." He turned to the wounded man. "Are you Brian Drinker?"

The man seemed to nod, but Hugo wasn't sure. Red bubbles appeared on his lower lip and the man groaned, then managed a whisper. "Yes."

"Brian, who did this?" Hugo said. "Can you tell me what happened?"

Drinker grimaced and his eyes slid down and to the right, to the object in his hand. Hugo looked and saw an open cell phone, the buttons slick with blood. "I tried . . . couldn't . . ."

"It's OK," Hugo said, his voice low and calm. "Help is on the way. I just need you to tell me what happened, can you do that?"

"He came here," Drinker gasped. "I wasn't going to let him in."

"Who?" Hugo urged.

"But he said . . . he apologized." Drinker suddenly gripped Hugo's wrist with his bloody left hand. "He said he was sorry."

"Harper? Are you saying Dayton Harper did this?"

Drinker groaned and looked away, then his hand fell from Hugo's wrist. He coughed once and then looked up.

"It wasn't meant to happen this way," Drinker said. "That's what he told me." He turned to Hugo, his eyes wide and brimming with tears, his voice rasping. "I don't understand. Why did he shoot me? I didn't do anything."

Drinker closed his eyes and his breath rattled in his throat. Hugo looked at the wound in the farmer's stomach but didn't touch it. The bleeding looked to have stopped and Hugo didn't want to restart it by adding pressure. He looked up at Pendrith, who shook his head and spoke quietly.

"We're in the country, an ambulance will take twenty minutes to get out here. Same for the police, probably."

"I don't mind waiting for an ambulance, but we don't have time to explain this to the police," Hugo said. "And Harper can't be too far away."

"You go," Pendrith said. "I'll wait with him. I can call some people I used to work with, make sure the police keep this wrapped up—for now, anyway."

Hugo stood and looked over Pendrith's shoulder to see Merlyn standing in the hallway. She was pale and her big eyes looked like those of a deer face-to-face with its hunter.

"What's happening?" she said.

"Buggered if I know," said Pendrith, as the two men moved into the hall. "Hugo, why would Harper shoot this man?"

"I wish I knew," said Hugo. "It doesn't make sense."

"He's gone stark-raving mad," said Pendrith. "Off his rocker."

Hugo nodded. "That's about all I can come up with, too. All the more reason for me to find him."

"Damn right," said Pendrith. "And the sooner the better."

They looked back into the room as Brian Drinker moaned and

opened his eyes. He was trying to speak, but Pendrith stepped into the doorway ahead of Hugo. The Englishman looked back at and nodded toward Merlyn, who had a hand over her mouth. "Go," Pendrith said to Hugo. "And you better take her with you."

"OK," Hugo said. "But for God's sake call me if he says anything else. If I don't catch Harper, I'll come right back for you." Hugo gave him a small smile. "Let's hope I don't see you for a while." He took Merlyn by the arm and steered her down the hallway and down the stairs.

At the bottom, Merlyn stopped him.

"I don't understand what's happening," she said.

Hugo looked at her, not knowing what to say. "I wish I could tell you."

"You mean you know and won't?"

"No," he smiled. "I don't know, so I can't. Come on, let's go."

She moved slowly after him. "Do you really think Dayton shot that man?"

"Don't you?"

"But why would he?"

"No idea," he said. "That's why we need to go, and right now. We need to find him and figure out what's going on before anyone else gets hurt. And if we do find him, you can be a friendly face, which he's gonna need."

She nodded and they moved to the front door. Just as he was about to open it, light cut through the window opposite the staircase, white flashes from the headlights of a vehicle passing the front of the house.

"The ambulance?" Merlyn said.

"No." Hugo stopped her. Whoever it was had come from behind the house and was heading for the main road. "It's gotta be him. Dayton Harper."

CHAPTER FOURTEEN

They sprinted out of the farmhouse and made straight for Hugo's vehicle, gravel kicking up behind them as they ran. As he opened the driver's side door, Hugo looked for the taillights of the Smart Car but saw nothing. A faint sound that might just have been the wind was the only suggestion as to which direction Harper might have taken.

The huge car's wheels spun for a second before gripping the loose surface, and they fishtailed away from the house and down the short driveway to the main road. Hugo had already decided that Harper would likely head back to London, and he was even more sure of that when a sign at the end of the driveway pointed to the town of Stevenage, a jumping-off point onto the A1, the main road from there to the capital. Hugo was sure that Harper had taken care of any business he had in the Hertfordshire countryside, here at the farm and at Braxton Hall, which meant that the only logical destination for Harper was London, a place the actor knew and where he could be relatively safe.

But as Hugo fought the car around the tight turn onto the main road, he knew that his theory relied on Harper acting logically. And there'd not been much evidence of that lately.

He punched *London* into his GPS device and saw Merlyn looking at him.

"You OK?" he asked.

"Sure. I think. I just don't get what's happening."

"Me neither, but I'm guessing he's on his way back to London."

"Why?"

He looked at her sharply. "Is there somewhere else he'd be going?"

"No," she said quickly. "Not that I know of. Do you think he's turning himself in?"

"No idea." He gripped the wheel as the car tore along the winding country road toward Stevenage. "No idea at all."

Hugo stared through the windshield, the road in front of him a ribbon of black that swept through villages, an empty track with no sign of his quarry. He went as fast as the car and the winding highway would let him, but it wasn't fast enough, and soon he felt like a greyhound chasing a rabbit that had already fled into its burrow.

They sped on for five minutes, long minutes, catching cars like fireflies, but each set of rear lights was a disappointment. Hugo's sense of desperation and pessimism increased with each.

Merlyn seemed to be thinking the same thing. "Shouldn't we have caught up with him by now?" she asked, as they raced up behind a cattle truck.

"Yes, probably." He'd been thinking the same thing. "This is the most direct route to London."

At the top of a steep hill, Hugo checked for oncoming traffic, then swung the Cadillac into the oncoming lane. He flicked on his high beams and gave them a view of at least half a mile, down the hill and back up the slope opposite them. No small car. He tucked back in behind the cattle truck and waited for the entrance to a field, which he pulled into and, with a reluctance that was almost painful, turned the car around and started back to the farm. Harper had gotten away.

When they arrived, the farmhouse was awash with lights, and Hugo had to park the car on the grass that bordered the driveway into the property. He and Merlyn walked toward the gaggle of police cars, Hugo scanning the small crowd for Pendrith. He saw him talking to one of the non-uniformed officers and decided against joining the group.

It took less than a minute for a uniformed officer to spot Hugo and Merlyn lurking on the edge of things, and when he approached them Hugo had his story ready. He had to assume that Pendrith had told them he'd gone there alone, been dropped off. He was smart enough not to escalate things by involving two more participants, one an armed US Embassy officer.

"Can I help you?" the officer said.

"Sure," said Hugo. "Constable . . . ?"

"Christie. You are?"

Hugo pulled out his credentials, and while the officer was inspecting them, Hugo motioned to Merlyn. "And she's with me."

Uncertainty clouded PC Christie's face. "Yes, sir. Do you need to speak to someone in charge?"

"No," Hugo said. "I'm just waiting for Lord Stopford-Pendrith. You might say I'm his chauffeur for today."

"Yes, sir. He's just giving his statement, he should be done soon. I'll let him know you're here." He started to move away but turned back, pulling a small notepad and pen from his breast pocket. "Excuse me, sir, but do you have any knowledge about what happened here?"

"No, can't say I do," Hugo said genially. "We just arrived, I'm sure there's nothing I can tell you that you don't already know."

Christie looked back and forth between them, then tucked his notepad and pen back into his jacket pocket. "Very well, sir."

They watched him walk back to the officers surrounding Pendrith, who turned and looked over toward them without giving anything away. Within a minute, the MP himself was striding toward them.

"I say, what a bloody mess," he said. "Poor fellow's unconscious but hanging on. For now, anyway. Local chaps don't get many of these, so they're calling the brass in."

Hugo grimaced. "What did you tell them?"

"Just that I was here on a mission of goodwill, sort of a liaison thing to sort out the mess with Harper. I told them that you dropped me off in front of the house, planning to pick me up or come by and meet with Mr. Drinker, if he agreed. I said that the door was open when I got here, and so I went in and found him. No mention of Harper being here, don't worry." Pendrith shrugged. "So far they're buying it, but once the big boys start arriving, the lid's coming off this little melting pot, I'm afraid."

Hugo looked at the activity around him. A man was gut-shot, a man who happened to be a prominent local farmer and the father of the man recently killed by two movie stars. Hugo shook his head at the thought of the senior brass lining up to demand a quick resolution. The chief constable himself would probably be arriving any minute.

"So," said Pendrith. "Back to London? Isn't that where you thought Harper was headed?"

"Yes," said Hugo. "That is what I thought." He eyed his companions for a moment. The left side of the house and gardens was surrounded by a brick wall, which separated the property from a field. A wooden signpost twenty yards away pointed into the field, and Hugo had walked enough in the countryside to know a public footpath when he saw one. With any luck, this path would lead them around the back of the property. "Anyone fancy a walk after all this excitement?" he asked cheerily.

"A walk?" Pendrith stared at him, bug-eyed. "What the bloody hell are you talking about? We need to get a move on, get back to London."

"He thought that Dayton was driving to London," Merlyn interjected. "Past tense. Looks to me like he doesn't think that anymore."

"Then where the hell is that bloody man going?" Pendrith asked.

"No idea." Merlyn shrugged, then jerked a thumb toward Hugo. "Ask the Yank."

"Follow me and I'll tell you," Hugo said. He opened the passenger door of the Cadillac and rifled through the glove box, pulling out a flashlight. He flicked it on, testing it, then off. "Let's go."

Ignoring Pendrith's mutterings, Hugo led them across the driveway toward the pasture. He pushed his way through a rusty kissing gate and waited for them to follow. When they did, he set off in the direction the sign pointed, parallel to the wall that surrounded that side of the farmhouse. They began walking.

"So what're you thinking?" Pendrith asked, as he trailed behind Merlyn.

"It's just an idea, nothing more," Hugo said, "but as Merlyn pointed out in the car, if he'd been going to London we'd have caught up with him."

"Maybe he took a wrong turn," Pendrith suggested.

"Maybe, but he doesn't seem to have done so yet. And a sign at the end of this drive points toward Stevenage, which is right beside the A1 that we all came in on. So even if he didn't know that was the right direction, the sign would have told him so. And in my experience, people who are not good with directions look extra hard for signs."

"So if he didn't accidentally turn the wrong way, you think maybe he went somewhere else on purpose?" Merlyn said.

"That's possible," Hugo said, "but where? Harper ran from us and came up here on the spur of the moment; he fled here. He didn't have time to plan an itinerary, to map out where he was going and when. And he can't now take the risk of showing up unexpectedly at a place where people will recognize him."

"Which is pretty much anywhere," said Merlyn.

"Right," Hugo agreed.

"So what?" Pendrith called from the back of the line.

"So maybe he didn't leave the farm," Hugo suggested. "Or even come here in the first place."

"Then whose car did we see?" Merlyn asked.

"I don't know. We've been assuming it was his, but it was dark and all I saw was a small car." Hugo smiled tightly, then said, "at least, I think it was a small car."

"But that chap Drinker," Pendrith insisted, "he said Harper had been here and bloody well shot him."

Hugo grunted, deep in thought, and the threesome trudged on as the night's quiet settled over them like a cloak. They walked for five minutes, their eyes used to the dark now, but even so they occasionally stumbled on the uneven ground. Once, Merlyn froze in her tracks, startled by the sudden call of a nearby pheasant. She was quickly reassured by Pendrith and they moved on in silence again. The path followed the outside of the crumbling brick wall, and sometimes Hugo wondered whether the three of them could just push it over. But the downside of the wall's fragility meant that any attempt to climb it could be dangerous.

After a quarter mile, Pendrith stopped. "Where the hell is this getting us?"

Hugo clicked on the flashlight. He ran the beam of light along the narrow trail, starting at his feet and directing it along the worn track. The smell of wet earth beneath their feet and the tumble of black trees ahead of them gave Hugo the sensation of being lost, a hapless wanderer in a strange land.

Which, he thought, *I pretty much am.*

Beside them, the dark silhouette of the wall curved off to the right, but the path went straight ahead, bisecting the lumpy pasture. Hugo turned the beam onto the wall and, twenty yards away, saw that it ended in a tumble of ivy that dangled down from the bricks and roped itself around a waist-high wooden fence designed to keep cattle from wandering onto the property.

"Here we go," he said.

He climbed over first, putting out a helping hand to Merlyn, who took it, and to Pendrith, who ignored it with a grunt of what Hugo took to be outrage. All safely over, Hugo looked toward the back of the house. They were standing at the edge of the garden, at least sixty yards from the house that sat as a gray hulk rimmed with white from the lights of the police activity out front.

Hugo led the way, flicking the flashlight on every few seconds, just long enough to know the way was clear. After just a few paces, Pendrith piped up.

"What the hell are we looking for?"

"An outbuilding with lights on," Hugo said, "or a tree house with people whispering in it. Use your imagination." For a former MI5 officer, Pendrith had a very blunt investigative edge, Hugo thought.

"I see a pond, how's that?" Pendrith said, stopping to point. Hugo ran the light to his left and saw a circular pond thirty yards across. A gentle bank sloped about two feet to a heavy-looking surface, and Hugo assumed it was covered in duckweed, or maybe an unbroken layer of lily pads. He moved closer, eyes straining in the dim light. A few feet from the pond, his ankle flexed as he stood on what felt like a dip in the lawn. He ran the light over the ground and his stomach tightened.

"Guys, stay where you are," he said, his voice low and urgent. He took two steps back and then aimed the flashlight at the surface of the pond. At the edge he'd just backed away from, the dark water sucked in the beam, telling Hugo there was a gap in the reflective greenery on its surface. He moved to his left, to the edge of the pond, and knelt. The weed-free patch of water was ten feet away, and he kept the light on it as he pulled a coin from his pocket. He took aim and lobbed it underhand toward the patch, following its flight with the beam from the flashlight. The coin arced over the green close to his feet and fell toward the dark water, landing with a gentle plink and seeming to hover on its surface for a moment before skittering away from Hugo, apparently along the surface of the water, before disappearing from view.

"There's something under there," Pendrith said from over Hugo's shoulder.

"There is," said Hugo. "And I'm afraid I know what it is."

"You do?" Pendrith said, as he helped Hugo up. They stood side by side looking at the pond, then Pendrith spoke again. "That was the roof of a car, wasn't it?"

"That's my guess," said Hugo.

"The question is, whose car?" Pendrith muttered.

"A car?" Merlyn moved forward and touched Hugo's arm. "Oh my god. Is there someone in it?"

"That," said Hugo grimly, "is the other question."

※

It took thirty minutes for the police to shift their battery of lights to the back lawn and for a tow truck to appear. Hugo, Pendrith, and Merlyn stood to one side, enduring the suspicious looks of the police who were busy orchestrating the extraction of whatever lay beneath the surface of the pond.

"You have some explaining to do," Detective Chief Inspector Clive Upton had told Hugo, happier to wag his finger at an American, Hugo thought, than at an MP or a frightened-looking civilian. A pretty, frightened-looking civilian. Upton had been furious at first, stalking across the lawn behind Pendrith, who had gone to fetch him. But the senior officer circled away from the tire tracks almost instinctively and directed his attention at the small amount of visible evidence before turning to Hugo. And even then, after the initial outrage that someone other than one of his men had found a crucial piece of evidence, a new crime scene maybe, Upton had calmed down and nodded along as Hugo explained why they were there, sticking as close to Pendrith's version as he could.

DCI Upton carried himself like a sergeant-major, ramrod straight and shoulders squared off with a ruler. His hair looked white in the dark, but his eyes were clear like a young man's, hard and silver though perhaps pale blue in daylight, his skin smooth enough to make even Dayton Harper jealous. And when Hugo had finished, Upton watched him for a moment, as if deciding whether or not to believe his story, ask for more, or go with what he had for now.

Hugo was relieved when he decided on the latter. Upton radioed for a line of constables to pick their way across the expansive lawn toward the pond, scouring the grass for further clues. Upton shouted at one young constable who wandered too close to the tire tracks, making the constable leap back into formation without a word other than, Hugo imagined, a quiet curse aimed at himself.

The thin blue search line pincered around the pond and stopped at the water's edge without finding anything, and everyone stood waiting and watching as two flatbed trucks drove around the side of the house and positioned themselves thirty yards from the pond, on either side. With a clicking sound followed by a *whump*, a dozen lights colored the scene in a yellowy green, forcing the night back to the fence that Hugo had crossed half an hour ago. A crime-scene specialist appeared and started photographing the ground around the pond, as well as the pond itself, a dozen men watching his steady progress around the scene.

Soon a lone policeman trudged across the lawn toward them, leading a tow truck whose diesel engine growled with impatience at the slow crawl along its safe path to the pond. When it got there, the driver shut off the engine and hopped down from the cab at his guide's behest. A short, round man in oily overalls, he wore a look of uncertainty that told Hugo he wasn't used to pulling cars out of water, especially when they might have bodies in them.

The crime-scene tech finally knelt to put his camera in its bag, and they all watched as he pulled out a video camera and walked to the far side of the pond. Moments after he'd set it atop a tripod, his voice crackled through Upton's radio that he was ready. Upton turned to the fidgeting tow-truck driver.

"Let's go, Mr. Crouch. Nice and easy, we'd like to keep whatever's in there as intact as possible."

The driver hesitated, then looked at the pond. "You want me to go in there, hook it up?"

"Correct."

"What if it's facing the wrong way?"

Upton smiled thinly. "You're the expert charging us a hundred quid an hour. So I want you to put your waders on, go in there, and hook it up."

Crouch licked his lips and nodded, then went to the back of his truck. He wrestled with a pair of fishing waders, losing his balance twice before getting them on properly. He leaned over some controls, and Hugo heard the clanking of metal on metal.

Crouch walked tentatively to the edge of the pond with a hoist cable in his hand, then stepped into the pond. He shuffled onward, feeling with his toes, but he slid forward anyway and stood there, suddenly waist deep in the water, eyes wide with the shock of the cold. Crouch looked around for a second, then shrugged as if giving in to the inevitable, and dipped his right side under the water as he felt around him. He stepped forward again, then stooped down so that the water rose to his shoulders and Hugo could hear him puffing away, his round chin brushing the frigid water as he worked. He seemed to stay like that for a long time, wrestling the cable and hoist pan with both hands.

Then he was out of the water and walking to his truck, leaning behind the cab and pulling a lever that tilted the flat bed to a forty-five degree angle. He pulled another lever and the cable went taut, the drum reeling it in with a grinding sound. All eyes turned to where the cable lifted out of the water and quivered, strands of weed dropping from the roped steel as it took the strain.

Then, with a lurch and a rush of water, the green top of the pond parted and a dark mass broke the surface. A murmur ran through the ring of policemen around the pond, but they soon quieted when progress halted. The winch motor changed pitch with the effort of dragging its load. The little pond, with its muddy floor and steep sides, didn't want to give up its prize. Hugo realized he was holding his breath, and he imagined everyone else was too. He looked back at the struggle going on at the edge of the water and heard a sucking sound, followed by a sudden whoosh, as the pond finally conceded defeat.

Hugo felt a hand on his arm. He looked down at Merlyn's pale face and watched the confusion and anger in her eyes as her little car was dragged over the rim of the pond. It sat there, plastered with weeds and bleeding pond water, a tiny capsule with opaque windows, a treasure chest or a coffin, pulled from the deep.

The winch fell silent and DCI Upton moved toward the passenger door. He shone his flashlight through the window but gave no indication of what he saw.

"Where's my crime-scene team?" he called, and nodded when the photographer and another officer appeared at his side. Upton reached for the door handle, then pulled it, swinging the car door open as he stepped back. A rush of dirty water spilled out and everyone on that side of the car, Hugo and Merlyn included, leaned forward to look inside.

Merlyn sighed with relief at the empty seats, no doubt glad her friend had not been under that turgid water. But she wasn't seeing what Hugo saw: a temporary victory and a sign that they needed to get back on the road.

"Thank God!" Merlyn whispered. "Screw the car, I'm just glad Dayton wasn't in there."

"And that means he's somewhere else," Hugo murmured. He looked at Pendrith, standing halfway between him and Upton, and read the relief on his face. Pendrith started toward them, the movement catching Upton's eye. The policeman leaned over to a burly officer beside him and gave a quick order, and the constable trotted over to the threesome.

"Not planning on leaving, are you sir?" he said to Hugo.

"Actually, yes," Hugo replied. "Places to go, people to find. You know how it is."

"Oh, I do, sir," the constable said cheerily. "Thing is, DCI Upton may not. Perhaps a quick word with him before you go." It wasn't a suggestion.

"Wait here," Hugo told Pendrith and Merlyn. "I won't be long." He strode quickly to where Upton was giving directions to his crime-scene technicians. "Chief, we need to be on our way. Lord Stopford-Pendrith has given a statement already, so I assume you won't be needing us."

Upton turned cold, gray eyes on Hugo, appraising him. "Right. Because all you did was find a recently submerged car in a pond in the middle of the night. How could I possibly have any more questions for you?"

"Look, I'll tell you what I can," Hugo said. "I'm looking for someone, someone who's been driving that car."

Upton jerked a thumb at the house. "Yeah, I think we're looking for him too, assuming he put that farmer into a coma. Who is it?"

Hugo shook his head. "I don't think the man I'm looking for did that. At least, I can't imagine why he would have. You and I are looking for two different people, Inspector."

"And I'm supposed to take your word for that?"

Hugo looked at him, trying to figure a way to convince Upton. "Look, I'll make you a deal. If I find the driver of that car, I'll bring him wherever you want for an interview. I can guarantee that you'll see why he's not your shooter."

"I need a name, Mr. Marston. Now."

"He's not your man, Inspector. Let me find him and bring him in, you start here and look for the shooter. The real shooter."

"Name. You have three seconds."

"Talk to Pendrith. You're making a mistake because all I'm trying to do is help you—"

Hugo stopped talking as his arms were grabbed from his sides and pulled behind him. He had no time to resist as the burly constable clicked handcuffs onto his wrists. Hugo looked over his shoulder at the startled look on Pendrith's face. The old man started forward, but his path was blocked by two constables much stronger and swifter. Hugo turned back to Upton and spoke firmly, trying hard to control the anger rising inside him.

"I'm a security agent for the US Embassy. I am on official State Department business, and I have diplomatic immunity. I don't like to pull rank, Chief Inspector, but we have two men out here somewhere, one trying to kill the other and happy to shoot anyone else who gets in his way. We don't have time for this shit, so take these handcuffs off."

Upton reached up and patted Hugo's shoulder, a smile playing on his lips.

"That so, Mr. Marston? Well, here's the thing. You're in Hertfordshire now, not your US Embassy, so it'll take a little while to confirm your immunity. In the meantime, we can get a nice cup of tea and talk about it down at the station."

CHAPTER FIFTEEN

Hugo sat in the rear of the police car, watching through the window as Pendrith talked with DCI Upton. Merlyn hovered in the space between, drifting close to the policeman and the politician only to receive "leave us alone" looks, which pushed her toward the car until one uniformed officer or another asked her politely, but firmly, not to get too close.

At first Upton stood there listening impassively, occasionally looking over one shoulder at Hugo, but more often looking over the other to check on the progress of his crime-scene techs. After five minutes of this, one of the techs interrupted Pendrith to make his report. Upton listened and apparently dismissed the man, then looked at his watch. He spoke now, and Pendrith nodded along. Finally, a constable was sent to the car and sat in the driver's seat. He waited quietly until Upton himself arrived, sitting beside his constable up front.

"What did they find in the car?" asked Hugo. He sat forward and spoke loudly through the plastic window that separated them, not sure how effective the little holes might be.

Upton half turned and looked at Hugo. "Don't you want to know where we're going?"

"You already told me," Hugo said.

"Change of plan. You're a lucky man, Mr. Marston."

"Call me Hugo. And you're referring to Pendrith's intervention?"

"No. The Rising Moon happens to be my local pub. We're going to have a beer and a chat."

Hugo sat back, not wanting Upton to see the relief on his face. "Works for me," he said. "Does this mean you didn't find a gun in the car?"

Upton raised an eyebrow. "Pendrith's right, you are a clever fellow. And he told me a little about your friend Harper."

Hugo cursed Pendrith silently, but knew he probably didn't have much option if he wanted Hugo free. Hugo turned his thoughts to what the absence of a gun meant, but spoke aloud. "Either Harper wasn't driving the car, or he didn't shoot Drinker, or he did both and . . ." The next option was his least favorite.

"Right," Upton finished the thought. "And unless he tossed it into the pond, and we'll look, he's out there with the gun in his hand. But whether he did it or not, we have a man with a weapon roaming the countryside. Someone perfectly willing and able to use it. Seems like cause enough for a drink and a chat, doesn't it?"

"No argument here," said Hugo.

DCI Upton and the landlord of the Rising Moon greeted each other like old friends, though there was a respect in Jim Booher's eyes that told Marston their encounters hadn't always been in the pub. They arrived as Booher was locking up, but he didn't hesitate to leave the four of them in the bar alone, trusting them to pay now or, should he need a favor from the men in blue, repay him later. Hugo liked that things still worked this way in the country, but he was interested to see that his initial evaluation of Upton was wrong. He wasn't a by-the-book cop as Hugo had first thought. The man was also results oriented.

Booher had gotten around to lighting the fire at some point that evening, and Pendrith kicked it back to life with his foot and two new logs. Then they stood around a nearby table and looked at Merlyn.

"She may know something that helps us," Hugo said, seeing Upton's desire to excuse her from the conversation. "She knows a lot more about Harper than we do."

Upton nodded his acquiescence, then played barman, not taking orders, just grabbing a bottle of whisky from under the counter and four glasses. As he moved to the table, Hugo was amused to see Upton shoot a questioning look at Merlyn, who looked irritated. *Yes, I'm a girl who drinks whisky.*

When he'd finished pouring, Upton took a sip without proposing a toast. "I'll tell you what I know; you fill in the rest," he said.

Hugo nodded. "Fair enough."

"I know that old Mr. Drinker is unconscious with someone's lead in him. I know that you guys are looking for Dayton Harper up here. I know that Harper and his wife ran over Drinker's son a week ago. The rest," he shrugged, "you're gonna have to help me with."

Hugo looked at Pendrith, who sat back, glass in hand.

"Fire away, old boy," Pendrith said. "He's your charge, not mine."

"Dayton Harper was supposed to be in my care," Hugo said, and he began with Ginny Ferro and her grisly end.

"That was definitely murder?" Upton said. "Any chance it was suicide?"

"Well, that's where things get complicated," Hugo said. "At first we assumed suicide, and then because of the situation with Farmer Drinker, we considered it might be murder. The cloth over her face helped with that. But now it's possible, just possible, it was an accident."

"An accident? She was hung from a tree in a graveyard by accident?" Upton looked around the table to see who else was laughing. When he saw nothing but straight faces, he added drily, "What was she doing, pruning?"

"Let me explain," Hugo said, holding up a calming hand. "As I said, I was supposed to take custody of Harper after his release, to make sure he was safe and to keep him out of the public eye while this mess with Drinker was sorted out. But then he found out about his wife and apparently decided he had business to take care of up here. We were close behind him and tracked him up here to a place called Braxton Hall."

Upton's eyebrows went up. "I've heard about that place, though God knows what's true and what isn't."

"Probably most of it's true, from what I saw and heard," Hugo said, shooting a smile at Merlyn. "Anyway, seems like he and Ginny Ferro, and a little cadre of their friends, were into asphyxophilia."

"Breath play. I've come across it a few times, but normally it's a solo activity," Upton said. "Or I thought so."

"It can be," Merlyn interjected. "I'm guessing most of your experience comes from finding people dead, right?"

"Pretty much," Upton said.

"Which explains why you think it's a solitary practice. Look, the only safe way is to have someone else there because if it doesn't go well, you end up on the front pages. With someone else there, you're much safer. Or," she said with a shrug, "several other people there. That heightens the safety aspect as well as the eroticism. For some people." Another noncommittal shrug, but this time a little smile went with it.

"So what does this have to do with anything?" Upton looked directly at her and nodded. "Harper and Ferro are into this?"

"Among other things, yes," Merlyn said. "Regular bondage stuff, mock incarceration. She was pretty wild even for that crowd."

She told Upton about the cemetery at Braxton Hall, the crypt that was designer-made for guests to enjoy any way they saw fit, including the recreation of death scenes through breath play.

"You have actual parties like that there?" Upton asked. Hugo thought he was trying very hard not to sound judgmental.

"Yes," Merlyn said. "I know it'll sound weird to you, but no one ever got hurt." That little smile again. "In a bad way, I mean."

"Which is why you wondered about Ginny Ferro's death being an accident. Seems kind of . . . unlikely, doesn't it?"

"Which part?" Hugo said with a smile.

"Well," said Upton, stroking his chin. "I can see now that she might get something out of a rope and a real cemetery. But the night of her release from prison?"

"Yeah, I thought so, too," said Hugo. "But think about it this way. She gains a certain emotional and physical satisfaction from mock incarceration, right? Well, if she's incarcerated for real yet treated well, which she was by all accounts, then she may have been on a high coming out of there. She may have wanted to extend the experience by acting out another fantasy in a real environment."

"But who with?" asked Upton. "Wouldn't she need someone else?"

"Not necessarily," Merlyn said. "All she needed was a ladder and the rope, pretty much. But she also had friends down there, friends into this. A quick phone call would have had a dozen people running out there to play with her."

"Play?" Upton said.

"Yeah, we call it playing. Because that's what it usually is." Merlyn took a swig of her whisky. "Look, the point is, she could have had someone meet her there in a matter of an hour, less. She's a famous movie star for fuck's sake, anyone in the scene, men and women alike, would have given their left nut to play with her."

"Literally, eh what?" Pendrith chortled, then stuck his nose into his glass when he saw he was the only one laughing.

They sat in silence for a moment, then Hugo looked up. "Shit, what about Walton?"

"Who's that?" Upton asked.

"Pain-in-the-arse reporter who followed us here," said Pendrith.

"He knows about Harper?" Upton asked.

"Yes," said Hugo. "Unfortunately, he does. He's agreed not to say anything if we help get him an interview when we get Harper."

"Very kind of him," Upton said. "Where is he now?"

"Hard to say," Pendrith chortled again. "We gave him the slip earlier, sent him on some phony errand. Probably crying in his fish soup. I'll trot upstairs and see if the bugger's still here."

"Good idea," said Hugo.

As soon as he disappeared through the door, Upton turned to Hugo. "If you don't mind me asking, what's His Lordship's role in all this?"

"I don't mind at all," said Hugo. "I think he has a crush on Harper, for one thing. Also, Pendrith's been a friend of the United States, as the ambassador put it, for some years. I'm told his background is in intelligence, which could sure be useful right about now." Hugo smiled when he saw the frown on Upton's face. "Don't be fooled by the upper-class-twit routine, Chief Inspector."

"All for show?"

"No, actually I think the upper-class bit is real. He's no twit, though, that bit is just to fool you."

"Well, we could use all the help we can get," Upton said, "though I see why you were so bloody evasive back at the farm."

Hugo nodded. "If it gets out that Harper is running around England, possibly armed and maybe dangerous . . ." He shook his head. "I was worried before when I thought maybe he'd just get mobbed to death by fans, or possibly strung up by a few villagers here. But now, well, it doesn't bear thinking about."

"Agreed," Upton said. "Every man, woman, and child in the county would grab a flaming torch and go looking for him."

They looked up as Pendrith reappeared. "All's well," he said. "Walton is sleeping like a baby."

"Good." Upton looked into his glass but didn't take a sip. "So we need to figure out who shot Drinker, what the hell Harper is doing, and whether or not we raise the alarm. And I think we're all agreed that there's no need for a public announcement just yet."

"Certainly not," said Pendrith. He turned to look at Hugo. "You said before you didn't think he shot Drinker. Still think that?"

"I'm not quite sure what to think." He turned to Upton. "Did the paramedics indicate whether Drinker is going to make it?"

"No. He was unconscious by the time we got to him. All we know is what he said to you chaps. I'll call in and see if there's been any change, but right now what he said points straight to Harper. Let me call."

Upton stood and moved away from the table, and they sat in silence as the policeman connected with an underling at the station. He asked about Drinker and listened quietly for a moment. Then he said, "Are you sure he was there? You're sure it was him?" He nodded at the response and hung up, then came back to the table.

"News?" asked Pendrith.

"Most definitely," said Upton, wrapping his fingers around his glass. But this time he took a swig. "He was conscious for a few minutes before they went into surgery. Conscious and coherent enough to tell his escort what he told you: Harper was in that house tonight."

"And?" pressed Pendrith.

"And then Drinker died during surgery," said Upton.

In the silence that followed, every glass was emptied.

CHAPTER SIXTEEN

The call that Hugo had dreaded came at six the next morning.

He was already up and in the parking lot, looking for a public footpath that might take him on a walk of a mile or two before the world awoke, a moment to let the country air run through his system and a chance to either escape or help resolve the mystery that had captured him.

He answered without thinking and without checking to see who was calling. "Hugo Marston."

"DCI Upton here. Where are you?"

All hopes of a morning walk vanished when Hugo heard his tone. "At the pub. Everything OK?"

"No, not by a long chalk. You know where the Weston Church is?"

Hugo almost smiled. *It's where Jack O'Legs is buried*, he thought. But he just said, "Yes."

"Good. I'm on my way there now, meet me."

"Sure, I'll grab Pendrith, though he may be sleeping still." Hugo looked at his watch and saw it was just after six.

"No time," said Upton. "Just get over here as soon as you can, I'll send a car for him later."

"What's going on, Clive?"

"This fucking situation is getting out of hand, that's what's going on. So do me a favor and hurry."

Hugo patted his pockets. Wallet and keys, that's all he'd need. He glanced back at the pub, a little guilty at leaving Pendrith behind and half hoping to see him at a window, gesturing for Hugo to wait. But the cottage-like pub slumbered in the morning mist, soundless and still.

Hugo turned right out of the parking lot and drove slowly toward the church, which he remembered being about two miles away. The road seemed windier and narrower than before, and twice he had to brake as rabbits darted in front of him, heading for safety in the road-side hedgerow, their breakfast foraging interrupted by the purring behemoth that was Hugo's car.

A small signpost warned Hugo of the turn toward his destination and he swung the car onto Church Lane, which angled sharply upward. He drove for forty yards and then saw the police cars, their rooftop lights curiously off considering this was, seemingly, an emergency. As Hugo found a place to park, he saw an ambulance in his rearview mirror, following him into the gravel lot. Two policemen detached themselves from the iron gate that was the entrance to the church, one heading for him, the other for the ambulance.

The constable held Hugo's door as he climbed out but blocked any further movement. He was Indian or Pakistani, Hugo thought, but spoke with the diction of an English gentleman. "Good morning, sir, I'm afraid I'm going to have to ask you to leave the church premises for a while. We have a bit of a situation right now."

A voice called out from by the gate, DCI Upton dressed in a green Barbour jacket and flat cap.

"He's with me, Agarwal, bring him over."

Agarwal waved an apologetic hand at Upton, then turned back to Hugo. "Sorry sir, I had no idea. This way."

Hugo followed the constable through the gates and looked around. The church lay ahead and to his right, occupying the top corner of the property. The rest was taken up by a large, full, and well-tended grave-yard, with a cinder path leading through it to the church doors. A low stone wall, as old as the church itself, kept the graveyard from spilling into a neighboring field that was ridged with recently plowed furrows.

He took a few steps in, looked to his left, and paused. There it was, the pride of Weston village, the final resting place of a legend still told.

"You've heard of Jack O'Legs, sir?" Agarwal said, stopping beside Hugo.

"People keep asking me that. Yes, I have."

"Bit of an amateur historian, I am. Great story, though I've always wondered why no one's dug him up to see how big he really was."

Hugo smiled. "I wondered the same thing and got yelled at for saying so."

"I've had the same reaction." Agarwal looked up. "We should get going, sir."

Ahead, at the far side of the graveyard, half a dozen police officers were milling around as if waiting for instructions or direction. A couple of officers leaned against the cemetery wall, which was higher there, looking as though they wanted to smoke but didn't dare. Near them, a tremendous oak tree towered over the wall, massive branches reaching out over the gravestones as if to provide as much shade and shelter to Weston's dearly departed as it could manage.

Upton was waiting by the entrance to the church, standing with a young woman dressed in jeans and a heavy sweater. She held a book in her left hand and held out her right for Hugo to shake as Upton made the introductions.

"This is Reverend Kinnison—she's the vicar here. She found him. Reverend Kinnison, meet Hugo Marston."

"Call me Kristi. How do you do?"

Her grip was firm, and Hugo saw that the book was a Bible. More interesting was the tattoo that encircled her wrist, a snake that looked like it slithered up her forearm. "Nice to meet you," he said, then turned to Upton. "Clive, what the hell—excuse me, what the heck is going on here? She found who?"

"You were right the first time, I think," Revered Kinnison said. "You guys go do your thing—come talk to me when you're ready. I have plenty to keep me busy." She turned and went into the church without looking back.

"Clive?"

"She's right, I'm afraid. This is getting worse and worse. Come and see for yourself." He started toward the gathering of constables, then turned to Agarwal, "I need you to go to the Rising Moon and fetch Lord Stopford-Pendrith. You know where it is?"

"Yes, sir."

"With any luck he'll know you're coming and be waiting in the car park. I left a message for him about three minutes ago. Hopefully woke the bugger up. And if you see a young lady there, she's not invited. Mr. Marston will be back for her later, got it?"

"Yes, sir." Agarwal nodded and started back down the path to the church parking lot.

"OK, let's go," Upton said, and led Hugo toward the back of the churchyard in silence.

They followed the path past the end of the church, then walked for another twenty yards before stepping onto the grass, weaving their way between gravestones. Like the ones he'd seen in Whitechapel, many were ancient and washed clean of identifiers, or had the names and dates covered with moss or lichen. But unlike those in London, these stones sat up straight and proud, like patient dogs watching over their fallen masters, waiting year after year for them to rise back into the land of the living. Bright sprigs of color lay at the base of many of the newer stones, flashes of remembrance or respect for the recently gone. To his left, a good distance from the police activity, an old woman stood watching them, her gray hair piled high on her head, both hands clutching a bouquet of blue flowers. *To the dearly departed, from the nearly departed*, Hugo thought.

As Hugo and Upton closed in on the crime scene, the constables stood to attention and moved apart, as if the senior officer were a pebble dropped into a pond, and they the ripples. He hadn't noticed it before, but blue-and-white tape cordoned off the scene, waist-high plastic strung between gravestones.

As soon as Hugo ducked under the tape, he saw the dead man. He lay with his back propped against the stone wall, hands on his lap, a bloody hole in his chest where his heart had once beat. A white, silk hood covered the man's head.

"Who is it?" Hugo asked.

"We haven't touched him, so we've not confirmed anything yet. Judging by the footwear, he's not local, so . . ."

So you're thinking the same thing as me. "Did your crime-scene people finish up?"

Upton snorted. "Lazy bastards aren't here yet. It'll be the same team as at the farm last night, probably, so a little hard to wake after a night's work. But that's why we haven't touched him. I feel like this is getting to be too big; I didn't want some clumsy copper screwing up the evidence by putting his paws where they don't belong. And I'm talking about me, of course."

Hugo smiled thinly. "Good decision. But we need to know who it is."

They both knew already, which is why, Hugo thought, Upton just nodded and said, "Then help yourself."

Hugo looked at the ground as he walked, eyes scanning for footprints or other evidence. He'd done this a thousand times at crime scenes, moving in and touching things before the techs arrived with their paper suits and plastic bags. But a dozen eyes watched him now, a foreigner operating in a foreign land.

Hugo moved in at an angle, leaving clear the most direct route to the body from the pathway, assuming that would have been the murderer's route, assuming there would be a shred of evidence to be found by someone with more time and a magnifying glass. Three feet from the body, he stopped and studied the area around the man. He was small, but the hands gave him away as a man, if only just. And the shoes: expensive and not from anywhere near here. Upton was right about the shoes.

On the other side of the body from Hugo lay the only piece of visible evidence, a gun. A .22 by the looks of it, but other than that, nothing. Confident he wasn't trampling on evidence, Hugo knelt by the body and placed his fingertips on an upturned wrist. It was a routine gesture, not a realistic hope for life, the first people to find him would have made sure of that.

Hugo reached into his pocket and pulled out a pen. Careful not to disturb the man's position, he slowly raised the front of the silk hood that hid his face. This, too, was a formality in large part. He and Upton had guessed, and up close Hugo knew before looking. But the visual identification of a body was a time-honored tradition and a ritual to be observed, no matter what.

Hugo knelt beside the man he had sworn to protect and looked into the eyes that had made him a star, that had captured the hearts of a million women, that in life had twinkled and danced across a thousand movie screens, but that in death held the cold charm of two children's marbles, unseeing, unfeeling, and soon to fade from memory, lost to the passage of time.

Hugo let the cloth fall back over Dayton Harper's face so the photographer could capture him as he was found, but he stayed on one knee for a few seconds before looking back at DCI Upton.

There merest of nods, a shared moment of sadness between two men who faced it daily but never quite got used to it.

CHAPTER SEVENTEEN

Hugo and DCI Upton returned to the church as the crime-scene team went to work filming and collecting evidence. It was the same pair as the night before, and they'd apologized for being late but also looked at Hugo and Upton quizzically, as if wondering about the American grim reaper who'd twice pulled them away from their usual crop of robberies and burglaries.

They got no explanations, because they didn't need them to do their job and because there were none—not good ones, anyway.

Hugo and Upton sank onto rough wooden benches in the porch outside the main door of the church, away from the other officers, silent for a moment as they processed as best they could. Finally Upton spoke, one word.

"Shot."

"I didn't see any other trauma," Hugo said. "Looked like one shot to the heart."

"Suicide?"

"Maybe."

"It fits. The love of his life is dead, he's wracked with guilt at killing young Quincy Drinker, and he's shot and killed the father for some damn reason. His acting career is over, he's looking at a long time in prison . . ." Upton shrugged. "Seems to fit."

"Yes," Hugo nodded. "It seems to fit." And yet it didn't. If Harper had shot Old Man Drinker it might. But he hadn't, and in Hugo's mind it made the rest of the puzzle fall apart.

"We'll know more soon. They'll swab his hands for gunshot residue—that'll tell us something."

"Not much," Hugo said. "Assuming your guys do it within about four hours of his death and they find something, it'll tell us he was in the presence of a gun that was discharged. Which we kinda know already."

"I've not had much experience with that particular science," Upton said sheepishly. "Shot plenty of weapons, but we don't get to enjoy the delights of GSR much in Hertfordshire. Thank God."

"Like all police work," Hugo said, "it ain't like on TV. As you know, I'm sure. We see it a lot at home, too much, where someone is shot and ends up with lead in their chest and gunshot residue on their skin. Had a case where a guy fired an AK-47 from the back seat of a minivan and killed two people. His buddies in front of the van also tested positive for GSR, setting up a nice defense for the shooter."

"Great," Upton said. "We'll see if we can trace the gun—that might get us somewhere. Where the hell would a Hollywood star get a gun in the middle of the English countryside?"

Hugo thought about that. "Well, given he's a movie star, he'd probably just have to ask. Who's going to say no? But he'd need to find someone who has a gun first."

"Those movie weapons," Upton said. "Are they real? If they are and just fire blanks, it seems like getting a few bullets might be easier than the gun itself."

"No idea," said Hugo. "Though I'm sure we can find out."

"Any problem with this getting out to the media?" Upton asked. "Even if these young coppers haven't figured out who he is, they will pretty soon, and it only takes one of them to talk."

Hugo shook his head, but in disappointment not disagreement. He'd been involved in his share of high-profile cases in the past, profiling and catching several serial killers, and helping unravel a plot to assassinate the Russian ambassador in Washington. But nothing like this. Politics and violence commanded headlines, he knew, but not like celebrities. And this story would have it all: sex, tragedy, love, and murder. Some of which he could have prevented. Should have prevented.

He rose. "I need to call Ambassador Cooper, let him know what's happened."

"Sounds like a fun call," Upton said.

"If you like being posted to Bangladesh, sure," Hugo smiled grimly. "Me, I'm getting used to the rain."

"Don't worry, they have rain there, too. Want me to talk to him?"

"I got it." He pulled out his phone but stopped when he saw two people striding toward them. Constable Agarwal was almost trotting to keep up with the figure ahead of him, making a beeline for Hugo and Upton.

"I told him she wasn't invited," Upton said, standing and moving into the path. "Agarwal, I told you—"

"It's OK," Hugo said. "No harm done."

Merlyn reached them, out of breath and seething. "What the hell's going on? If it wasn't for me, you'd be chasing your fucking tails still." She noticed the activity at the far end of the graveyard. "What's that about?"

Hugo took her by the elbow and steered her into the porch, pulling her down to sit next to him. He told her slowly and gently, taking her hand when her face paled, waiting quietly for a moment, holding her hands as she sobbed. After a moment, he stood and moved over to where Upton and Agarwal were deep in discussion.

"Pendrith taking a leak in the trees or something?" Hugo asked.

Upton turned and looked at him, no trace of a smile on his face. "He wasn't at the pub."

"What?"

"He wasn't there, sir," Agarwal confirmed. "The landlord hadn't seen him, nor had the young lady. No one's seen him since last night."

"You checked his room?"

"Yes, sir. Cleaned up and cleaned out, nothing there at all. He even made the bed before he left."

The landlord told Hugo and DCI Upton the same thing he'd told the constable, adding for Hugo's benefit the observation that just because a guest had walked off into the sunset, or sunrise, as the case may be, and just because the cops were all worried, didn't mean those rooms didn't need to be paid for.

Hugo dug out his wallet and handed the man cash, then dialed Pendrith's phone for the third time in ten minutes. When it went to voicemail, Hugo climbed the stairs with Upton and stood at the entrance to Pendrith's small room. The landlord assured them that the rooms hadn't been touched, what with his wife being sick, which was the first good news Hugo had heard in hours. The bed had been made, as Agarwal had said, and a cursory search also confirmed what was obvious from the outset: no indication of where Pendrith had gone or why he'd left.

"No signs of a struggle," Upton said. "That's something."

"I guess." Hugo stood at the end of the bed and ran his hand over the blanket. He looked down at it. "Did you go to boarding school, Clive?"

"Boarding school? No, why?"

"How about the military?"

"Nope. Local grammar school, local university, local police. My life in a nutshell. Why?"

"Look at the bed, the way it's made."

"Like a maid did it," Upton shrugged. "A nicely made bed, your point being that he wasn't in a hurry?"

"My point being that perhaps he didn't make it."

"Explain."

"The FBI is famous for its training and application of the behavioral sciences, right?"

"Profiling, you mean. Yes, that's right."

"But you Brits are pretty good at it, too. I came over here a few years ago and took a course with a guy from Scotland Yard. Anyway, profiling courses and training are naturally full of examples, real-life examples, that show a little about the unsub."

"*Unsub?*"

"Unknown subject, sorry," Hugo smiled. "Anyway, one example this Scotland Yard guy gave us really stuck in my head. There had been a few murders in a town called Colchester, women raped and strangled in their beds. The locals didn't have any idea who did it or why, so these guys from Scotland Yard came and looked at pictures of the crime scenes. This detective saw what the local police had seen, that the unsub killed these women and then left them in their beds but remade them, tucked them in almost. But what this Yard detective saw was the way the beds were made. The corners had been tucked a certain way, I think he called them hospital corners."

"Hospital corners, right. So . . . ?"

"So we know that people are creatures of habit, especially when carrying out an action they can do without thinking, an action they've done thousands of times before. Pendrith went to boarding school and was in the military. For years the guy made his own bed, and every time the same way, which means that he'd make his bed with hospital corners no matter how much of a hurry he was in because it'd be easier and quicker for him. He'd probably not even think about it."

"And these are not hospital corners."

"Correct."

"Meaning someone else made his bed for him." The men looked at each other, and Upton raised an eyebrow. "You think he was kidnapped?"

"I think he had company of some sort. Let's not jump to conclusions about kidnapping, though."

"I'm open to suggestions."

Hugo stroked his chin. "Well, first we should make doubly sure he's not around here somewhere."

"OK, I'll have my men search the pub grounds right away."

"Good." Hugo frowned. "And have them canvas the houses around here. Pendrith didn't have a car, so maybe someone saw him walking along the main road, down one of the public paths, or maybe even gave him a ride."

Upton nodded and started down the stairs, leaving Hugo to stare into Pendrith's room. As always, when he failed to come up with a definitive, helpful clue, he knew he was missing something. And while the hospital corners were definitive in his mind, he didn't see them as a helpful clue, simply because a clue should answer part of the riddle, not make it more complicated. Who would have wanted to kidnap Pendrith? More to the point, who would have been able to? The old boy would not have gone quietly, Hugo assumed, nor would he have fallen for some trick. He was too wily for that.

He turned in the doorway and walked across the sitting area to Walton's room. The reporter had not been seen since the previous day, and Hugo couldn't think of a single reason in the world why he'd want to take Pendrith. And how the hell would such a scrawny little weasel manage it? A gun?

Possibly. All things were possible when you were at the right end of a gun, Hugo had seen that time and again.

He walked slowly into Walton's room, lifting the pillows from the bed, then the top blankets and sheet. They had been pulled up rather than made, as if straightened by the occupant rather than made by the landlord or his wife. No hospital corners here either, Hugo smiled to himself. He opened the dresser drawers and saw nothing, even looked into the two wastepaper baskets. Empty. Had he disappeared into the same vortex that had swallowed Pendrith? Had they gone together willingly or was one of them the coercer? Or someone else . . . ?

Hugo walked back out to an armchair and sank into it, wrinkling his nose at the musty odor that enveloped him when he sat. He pulled out his cell phone and called his office, asking to be put through to the agent who'd been at the pub watching over Cooper, Bart Denum.

"Bart, it's Hugo. Busy?"

"Nope, all quiet on the London front. I hear you've been a little preoccupied, though."

"You could say that. I need your help with something. Lickety-split, if you can."

"Sure, whatever you need."

"Pen and paper ready?"

"Always."

"Good." Hugo read off Pendrith's phone number. "I need you to start pinging towers to see if we can locate the owner. I also need you to dig up as much as you can on a reporter called Harry Walton. He's about sixty years old, a freelancer. Can't give you anything more than that, I'm afraid."

"No problem. OK to use one of the other guys here, or you need this to stay hush-hush?"

"Use whoever you can of our people, sure. Speed is the key here."

"Will do. And boss?"

"What is it, Bart?"

"Been online lately?"

"No."

"Our wandering minstrel is all over the news sites—the story is out."

Hugo grimaced. "It was bound to happen. Thanks Bart. Call me when you get anything on that number, or anything interesting on Walton."

"Will do. Oh, Ambassador Cooper asked me to tell you about the Ferro autopsy."

"Good, what have you got?"

"That's the thing," Denum said. "Nothing. Seems like there's a bit of a jurisdictional battle here. Brits want to do it as she died on their turf and, I gather, was once a British citizen. We want to do it because she's now a US citizen and because we don't trust anyone who's not American to get it right."

Hugo heard the smile in his voice but knew he was only half-joking. Nevertheless, this kind of bureaucracy was precisely why Hugo got nervous every time he was promoted. And in the State Department he'd seen even more red tape than he had in the FBI, which he'd never thought possible.

"In the meantime," Hugo said, "she's on ice and the investigation goes nowhere. That's absurd, Bart."

"Yeah, I agree. But I don't think it's Cooper making the call, to be fair."

Hugo was pleased to hear that, at least. "OK, let me know if anything changes." He closed his phone, then looked up as DCI Upton crested the stairs. "Any luck?" Hugo asked.

"I'm afraid not. No word from or about Pendrith at all."

"And no sign of Harry Walton?" he asked.

"Nothing." Upton sank into the empty armchair and looked at Hugo. "What the hell is going on?"

CHAPTER EIGHTEEN

Hugo held the car door for Merlyn, looking over her shoulder to see DCI Upton saluting a tall and powerfully built woman in police uniform bearing the crown on her epaulet. The chief constable, Upton's boss, who'd come running when Dayton Harper's name hit the headlines. He'd been dead a matter of hours and everyone knew that this crime, if that's what it was, had to be solved immediately.

Inside the car, he turned to Merlyn. "You doing OK?"

"Fuck no, what do you think?"

"That's what I thought." He started the engine. "I also think we need to talk."

"OK."

"I need to fill in some gaps, make some connections . . ." He waved a hand. "Whatever you want to call it."

"Where are we going?"

"To the church." He felt her stiffen beside him. "It's OK, they took him away an hour ago. I just do my best thinking at crime scenes."

"That's weird, Hugo." The vague hint of a smile in her voice.

He looked over and winked. "From you, missy, that's a compliment."

They drove in silence for the five minutes it took to get to the church. A police constable stood guard at the entrance but recognized Hugo and let him through with a polite "Good morning, sir."

Merlyn shivered and wrapped her arms around herself as they started up the path to the church. For the first time in days Hugo looked up and saw blue sky, but the cloudless night had brought with it a frost that painted the grass in the churchyard a silvery white, dusting also the gravel beneath their feet. Hugo looked ahead to the high stone wall against which Dayton Harper had either propped himself or been left by another. The sturdy branches of the oak tree held still, but at their tips the bare and brittle twigs bobbed up and down, rubbing against each other as if for warmth. They stopped by the entrance to the church, and Hugo turned to Merlyn.

"I need to ask you something," he said.

"Sure," she said with a glance.

"Did either Pendrith or Harry Walton ever go to Braxton Hall?"

"You mean as guests? Or breaking and entering, like you did?"

"As guests."

"Not that I know of."

"Are you sure? I know you need to protect the place, but this is bigger now; whatever secrets you have I can try to keep, but people are dead, Merlyn, and it may not be over. Walton and Pendrith are both missing, and I don't know why."

"And you think Braxton Hall has something to do with it?"

"I have no idea. I'm just trying to find connections between everyone and everything. Braxton Hall may be that connection."

"I don't know everyone who goes there, Hugo. How could I? And I know this is important, more important than anything." She shrugged. "I'll help as best I can, but I don't know the answer to your question. All I can say is, I've never seen them there."

"Does the guy who runs it keep records?"

"His name is Nicholas Braxton. And yes. Actually, he asked me to work for him once, as kind of hostess-cum-secretary. I declined because I didn't want to leave London. Plus he's a little creepy. Anyway, he showed me the office, and I know he keeps records because whenever you first go there you have to give your real name and show some sort of identification, which he copies and locks away. He also makes everyone sign confidentiality agreements and a legal waiver."

"A waiver?"

"All BDSM dungeons do it, in case someone plays too rough and gets hurt. Also, he uses people's initials to identify them at the door and for stuff like place settings and room reservations. I'm guessing he has the master list in a safe somewhere, and I'm also guessing he won't willingly hand it over."

"That's a safe bet," Hugo said.

"Search warrant?" she suggested.

"I think under English law they're easy to get if you have someone in custody. We don't. In fact, we don't even know who we're looking for, and no judge or magistrate would give us a search warrant to poke around someone's house on the off chance we'll find something."

"Especially if a judge or a magistrate is a guest at Braxton Hall," Merlyn said.

"Precisely. Is that the case?"

"I'm not telling," she said with a smile. "Anyway, why not ask Upton about the warrant?"

"Because I don't want him to know. I'm pretty certain we wouldn't get one, which means we need to poke around some other way. And I don't know how it works here, but in the States, any evidence obtained by law enforcement without a warrant, like we're talking about doing, is not admissible in trial."

"If you say so. I don't know anything about that stuff."

"I'm just thinking aloud." He smiled. "And I'm getting ahead of myself. The point is, we're not law enforcement, so if we happen to find anything at Braxton Hall, it can be evidence in court."

"And you think that if Upton knows we're about to go poking around . . ."

"Exactly," said Hugo. "If he knows, we become law enforcement in the eyes of the law, and the evidence gets excluded."

"It works that way?"

"In England? I have no idea. But it does in the United States, and our system is based on yours, so better to play it safe."

"OK then," she said. "But how do you expect to get into Braxton Hall?"

"That's where I need your help."

"To break in? You expect me to break you in? No chance, mate. Not happening." She shook her head emphatically. Then she turned to face him. "Unless ..."

"Unless what?" A smile had spread across her face and mischief danced in her eyes. "What are you thinking?" Hugo asked, suddenly wary.

"Once a month, on a Friday night," she said, "there's a party."

"A party?"

"Not the kind you're used to."

"You're proposing taking me to some kind of ..." He didn't even know what to call it. "This Friday? Wait, that's ..."

"Yep," she said. "Tonight. Got any assless chaps?"

"Great," he said, rolling his eyes. "I can see this is going to be an experience."

"You're doing it for king and country. Or whatever the American version is. And yes, it certainly is going to be an experience."

"This doesn't sound like the best idea, so let's see if we can think of something else," he said. "In the meantime, I need to walk over to the crime scene. Stay here if you want."

"No, it's OK, I'll come. But what if we touch something we shouldn't?"

"You mean contaminate evidence?" He smiled. "Good thinking, but they've processed the scene by now. Or should have. We can touch what we want."

"Which ain't much," she muttered.

They left the protection of the church and headed for the blue-and-white tape that was still strung among the gravestones, and for some reason, the combination made Hugo think of dental floss. He led the way between the markers and stopped at the tape to check on Merlyn. She nodded that she was OK, and they ducked beneath the blue-and-white cordon and took three steps forward, Hugo's eyes sweeping over the earth. He walked in a zigzag route in what he suspected would be a fruitless search. But thoroughness was a habit, a lesson learned after small clues had been missed at crime scenes years ago, thousands of miles away, embarrassment forged into a routine of painstaking care. Once he'd finished scouring the place for physical clues, he could settle in to absorb the feel of the place, let it speak to him in its own weird way. His own weird way, maybe.

"It's odd, isn't it?" Merlyn spoke in an almost-whisper, standing on the spot where Harper's body had lain.

"What is?"

"That a man can die here, just hours ago, and there be no sign other than a few strands of police tape. If you didn't know it had happened . . ." she shrugged, "you'd never know, would you?"

Hugo didn't answer, instead putting a hand on her shoulder. She was right, there was nothing here, no clue, no sign, not even a feeling. The only thing he could do was walk, so he pointed to the old wall and walked toward it. They ducked back under the tape, crossing out of the crime scene, and Hugo started his clue hunt all over again, expanding it to the entire graveyard.

They'd walked less than twenty yards when he stopped. Ahead, the ground had been disturbed, leaves and sticks piled on the grass in a rectangular shape. About the size of a human grave. Hugo looked around him, senses on high alert, but the place was silent. He held out a hand, silently telling Merlyn to stay put. He briefly considered calling Upton to get his crime-scene team here, but maybe it was nothing. He moved closer and saw that the leaves and other debris had been scattered over a green tarpaulin that had, in turn, been pegged to the ground. He knelt by a corner of the tarp and tugged at the metal peg, which slid easily from the wet earth. He lifted the canopy six inches, and the gentle smell of wet soil rose up to greet him.

If there's something dead in here, he thought, it's not been dead long.

He raised the tarp higher and peered into a coffin-sized hole, two feet deep. He was no expert on grave digging, but this didn't look like it had been professionally cut. Roots and twigs poked out from its steep sides, which were jagged and uneven, and the bottom was rounded, not flat, as if earth from the sides had tumbled in and been trampled down. He lowered the covering and stood, looking around. No shovel. No other graves within ten feet, either, just an ancient oak tree standing guard over it, a heavy bough as thick as his waist extending into the graveyard, and no more than eight feet above his head. Shelter? Hugo wondered.

"It's OK, no one inside," he told Merlyn, and he saw her shoulders sag with relief.

She moved a little closer, eyes on the tarp. "What is it?"

"Looks like the beginnings of a grave," he said. "Pretty fresh but not finished, I'd guess. On the other hand, could be a hole dug by kids to bury pirate treasure."

"Wait. Do you think it's a real grave or not?"

"No idea," said Hugo, reaching for his phone. "I'll let Upton and his men figure that out." He was through in a matter of seconds. "Clive, Hugo here. Did your guys search the graveyard before clearing out?"

"Of course," Upton said. "Why?"

"They didn't mention finding a new grave about fifty yards from Harper's body?"

"No," Upton said slowly. "Unless there was another body in it, I'm not sure I would expect them to. It's a graveyard, after all."

"Yeah, it is. But this one looks unusual."

"How?"

"For one thing, it's covered with a tarp, which may be something they do here to keep out the rain. But the tarp itself was covered with grass and leaves, as if to hide it."

"People don't like looking at fresh graves, Hugo."

"They don't. But this one wasn't finished. Just a couple of feet deep. It just feels wrong."

"Well, it's easy enough to check on. I'll have someone call Reverend Kinnison and see if the cemetery is expecting any new occupants. She can probably put me in touch with whoever digs graves and I can see if he dug yours. Where is it exactly?"

Hugo explained its location as best he could while Upton grunted on the other end of the phone, presumably taking notes.

"Got it," said Upton when Hugo had finished. "So what are you doing over there exactly?"

"Nothing in particular. Just trying to figure out what's next."

"Well, my boss thinks that what's next is you heading back to London and leaving this investigation to us."

"Seriously?"

"Yes. As she put it, the guy you were chasing is dead so there's no longer anything you can do for him. If this is suicide, which is what she suspects, then we'll handle the inquest. If it's murder, then the guy who killed him is, presumably, alive and hiding, and we're the ones who should be chasing him."

"So you think suicide?"

"I don't know what to think, and neither does she. How about you?"

"I didn't think it likely for Ginny Ferro," Hugo said. "But Harper, I don't know. He was pretty devastated by her death and has been acting crazy ever since. I think it's a possibility."

"Assuming no jurisdictional disputes, we'll do the autopsy this morning. That may tell us something."

"I doubt it," Hugo said. "We already know the cause of death. Make sure they run a tox panel—he could have been on something to make him act weird."

"We will. I'll call you when I hear from the coroner's office. What are your plans?"

"I'm not sure." Hugo looked at Merlyn. "I suspect I'm going shopping."

"Shopping? What for?"

"I have a party to go to," Hugo said. "And absolutely nothing to wear."

CHAPTER NINETEEN

On a sweltering Chicago evening, back in August of 1999, Hugo donned a cropped leather jacket and glittery leather pants, glued a pointy black beard to his chin, and walked out of a motel with a hooker on each arm, swaggering like the pimp he was meant to be.

He'd set up in a nightclub, knocking back fake whisky and thinking very hard about his first wife, Ellie, who wouldn't have minded the girls gyrating around him, would even have found it funny. He'd never thought of himself as uptight, but as his companions, the youngest and freshest agents out of the academy, strutted their stuff around the club and as the target of the investigation brought him a succession of beautiful, half-naked, and apparently very eager-to-please women, he found himself shocked at the variety of sexual delicacies he was being offered. He was supposed to try them for himself, then broker deals between the Chicago guys and some flesh dealers in Las Vegas, keeping the stream of women constant and ever-changing. To keep the customers happy, the cash flowing, and the girls disoriented. He'd refused to sample the merchandise, though, telling his seller that he wanted something younger, fresher. And when something younger and fresher appeared by his side, he'd tried not to strangle the man who sat across the table, grinning like a chimpanzee, licking his lips as though the teenage girl was a steak to be devoured. No, Hugo had played it cool and touched the little girl's chin, looked into her heavily painted eyes, and recognized the fear hiding behind her smile.

"She doesn't speak English," the man had said. "Which makes it better, as far as I'm concerned."

"Where from?" Hugo asked him.

"Eastern Europe somewhere, does it matter?"

"No. But you only have one?"

"Shit no. We get them in batches of two and three. How many you want?" The man leaned forward, earnest now. "I gotta tell you, they are expensive. This one's a virgin, most of the little ones are." They called them "little ones" instead of "young ones," Hugo had noticed. He wondered why—it wasn't as if these men had a conscience. "You want three, four?" the man was asking.

"I don't care. Whatever I pay you, I charge my clients double," Hugo told the chimpanzee. "Give me as many as you've got."

"Tomorrow morning," the ape said. "I can bring you nine. Nine virgins. Sounds almost biblical, doesn't it?"

Hugo took the twelve-year-old, named Masha, with him that night, making the ape happy and trusting, handing her over to a bureau translator who introduced her to a counselor and a safe bed in the motel in South Chicago where the team had staged. She slept two doors down from Hugo, who felt good having her that close, that protected.

They took down the ape in the morning outside the motel, and Masha watched from inside, nose pressed to the second-floor window, she wept silently as her friends and little sister were led from the van into the care of the federal government.

The trafficker had stopped grinning pretty quickly and had done his best to spill his guts to save his own hide, but Hugo and his colleagues knew whom they were after, and all the snitching in the world hadn't kept that bastard from the pen. A very long time in the pen, if Hugo remembered correctly.

He thought about this operation, made a point of remembering the ape's evil face and the wretched feeling those young girls gave him, because it had been his last undercover operation, and because it was so different from this one. And remembering the girls he'd helped rescue back then made this undercover excursion a little less . . . humiliating.

Merlyn took him to Stevenage, a drab and concrete town, leading him to a quiet row of unkempt stores that sold the kinds of books and magazines he'd not sought since he was a teenager. He was relieved, slightly, when she led him into the newest, and largest, halfway down the row. He was less relieved when she showed him the racks of clothing he'd be required to choose from in order to be let into the party.

"They have an eighty percent rule," she said. "You have to be in eighty percent leather."

"And you?"

"Same rule. Which means you'll be buying for me, too." She winked. "You'll be able to expense this, right? So no worries."

"Able to, sure. Whether I'll dare to is another matter."

As if choosing wasn't bad enough, she made him try on everything, though he wouldn't let her look. He rejected the chaps-and-thong outfit, advocated by Merlyn, and went with the leather pants and a matching vest, though unfortunately they had only the tasseled version in his size.

"Your cowboy boots match perfectly," she said. "Who'd have thought it?"

She then left him by the "toys" and disappeared into the ladies' dressing room with an armful of clothes to try. When she reappeared in her own clothes and he asked what she'd be wearing, she gave him a "wait and see" look.

Hugo decided not to return to the pub, instead renting a room at a motel on the southeast side of Letchworth, nearest Weston. They ate at an Indian restaurant in town, a late buffet lunch that was probably quite good an hour or two earlier. There were two other tables still eating, both foursomes of men and women in work clothes, and as they sat opposite each other in a booth, Merlyn thanked him for the meal.

"I'm also curious about your wife," she said. "We've been together a couple of days now and you've not phoned her once."

"That you know of." Hugo grimaced as he remembered the call he'd ignored in Braxton Hall's mock graveyard.

"So you have phoned her?"

"That's none of your business, now is it?" He had, but they'd spoken for no more than a minute, coldness on her end, brusqueness on his.

"Oh, come on. What's the deal?"

Hugo thought for a moment. He didn't really know what the deal was himself, so explaining it wouldn't be easy, but he didn't mind trying. "She's in Dallas right now. She's . . . an interesting person, likes to travel, likes to shop." He shrugged. "I don't know what you want to know."

"We could start with her name."

"Christine."

"And how long have you been married?"

"Since May of last year." He saw her mouth open for more questions, so he gave her the rundown. "We met in Washington, DC, and got married in Dallas, where she's from. I'm from Austin, which is about three hours south of Dallas. She's my second wife."

"A new and shiny trophy wife?"

"Not really, no." Hugo tried to bend a piece of naan bread, but it snapped. "Kind of old, some of this food."

"Don't change the subject. Why did you divorce your first wife?"

"I didn't."

"She divorced you."

"No, she died in a car accident. Four years before I met Christine."

"Oh." She looked down at her plate. "I'm sorry, that was insensitive." She looked up again, her voice softer now. "You have any kids?"

"No," said Hugo, and he was surprised to feel the regret in his voice. He cleared his throat. "How about you? What's your story?"

"Born and bred in London. Only surviving child; my mother's the daughter of a banker in Hong Kong and my father's a banker from Putney. No idea what I want to be when I grow up. Not a banker."

"How old are you?"

"Twenty-five. No kids, no boyfriend, no pets."

He smiled. "And no car."

"Thanks for the reminder. Shit, will the police keep it?"

"For a while, I'd guess. Until they've processed it for any evidence."

"They can keep it." She shuddered, then reached for her Coke. "Do you think I'm pretty?"

She isn't seeking a compliment, Hugo thought; she'd asked the way she'd ask him to pass the salt, or if he liked the Beatles.

"Yes, I do."

"I can never decide. The whole mixed-race thing is kind of a curse sometimes." She shrugged. "Oh well. We should talk about tonight, so you know what to expect. It could get pretty wild for you in there, Mr. Vanilla."

"That's OK, I'm not planning on staying long. And I'm certainly not planning on partying for long."

She cocked her head and pointed her fork at him as a smile spread across her face. "That, my friend, is a great shame."

As they passed through the gates to Braxton Hall, Hugo suddenly worried that someone would recognize his car. Maybe Nicholas Braxton had written down his license number, or remembered the diplomatic plates, and was on the lookout.

But there was no one checking plates, as far as he could see. Three cars followed him up the driveway, and Merlyn directed him to an empty spot in a line of parked cars.

"Popular party," he said.

"Yeah, people come from London, Cambridge, all over."

"How the hell does he keep it so quiet?"

"It makes sense if you think about it," she said. "If you know about the parties, it's because you come. And if you come, you don't want some reporter or clown with a camera snapping pictures of you."

"I guess that much is a relief," Hugo said, looking down at his leather-clad legs. "Do we leave our coats here?"

"No, silly, they'll have someone checking them at the entrance."

"Which is where they do the eighty percent check, I assume."

"Right. You're fine, you're a hundred percent, you get a gold star."

"Not a hundred percent," Hugo muttered. "Just for the record."

"Underwear? Not a problem in my case."

"I was thinking about my socks," he said. "But thanks for the info. And stop thinking about my underwear—I'm married."

"Yeah," she said, rolling her eyes. "To a chick in Dallas."

They crossed the gravel driveway and went up the stone stairs to the main entrance where a woman in a black PVC catsuit stood with a clipboard.

"MHS from Putney," Merlyn told her. "And guest."

"Handsome guest," the woman purred. "Both eighty percent? Coats over there." She pointed over her shoulder with her pen, eyes still on Hugo.

As they approached the coat check, Hugo felt a flutter in his stomach. He'd still not seen Merlyn's outfit and he'd do his best not to look, and then to act nonchalant when he did look. She'd slipped her long coat from her shoulders and handed it to a young man sporting what looked like rubber shorts. Merlyn wore a black leather bra, plain and well-fitting, and a matching skirt that clung to her body and ended just, and only just, below the curve of her bottom. A pair of plain black knee boots finished the look, and Hugo was relieved not to see stilettos, but for no reason he'd be able to articulate.

His covert admiration of Merlyn ended when the young man moved to help Hugo off with his coat, the American suddenly aware of his own attire and how ridiculous it felt. He shot a look at Merlyn and saw her fighting a smile. He frowned at her and then realized that if he was going to tussle with his ego all night, he was fighting a losing battle. He changed his scowl to a sheepish grin and shrugged. *After all, undercover is undercover*, he thought. *No matter the cover.*

"Along the corridor and down the stairs," the young man was saying, camping it up with a lisp and wave of the hand. "I think I've seen you before, young lady. You know the way."

"Sure do. And it's Merlyn," she smiled. "Remember the name because you'll see me again. See us again, maybe." Without waiting for a response, she took Hugo's hand and dragged him through a dark archway and

along a short passage. Their feet rang on the red tile floor, the sound captured and thrown back at them by the narrow and low-ceilinged hallway.
Ahead, the floor disappeared down a staircase, and the heavy beat of
music rolled up to meet them. Hugo realized he was still holding Merlyn's hand, but he didn't let go. *Undercover*, he reminded himself.

They descended the stairs slowly, the music growing louder and
louder, an orange glow lighting their way and guiding them into what
Merlyn called the "Cellar." Another stone arch marked its entrance,
and once inside Hugo moved to one side to look around. To his left,
a long bar stretched the length of the room, which was at least a thousand feet square. To his right, and opposite the bar, a series of arches led
into another space that Merlyn had warned him would be set aside for
playing, watched over by DMs, or Dungeon Masters, who made sure
everyone played safely. He'd need a drink before going in there, he suspected, though he was definitely curious. Merlyn had said it wouldn't
get busy in the play space until later, once people had socialized and
made connections, and right now he could see a few people wandering
through to have a look at the area, a good time to sneak a peek at the
equipment before getting to work, he thought.

But he couldn't work yet. Despite the row of cars out front, there
were not more than twenty people in the Cellar, and he assumed many
of the party-goers were staying overnight in the rooms upstairs, still
getting ready. He looked closely at those already downstairs, interested
in the profile, and even more interested when he didn't see one. They
were a good mix of ages, a few more men than women, and all abiding
by the leather rule, though there seemed to be a PVC and a rubber
exception. One older man wore an ankle-length leather coat. Hugo
nodded in appreciation. Wish I'd thought of that.

He turned as a young couple entered the room beside him, the
man in immaculate evening dress, a black tuxedo and bow tie, crisply
pressed pants and shoes that reflected the little light that shone in
the room. His date was a beautiful brunette in a flowing, strapless red
dress that exposed milky-white cleavage. Her throat was adorned by a
crimson velvet collar, emphasizing the whiteness of her skin and com-

plimenting her thick, bloodred lips. Her black-lined eyes lingered on Hugo, then drifted to Merlyn, and the two women exchanged muted smiles. The young couple swept into the room and the man steered her toward the bar, his left hand on the small of her back.

"Beautiful dress," Merlyn murmured to Hugo.

"You mind telling me why they're not wearing leather?"

"Sure." A mischievous smile crossed Merlyn's face. "You don't have to wear leather if you wear a tux. Didn't I tell you that?"

Hugo put his hands on his hips and shook his head. "No. You didn't tell me that."

"Oh, sorry." She shrugged and looked away. "I thought I had. Must have slipped my mind."

No doubt, Hugo thought, but smiled to himself in the dark. "You want a drink?" he asked.

"I thought you'd never ask."

Hugo took a bottle of water from the bartender as Merlyn took a gulp from her gin and tonic. He nodded toward the play area. "Let's take a look," he said.

"Oh yes?"

"Yes. I'm looking for exits, or other doorways. I'm not seeing another way upstairs from here."

They walked through one of the arches and stopped. There looked to be four distinct areas, each with a different piece of equipment. Merlyn saw him looking.

"Want some explanations?" she asked.

"I'm not sure."

"Don't be silly, everything that goes on is between adults and is fully consensual. So, over there." She pointed to the area on the far right, which was dominated by a large wooden cross in the shape of an X. "That's a Saint Andrew's Cross. It's cool because there are wrist and ankle straps on both sides so two people can use it at once."

"Very cool," Hugo agreed politely.

"No, the cool thing is the platform it sits on. It revolves, which makes for a great show."

"I bet."

"Next to that, a set of stocks, which you probably recognize."

"Where are the rotten tomatoes to throw?" Hugo asked.

"Very funny. Now, those two things beside the stocks are saw-horses, they'll get plenty of use. And last of all, a Houdini's box."

"All looks a little medieval, if you ask me."

She nudged him in the ribs. "That's the point."

They turned as the music went up a few notches. A stream of people had come into the bar in the last few minutes, and the place had started to fill up. Most were in leather, and there was a lot of bare skin on display, but setting and dress aside, it looked like any other party. People held glasses of wine, beer, and mixed drinks and leaned in to hear each other, laughing at jokes and complimenting each other's outfits. A couple of people held leashes that were attached to collars around their partners' necks, but even these people smiled and laughed as if they were at their local pub or at a friend's for drinks.

"I need a refill," Merlyn said. "Can we?"

Hugo nodded, but before turning away he quickly scanned the play area again, looking for doors. He saw one on the far-left wall and one on the right. Both had exit signs above them, but there was no way to tell whether they led straight outside or to another part of the building. It didn't look like they'd set off any alarms if opened, which was a relief.

They nodded and smiled their way to the bar and waited patiently as the topless bartenders wriggled and flirted with their customers, making their way to Hugo's twenty-pound note in their own sweet time. Hugo didn't mind the delay; he was worried that once she had a drink in her hand, Merlyn would want to meet people.

He felt pressure on his left arm and turned to see the brunette in the red dress.

"Hi, mind if I squeeze in next to you?" she asked, already there.

"No, not at all." He suddenly felt out of his depth, like a high school senior at his prom, wearing his first tuxedo and suddenly face-to-face with the prettiest cheerleader in the school. Beside him, Merlyn nudged him with an elbow, but when he glanced over, she was smiling into her drink. Hugo was sure that she knew exactly how he felt and was enjoying it.

"I'm Annabelle," the woman in the red dress was saying.

"Hugo," he said, automatically extending a hand. "Nice to meet you." *Are we supposed to shake hands? Use our real names?* But she took his hand and smiled.

"You're American?"

"Yes."

"Neat. Dom, sub, or switch?"

"Excuse me?"

Merlyn leaned around him and grinned at Annabelle. "He's vanilla. Humoring me."

"I see." Annabelle arched a delicate eyebrow, then leaned in toward Merlyn, her voice conspiratorial. "Think we could convert him?"

They laughed and Hugo smiled along with them, the tolerant outsider being tolerated.

Hugo noticed him almost immediately, the worried look on Braxton's face sending alarm bells ringing in Hugo's mind. The man was dressed in a tuxedo that was too small, his fat little head popping out of a shirt collar that squeezed his neck like a noose. The man waved a hand at the female bartender to turn the music down as he went between groups and couples, speaking a few words to each, but not words of welcome, Hugo was sure.

He turned to Merlyn. "The car. He's recognized the car from when we were here the other night."

"How do you know?"

"I don't, but when I'm on someone else's property under false pretenses, I assume the worst. Plus, there's a downside to having diplomatic plates."

"People remember them," Merlyn said.

"Right."

"You think he's asking people if it's their car?"

"That's my guess." He looked toward the play space. "I need to get poking around. Once I get upstairs, where is his office?"

"At the west end of the building. His apartment is that end of the house, too."

"OK, better that you're not seen with me from here on. I'll meet you on the front steps in twenty minutes, OK?"

"Let me come with you."

"No, you've been here before and can't play dumb, I can."

"Oh yeah, the stupid American," she grinned. "Twenty minutes."

He left Merlyn in the company of Annabelle and her boyfriend, Jensen, and started toward the play space, which was now in full operation. He stopped under an archway to decide on which door to take. To his right, the exit was already open and he could see people coming and going through it, pulling out packets of cigarettes as they headed outside, popping in gum as they came in. The door to the left, by contrast, remained closed. *That's mine*, he thought.

On his way to the door, he couldn't help but take in the scenes unfolding in front of him. The Saint Andrew's Cross was occupied by a muscular young man, entirely naked, and a ring of people stood watching as a svelte woman in bright-red leather adjusted wrist and ankle straps. It was as if they were watching the unveiling of a painting, or admiring a sculpture, he thought. In front of him, an elderly man helped his wife onto what Merlyn had called a sawhorse. A paddle hung from a strap on his wrist, and as Hugo watched, he gave her a playful swat to hurry her into position.

Hugo smiled and angled left toward the door. When he got there, he paused to check for curious eyes and, seeing none, pushed open the door and slipped out of the Cellar.

He found himself in a small alcove. The door to the outside was on his right, and to his left was a set of stone steps—the fire escape, he assumed. He trotted up the stairs, feet scuffing against the stone, his ears pricked for sound. He went up to the first landing and paused by the door, which bore a sign that read: "Private Residence. Keep Out."

He put his ear to the door. All was quiet, so he pressed the metal bar and opened it. This was Nicholas Braxton's side of the house, according to Merlyn, and while the fat little man himself was in the Cellar, friends, family, or guests could still be here.

Hugo stood still for a moment, watching, listening. A hallway extended to his left, opening into what looked like a living room, and to his right, where it ended in large double doors. Hugo guessed the doors opened into the more public area of the house, which meant they could be his escape route into safer territory, even to the front door.

He moved to his left, walking on the rug that ran down the center of the wooden floor. A half-open door to his right made him pause, but it was dark as well as quiet. He poked his head in and waited for his eyes to adjust. Beginner's luck, Hugo thought, as he found himself looking into Braxton's study. If there was going to be a list of the hall's members, or a stack of waivers, this is where they'd be.

And something was bothering him. He had no real reason to think Pendrith was connected to this place, but coincidences always made him hesitate. Sure, it could be chance that Pendrith had inserted himself into this investigation without knowing any of the players, but his interest in Harper had seemed . . . unusual. And here Hugo was, in a secretive mansion in the very territory Pendrith claimed to know so well. And if Pendrith was indeed aboveboard and not hiding anything, how come he'd disappeared in a puff of smoke? Hugo wondered if an answer to one of those questions, or at least the hint of an answer, lay filed away in this room.

What of Walton? Had he decided on his story and left for London? Somehow Hugo didn't think so, though again he couldn't come up with any reason why Walton should be up to no good. *A gut instinct*, Hugo thought, *no more and no less*. And he never dismissed those instincts entirely, not until he was sure they were leading him astray.

He closed the door behind him before flicking on the overhead light. Tall filing cabinets flanked the door, while directly opposite was an impressive wooden desk. Heavy green curtains covered a bank of windows to his right, and in the far corner, behind the desk and opposite the windows, a shoulder-high safe squatted in the corner.

He ignored the safe, knowing he didn't have time to mess with it and almost certainly didn't have the skill to open it. An image of a good friend, one he'd not seen in a while, in far too long, popped into his head; Tom Green, his roommate at the FBI Academy and close friend ever after, would be able to get into the safe, one way or another. Hugo rounded the desk and pulled open drawers, rifling through papers but not seeing anything resembling a member list. He turned his attention to the filing cabinets, starting at the top and working his way down. He found copies of bills and old legal documents, brochures for real estate in London and others for the kind of equipment Hugo had seen in the Cellar.

But no list of names.

Hugo stood by the door, his hand on the light switch, when he spotted a leather-bound ledger sitting on top of the safe, near the back edge. He went over and opened it, smiling to himself when he saw a long list of initials.

What was it Merlyn had said when they signed in? *MHS from Putney.* The list was three pages long and written in the same format as Merlyn's self-description to Cat Woman at the door. Just a column of initials, followed by a list of towns. He checked to make sure he was looking at the right thing by locating Merlyn's initials. A thought occurred and he looked for Harry Walton's initials, knowing that the reporter came from the Hertfordshire area. But no *HW* on the list. He then scoured it for Pendrith.

There it was, surely. *GSP. Chelsea/Paris.*

Paris? Hugo knew Pendrith lived in Chelsea, he'd said so during the brief car ride with Harper. But Paris? No surprise that he had the money to buy a place there—wealth being another indication that maybe this *GSP* was indeed Graham Stopford-Pendrith. *No wonder he'd inserted himself into this investigation*, Hugo thought. He remembered the MP's obvious sincerity, the gentleness in his voice when he expressed his sympathy to Harper for his wife's death. *They knew each other.*

He turned as the door to the study opened behind him. The doorway was filled by a bald and very muscular man in a tight, black T-shirt and jeans, about an inch shorter than Hugo but forty pounds of solid muscle heavier. Not dressed for the party, Hugo noted. Dressed like security, with a clipboard in his hand.

"Who are you?" the man said.

"Michael Sudduth," Hugo lied, intentionally disguising his accent. Instinctively the man looked down at the clipboard, and Hugo knew he'd guessed right about it being the guest list. "Middle name, and where from, please."

"Harry, from Putney."

The man grunted and looked up, apparently satisfied with the *MHS Putney* that Hugo knew was on the list. "What are you doing in here?"

"Looking for something," Hugo said. "But I found it, thanks." He started toward the doorway but the man didn't budge.

The man's eyes narrowed. "You American?"

"Texan, actually. You?"

"Funny man, eh?"

Hugo shrugged and smiled. "I try. After all, look at what I'm wearing."

"Stay where you are pal, I don't want to hurt you."

"That makes two of us," said Hugo. "But I should be getting back to the party."

The smile on Hugo's face disappeared as the man reached behind his back and tugged at something in his waistband. The man pulled out a walkie-talkie, his eyes never leaving Hugo. "I got him. Mr. B's study." A crackle of noise and the words "Hold him there" came through. The man nodded to no one and tucked the walkie-talkie away. He stood in the doorway like a sentry, arms crossed over his chest, feet planted wide apart like the roots of an old elm tree anchoring him to the ground.

"Here's the thing," Hugo said. "I have no beef with you, your boss, or what you guys get up to here. None at all. But I'm looking for someone who has gone missing, and I'm responsible for his safety." Not a literal truth, but Hugo did feel that he should have foreseen or somehow prevented Pendrith's disappearance.

"You can tell it to the boss."

"Yeah, except I don't have time for that."

"Oh?" A sardonic smile touched the man's lips. "Gonna throw yourself out a window? I wouldn't bother, they're reinforced glass."

"That's OK," Hugo said, walking to within two feet of the man. "I think I'll play it conventional." Hugo wafted his left hand in the air, a simple but effective distraction that gave him the split second he needed to drive his first and second knuckles into the man's sternum. Size didn't matter when you couldn't breathe, a lesson Hugo had learned for himself in the past.

As the bald man doubled over, gasping for air, Hugo gave him a follow up blow to his side, up under his ribs, and the man fell like a log onto the floor. Hugo stepped around him and looked through the doorway. He assumed the reinforcements would come charging through the main door to Braxton's apartment, so he headed back the way he'd come, trotting along the hallway and barging through the fire door into the stairwell.

He slipped back into the play area and let the beat and dark of the Cellar wrap a protective shield around him, turning him into just another anonymous set of initials in a sea of leather bodies. He drifted through the room, which had filled considerably in the ten minutes he'd been upstairs, looking for Merlyn. He found her chatting with the handsome Jensen, who was tightening a heavy strap around the Annabelle's waist as she lay facedown on one of the sawhorses.

"Hi," Annabelle said, looking back over her shoulder. "Come to play?"

Hugo smiled but didn't know what to say, unsure exactly which game was afoot. He took Merlyn by the arm and spoke into her ear.

"I found something. Not much but something. Trouble is, they found me, so I have to split."

"I'm coming too," she said.

"Bad idea. They don't know you're with me, so you're safe to stay here."

She looked down at Annabelle and then back to Hugo. "Tempting, but no. I want to know what's going on."

"Well, I can't tell you that yet," said Hugo. He didn't have time to argue, so he waved a hand at their new friends and started for the exit. Jensen called out to them, but his voice was lost in the rising tide of music that swept them toward the door.

"What about our coats?" Merlyn asked.

"We'll have to come back for them." He patted his vest. "I'm finally glad for all these pockets and zippers."

"Keys and wallet?"

"Exactly." Once outside, Hugo put his arm around Merlyn. "Two lovers out for some fresh air."

"A little chilly for that, isn't it?"

She was right. Whatever warmth had been generated by the day had fled into the night, leaving the air with a vindictive chill that bit at Hugo's bare arms.

As they approached the row of cars, Hugo saw a man standing by the passenger side of his Cadillac, in much the same arms-crossed position the bald man had adopted while blocking Hugo's exit from Braxton's study.

"Time to make yourself useful," Hugo said.

"How so?"

"Simple. Act as if you're getting into the car next to mine. Make like you dropped the keys and can't reach them under the car. Show some flesh if you want."

"Hugo, as if!"

"Yeah, I know. Anyway, once he's helping you look I'll hop into my car and drive slowly enough that he'll run after me. You head the other way, I'll just loop around and pick you up."

"You think he'll be that stupid?"

"No, it's psychology. Everything he does will be based on instinct, and if we keep changing the stimulus, he won't have time to figure out he's being played." He pulled out his keys and took off the one for the Cadillac. "Wave these at him as you approach. And if you can just pretend to lose them, I'd be grateful."

Merlyn took the keys and smiled up at him. "You giving me the keys to your apartment, mister?"

Hugo wagged a finger. "Married, remember."

Merlyn kept smiling, but shrugged as she walked toward the lone guard. Hugo moved into the row of cars to stay out of sight, working his way to the Cadillac, keeping his head down. As he got close, he heard Merlyn's voice and the low, unintelligible response of the guard. Hugo dropped to one knee and peered under the two cars between him and them. He saw Merlyn's shins and the soles of a man's shoes. He got silently to his feet and moved past the remaining cars to his, putting the key in the lock as quietly as he could. He couldn't tell whether the man heard the loud click, but he didn't wait to find out. He pulled himself behind the steering wheel and started the engine, surging out of his parking spot into the driveway, heading across the front of the house.

He looked in the rearview mirror and saw the silhouette of a man closing in on the rear of the Cadillac. Hugo touched the gas pedal and the man shrank away, so he slowed again, too much, and the man caught up and slammed his fists against the rear window. *Good enough*, Hugo thought, swinging the car off the driveway into a sharp U-turn on the strip of lawn fronting the house, spinning the wheels on the grass and leaving his chaser standing in the light of the security lamps, flat-footed and no doubt furious.

Hugo gunned the engine as four people tumbled down the stone steps of the house's main entrance, fanning out on the gravel drive, threatening to block his path to freedom and, more importantly, to Merlyn. He flicked his lights to bright, making the foursome think he'd turned toward them, delaying them for the second it took to get the lead on them and get to the curve in the driveway before they could. In moments he was past them, barreling toward the main gate, and ahead he saw a slim figure jogging along the grass, waving a hand. He pulled past her and then hit the brakes, and in a second she was beside him, breathing hard, smiling, her first high-octane experience of connivance and deceit in the furtherance of their mission.

"That was fun," she said, breathless and grinning. She reached for her seatbelt as they passed through the gates and onto the little road to Baldock. "Where to now?"

"London for a quick stop, and then Paris. First thing in the morning."

"Paris?" She sat back and Hugo recognized the excitement in her voice. "Now that's cool. We flying or taking the train?"

"The train," he said. "And it's not 'we.'"

"What do you mean?" She turned in her seat to glare at him.

"I'm going by myself, I'm sorry."

"Oh, no. No way. I took a lot of risks getting you in tonight and you're not dumping me now. I've played along every step of the way and I deserve to see this thing through." She was still glaring at him. "So let's just make our quick stop in London and get going. I'll call for tickets, just to show that I can still play my part."

"This isn't a game, Merlyn." He glanced over and saw anger in her eyes. "I'm sorry, but dropping you off *is* the quick stop in London."

CHAPTER TWENTY

At seven the next morning, Hugo arrived at the refurbished Saint Pancras station. Newly open for business, the Victorian Gothic building had replaced Waterloo as the departure point for trains heading out of London to the English Channel and on to France.

He set up on the small patio outside Carluccio's Caffé with some panettone, a plate of parma ham, and an oversized latte. He watched the crowds ebb and flow before him, tides of scurrying feet that flooded the platform when a train arrived, then receded as another departed. He was amused by the range and easy predictability of expressions; the drawn faces of suitcase-bearing travelers, tired but intent on reaching their destination, flashing dirty looks as their rapid steps were impeded by wide-eyed youngsters sporting backpacks. The calm and determined elderly couples in town to shop, or perhaps for a medical appointment, bound to each other with interlocked arms, drifting through the terminal when the current took them, standing patiently to one side when it went the wrong way. The most worried faces, harried perhaps, belonged to the parents and their children who clung to one another as if afraid the tide would sweep the little ones onto the tracks or under the wheels of the lumbering luggage carts, those whales of the station, propelled by the tired but cheerful porters who leaned as they pushed, wending their way through the squalls of travelers with the plodding precision of experienced tugboat captains.

As he sipped his coffee, Hugo half expected to see Merlyn appear in front of him, her almond eyes laughing at him for thinking he could get away with making the trip alone. She'd been unhappy the whole way down from Hertfordshire to London, and they'd driven in almost total silence. After dropping her off, Hugo had called the office and sent two men to Pendrith's address in Chelsea, getting a phone call twenty minutes later to tell him what he expected: no one home, and no sign anyone had been home. A quick look through his mail slot at the mail piled inside his door, using a handheld snake camera, had told them that.

So maybe, just maybe, the old man was in Paris.

Hugo left his table and checked in at the Eurostar terminal thirty minutes before the train's departure time, picking up a paperback from an open kiosk en route. Not happy with his reading choices, he was pleased to get to his seat and find an almost-new copy of the *Bookdealer*, the trade journal for the book trade. A knowledgeable, if infrequent, collector of old books, Hugo sank into the thin pages of the magazine with the same delight his wife took in her shopping catalogues, the long articles and old-style ads from antiquarian dealers beckoning him into a world that was familiar and safe.

But Christine was on his mind, had been since they'd spoken a few hours earlier, just briefly, as he waited outside the embassy grounds for a taxi. She'd been busy and sounded happy, doing more talking than listening, and Hugo knew without asking that these were signs she had no immediate plans to return to London.

She was and always had been, without doubt, his most interesting study. Serial killers, psychopaths, and arsonists had always presented a challenge, held a fascination for him. But while their specific acts were different, they all had strings of similarity that tied them together, familiar tales of neglect as babies, abuse as children, abandonment as teens.

Christine, on the other hand, presented a multitude of contradictions that he'd yet to figure out, but that had initially attracted him to her. She'd been the Dallas socialite with a soft spot for the underprivileged, her charity work coming from the heart, not for show. She'd traveled, too, shown an interest in the world and perhaps from that she possessed a confidence in her place in it that was rare among her spoiled friends. Ultimately, Hugo knew that her place was in Dallas, near her family, her work, those same friends. She loved shopping and so should love London and Paris, at least that was the logic he applied to the situation, and one that he used to appeal to her. But logic and Christine were occasional friends, meeting up when the circumstances were right, not seeking each other out at the behest of others, including Hugo. She enjoyed London only a little, Paris even less.

He tried to keep his mind on the magazine, scanning the reviews and an article about French poet Arthur Rimbaud and his love affair with Paul Verlaine, a brief relationship fueled by passion, absinthe, and hashish. But Hugo couldn't entirely escape the present, his eyes wandering to the platform outside his window, the soft hiss of the doors whispered reminders that Pendrith and Walton were out there somewhere, perhaps watching him or perhaps being watched by someone else, by some faceless person responsible for a growing list of dead and disappeared.

The voice of the station announcer echoed from the platform, giving his rendition of the traditional "All aboard!" Hugo looked over his shoulder as he heard chatter behind him and saw a handsome couple in their fifties checking their tickets for seat numbers.

All well in their world, he thought, suddenly conscious of where he was going, and why. With no sign of Pendrith or Walton, despite police inquiries into both men, that alarm bell ringing in the back of his mind had grown only louder. His chest tightened with a sudden and powerful unease. Maybe he should have let Merlyn come. What if she, for some reason he couldn't yet fathom, was the next person in this bizarre case to disappear without a trace?

Hugo didn't notice when the train began to move out of the station, so smooth, like the caress of a mother's hand on her child's sleeping brow, and he was momentarily disoriented by what he thought was movement on the platform.

Almost immediately, though, he felt the familiar nudge and pull as the train picked up speed, heading north out of the station before making a firm right-hand turn past the towering and unsightly gasometers behind the King's Cross rail station, and then burrowing into a covered bridge that funneled the sleek train into the ground, lights flickering past the dark windows.

Hugo blinked at the sudden return to the surface, feeling like a mole, or better yet a long worm, appearing out of the earth into daylight. *A disappointed worm*, he thought, as the dirty brick and stone buildings of east London passed by, the view full of warehouses and run-down housing estates, depressing and drab until he spied the magnificent Queen Elizabeth II suspension bridge, which bore the M25 motorway, the road encircling the city, across the River Thames. The train dipped down, though, not up, burrowing again to get them under the Thames, bursting back out the other side into the countryside, trees and hedges now a blur and the motorway traffic beside them sluggish, unhurried.

As the train rocketed south through rural Kent, Hugo felt himself relax into his seat, the greens and browns of the countryside massaging his mood, the villages tucked into the chalky hills appearing and disappearing like reassuring mirages in the desert, but offering him real, not imagined, comfort.

Feeling better, Hugo set about putting his travel time to good purpose. He'd already phoned Bart Denum, his subordinate at the embassy, and given him some research. He wanted to know more about Ginny Ferro's life and also get some background on Pendrith and Walton. In his experience, people's actions were rooted in the past, their motives connected to events they might not even remember. Even though he was bemused by most of what was happening, Hugo thought maybe he could reach back in time and grasp one of those roots and grope his way to some solid answers.

While he waited for Bart's return call, Hugo reached into his overnight bag for a pen and paper. If he'd had the resources, he would have created a literal jigsaw of the puzzle that had him stumped, squares of paper he could spread out and connect physically to build a picture of what was happening. And, more importantly, why it was happening. But for now, a few notes would have to do. The words he wrote were, for the most part, unimportant, acting as reminders of the major issues and questions, and also as triggers for his thought process. As he began, it struck him forcefully that the missing pieces were different for each case.

He began with Ginny Ferro. She was dead, but it was not clear why. Suicide seemed unlikely, but possible. Accident seemed equally unlikely, yet possible. And if it wasn't either of those, he was left with murder.

But who would kill Ginny Ferro? And why?

Hugo skipped to Harper's own death in the churchyard. Certainly, it could have been self-inflicted. Hugo had seen many suicides that looked just like that. And given the movie-star couple's penchant for cemeteries, the place seemed ideal. But it didn't *feel* right to Hugo, even though he couldn't say exactly why.

And where the hell were Pendrith and Walton?

Hugo tapped his notebook in frustration, irritated that he was unable to make the right connections, really make any at all. He was interrupted by his phone, the number coming up as the embassy. He silently hoped it wasn't Ambassador Cooper.

"Hugo, it's Bart."

"Hey, Bart, get some sleep?"

"Not much, you?"

"None. So what did you find?"

"You're not going to like it, I'm afraid."

"Try me."

"First you should know that the English cops are trying to cut you out of the loop. They found something and apparently haven't told you."

"I haven't heard from them, so you're probably right." Hugo instinctively leaned back as the train flew into a tunnel with a loud *whump*. "I think we hit the English Channel, so I'll call when we get to France in about twenty minutes."

"OK, but before you go, you might want to know what they found."

"You're being a tease, Bart. What is it?"

"Not just what, but who. They found that reporter's car with a body in it."

"Whose body? Harry Walton's?" When he got no response he looked at his phone. The signal had gone. He snapped it shut with a silent curse and settled back for a tortuous twenty minutes. His scribbled notes sat on the table in front of him like an unfinished crossword, a crossword where even the clues were starting to be withheld.

The train hit France at a hundred miles an hour, climbing into the lap of the French countryside only to accelerate onto the specially designed high-speed rail line, keeping the train tight to the contours of the land, sweeping up over rises and swooping down through its shallow valleys.

Hugo got Bart back on the line.

"Sorry, boss, wasn't meaning to play games with you; I figured they'd have routers on the train and we'd be able to talk."

"No problem. So tell me about Walton. I assume it was him in the car?"

"They think so. He'd been burned to a crisp, so they'll be running dental matches, maybe a DNA check if they can. But the body size was right."

"Any other signs of injury?"

"Like bullet wounds?"

"Anything."

"Not that I know of." Bart hesitated. "Boss, what exactly is going on?"

"I wish I knew. Too many people disappearing and dying, I can tell you that much. Where was Walton's car found?"

"In a church parking lot, in Wakefield."

"A church?"

"Well, not exactly a church. They were buildings owned by the Church of England."

"But not an actual church or graveyard?"

"No. I looked at some photos, knowing about your little incident in the country, and you wouldn't even know they were owned by the church. Sorry."

"OK, thanks," said Hugo. "Let me know as soon as they confirm the ID."

"Will do."

"And not that it matters, probably, but did you find much about Walton?"

"A little. Let me get my notes here. You writing this down, or want me to send these to you?"

"I'll make notes, so just run through it for me."

"OK. His father was a soldier in the first part of World War Two, sent home when he lost a leg. Mother a housewife who died when he was five. He had no siblings, grew up with his father, religious about going to church. And his dad had an interesting job after the army thing. He was an executioner, how about that?"

"Delightful," said Hugo. "A grim reaper with a wooden leg."

"Right. Seeing that got me reading about the process, and apparently they had two at every execution, and half a dozen on the Home Office books. They'd call them up when they had a neck to stretch."

"Delightful, as I said. And Harry Walton, what was his career path?"

"Started work on the *Hitchin Gazette*, stayed there a few years before moving up to London to work shifts at the tabloids. Kept a roof over his head by working at some of the tourist attractions like Madame Tussauds, where there's a wax figure of his dad, the last executioner, and the Tower of London. A whole year at Tussauds, actually, but he's been freelancing for a few years."

"No dirt or criminal history?"

"Nope, at least not as such. Only one odd thing, maybe not even that odd. Lucky, I guess you'd call it. He was a lottery winner a couple years back, which means he doesn't have to work much. Must have taken some time off after the win because he wasn't writing. Quit for about a year, best I can tell."

"Can't blame him for that. And Pendrith?"

"Hard to find much on him, I guess because of his background. Most of his official stuff is under wraps, but from regular web searches I didn't see anything of interest. Not that I know what I'm looking for."

"Me neither, Bart, I'm sorry. What are his major issues?"

"Politically? Well, he's big into law and order. But then, who isn't? Before he was elected, he was all about reinstating capital punishment but apparently read a bunch of studies and converted, said it was a waste of money and barbaric. Some thought it was a cynical switch of opinion to get elected, some thought it was real. I guess the electorate thought it was real and he's stuck with the new view ever since, always voting against reinstatement. Let's see, he also favored the recent wars in the Middle East, but he doesn't like how much they cost. If I had to guess, I'd say budget issues were his next main concern. Tight bastard."

"Not a bad trait for a politician," smiled Hugo. "Anything else?"

"Not on him. But I spoke to your buddy Upton, he called for you. On the down low, it seemed like. Anyway, he faxed me a copy of Dayton Harper's autopsy report."

"He did?" Hugo was suddenly excited. "And?"

"Dead from one shot in the heart. No drugs in his system, no other signs of physical harm. GSR on his hands, and his fingerprints on the gun."

"That can be done postmortem," Hugo said. "What else?"

"I'm looking at it now. Nothing except minuscule bits of clothing and . . . huh, paper, found in the wound."

"Paper?"

"That's what it says. Maybe he had a notebook on him, bullet went through it?"

"Maybe." Hugo thought back to their conversation in his apartment. "You know, you might be right, I'm pretty sure he carried one with him. Do you have a list of his belongings, stuff found on him at the churchyard?"

"No, just the autopsy report."

"OK. Any other news?"

"Nope. Oh, they resolved the Ginny Ferro debacle. The ambassador stepped in and told our people to stop being silly, so the Brits are doing the autopsy. Or have done it, I have no idea which."

"Can you find out?"

"I can try."

"Good enough. Thanks for your help, and keep your cell phone charged, I may need you again."

Hugo hung up and sat back. He looked out the window, the new information percolating as the rolling lands of northern France flashed by. He was far from any real answers but was beginning to see the ends of a few roots, to recognize patterns that might be coincidences, or might be meaningful. He checked his watch. Thirty minutes to Paris, so just enough time for a cup of coffee. Maybe even enough time for Bart to call him back about the body in the Mini, a call that he was fairly sure would confirm a growing suspicion: whoever had burned up in that car, Hugo had a powerful feeling it wasn't Harry Walton.

CHAPTER TWENTY-ONE

Pendrith's address had taken some finding, but Bart had managed it, giving Hugo a street name and number for an apartment in the Latin Quarter, on the second floor of a four-story building on the busy Rue Monge, just south of the River Seine.

As the train pulled into Gard du Nord, Hugo thought about walking or taking the metro so he could see and experience something of the city. It was a fleeting thought; he just didn't have time for that. Instead, he took a cab from in front of the train station, asking the driver to drop him at the metro stop closest to the Sorbonne University. He settled into the back seat, a few minutes at least to watch the city pass by.

Something about Paris had grabbed Hugo the first time he'd come ten years ago, and he'd been back every chance he got, even if for a day or so. It was, to his mind, the most visually appealing of the world's cities, its center devoid of the ugly concrete blocks that passed for buildings in cities like London and New York. He loved the language, too, and had taught himself to speak it to the point where he was a notch or two below fluent. And he liked the people, despite what others said about them being rude, not minding their insularity because he liked his space, too. His favorite pastime in Paris was to sit at a café and people watch, amuse himself by making up stories about those who passed by, using the clues people carried with them or wore on their back.

Today, though, the romance of Paris was tainted. The pedestrians scuttling across the road in front of the taxi and the weaving cyclists were impediments, not Parisian flavor.

The taxi pulled to the curb with a squeak of its brakes and Hugo climbed out, paying the driver and turning up the collar of his overcoat against the cold. A heavy, gray sky sat low overhead, and two large drops of rain hit his cheek as he started to walk south along Rue Monge. He had no specific plan other than to see whether Pendrith's place was occupied or had been recently. He felt like he was at a dead end, and this was his last chance to find the politician.

He checked the numbers written high on the buildings and saw he was close, realized that he had no real plan of action. Ringing the doorbell no longer seemed like much of one, and he was sure there was a better way, if he could just come up with it. He was relieved to see a café on his side of the street, almost directly opposite the entrance to Pendrith's building. A place to think.

It was busy but warm inside, and he took a seat at the only free table by the window, giving him a view across the street to the apartments. He ordered a café crème and a sandwich, less worried about time now that he had an eye on the place, happier to be able to think for a few moments and, maybe just a little, soak up some of Paris.

Even so, he remained watchful, scanning the sidewalk across the busy road for the familiar shape of Pendrith, knowing he was grasping at straws.

And then he saw him.

He'd missed the portly figure because he was on the same side of the street as the café, not his apartment, and he was now feet away from the window. Hugo lifted his cup to cover his face, and swiveled in his seat to put his back to the sidewalk. Seconds later he heard the door behind him open.

Of course, this is his neighborhood café.

Hugo didn't know whether to leap up and confront him or sit tight, see whether Pendrith was here alone. That decision was made when the houndstooth coat of the Englishman brushed against Hugo's table. He'd not seen the American, wasn't expecting to, intent only on finding somewhere to sit.

"Pendrith."

The Englishman whirled around, his mouth falling open at the sight of Hugo looking up at him, and when he spoke, his voice was a croak. "Marston. What . . . what are you doing here?"

"Looking for you. Sit down." Hugo waved a hand at the empty seat opposite him.

Pendrith looked around the café, as if checking for other surprises. "How did you find me?"

"A little luck and a little ingenuity."

Pendrith nodded. "You probably want to know what's going on."

"Good guess."

Pendrith had regained his composure and sat watching Hugo, his lips pursed as he thought. "Here's the deal, old boy. Graham Stopford-Pendrith got in over his head. Has some people looking for him and needs to disappear."

"Who? And why?"

"Can't tell you either of those things." Pendrith looked up as the waiter appeared at his shoulder. "*Rien, merci. Je pars.*"

"Leaving already? I don't think so, Pendrith; you have a lot of explaining to do."

"I'm sure you think so. I'm not one of the bad guys, Hugo, I'll tell you that much. I'm really not. I hope you realize that."

"Explain it to me."

"I don't have time. I have some bags to pack and a plane to catch."

"And you expect me to just let you disappear?"

"I do." Pendrith cleared his throat, then leaned forward. "I assume you didn't bring your weapon? You're a bit of a cowboy but basically a rule follower, and I suspect you'd lose your job if some Frog caught you with a gun over here, am I right?"

"Maybe."

"Then I have the advantage. And it's pointing at your groin."

Hugo hadn't noticed Pendrith slipping his hands into his pockets, but they were there now. He may be bluffing, Hugo knew, but when it came to guns, he didn't take chances. As long as he stayed in a public place and did as he was asked, Pendrith wouldn't do anything. "So you're pointing a gun at me and you're one of the good guys?"

"In self-preservation mode. As your Thomas Jefferson said, 'We have the wolf by the ears, and we can neither hold him, nor safely let him go. Justice is in one scale, and self-preservation in the other.'"

"That's a riddle, Pendrith, not an explanation."

"Think about it." He sat back. "I assume you know where my apartment is?"

"Correct."

"And I assume once I'm no longer pointing this gun at you, you'll head over there?"

"I want to know who killed Ginny Ferro and Brian Drinker. And, I assume, Dayton Harper." Pendrith's eyes gave nothing away, so Hugo played another card. "I also want to know who killed Harry Walton."

A shadow passed across Pendrith's eyes, but only for a second. "Walton?"

"Yeah, they found his car burned out, a body in it. Fits his description."

Pendrith smiled. "But they didn't make a proper ID yet?"

"Not yet, but they will."

"Hope springs eternal in the human breast."

"Yes, Alexander Pope, very clever. You don't think Walton's dead?"

"Do you?"

"No, I don't. I think he's the one trying to find you."

"That so? What's your theory?"

"Unfinished. But I'm pretty sure you two know each other. Maybe from Braxton Hall, maybe not. But you both put yourselves squarely into an investigation that didn't concern you. Walton even risked losing a story when he could have had a front-page, national headline. Journalists don't do that."

"So what makes you think we know each other?"

"Two things; one big, one small. The obvious one is that you had no way to leave the Rising Moon. You didn't seem to like each other, so when you both left about the same time I didn't even think you might have gone together. But you did, didn't you? You had no other way to leave the village."

Pendrith didn't respond at first, then asked, "And the small thing?"

"Something I should have noticed, or paid attention to, also at the pub when Walton brought us beer."

"What about it?"

"If he'd asked the publican what we were drinking, the man wouldn't have remembered. He told us he'd forgotten who had which drink when he delivered the food. And if Walton had paid attention to what we drank, he would have brought me a pale ale. I think he knows your strong feelings about beer and defaulted to that, brought two pints of what he knows you like."

"Bit of a stretch, old boy."

"Then tell me I'm wrong."

Pendrith studied Hugo for a moment, as if deciding. "It's a long story. Long and sordid and, God willing, it's a story that will never be told. Certainly not by me."

"That's why you're disappearing. So you don't have to face him or tell this sordid story?" When Pendrith didn't respond, Hugo asked, "So where are you going now?"

"To pick up a few belongings and then tallyho."

"You're leaving your whole life behind, just like that?"

"The alternative, according to my analysis, is a life behind bars. One I can manage, the other I cannot. So yes, I'll take my chances on the run."

"New identity in your bag, I assume?"

"That's the wonderful thing about Europe now. One can flit about from country to country and not worry about passports and such."

"You'll need one to get into Switzerland."

Pendrith smiled. "Oh, you are a clever chap."

"I don't know where else a man on the run would keep his money. They will find you."

"Probably, sooner or later. But if it's later, then all to the good. Gives me time to write my memoirs, set the record straight." He stood. "I want you to know, Hugo, I didn't kill any of them. Not one."

"Then why can't you tell me what's going on? If you're innocent, I can help you, Pendrith, for God's sake—"

Pendrith shook his head, a sad smile on his face. "I didn't say I was innocent, now did I?"

"Then—"

"Don't be the first, old boy. I don't want your blood on my hands, any more than I wanted those others. Don't follow me, you know perfectly well that I'll see if you do." He patted his pocket. "And I really don't want to see you."

"Pendrith, two movie stars are dead. Every cop on the planet will be hunting for you. God knows what kind of reward, or even how many rewards, will be offered for your capture. If you didn't kill anyone then you know as well as I do there is a very good chance—"

"Fine." Pendrith held up a hand. "You're right. Look, I have to take care of some things first, though. Meet me back here in an hour."

"How do I know you'll be here?"

"You don't. But it's the best offer you're going to get."

Hugo nodded, then watched through the large window as Pendrith passed in front of the café and headed north toward the River Seine, away from his apartment. The old man walked with his hands thrust deep into his pockets and his shoulders hunched forward, as if trying to make himself smaller, as if afraid a pair of eyes other than Hugo's might be watching.

Hugo waited for five minutes, then paid for his food and left. He walked the same way Pendrith had gone, cursing when he saw a side road that curved back toward the old man's building. *He did go there, after all.* Hugo kept straight, though, intending to keep his word and be back at the café in one hour. He thought about staying put, keeping his vantage point over the front of the place. But to what end? Hugo was sure there'd be a back exit, which Pendrith would use now that he knew Hugo was there. And if he did have a gun, there was an outside chance he'd use it.

In any case, an hour sitting and waiting would be torture. Better to get his Paris fix, to exercise his legs and his mind and let the chill November air work its magic on his senses. He crossed the busy intersection with Boulevard Saint-Germain, where the aromas of Paris welcomed him as he passed by, the warm smell of baking, the mustiness of the cheese shop, and the fresh, almost metallic, smells of the poissonerie, the fish shop, and its neighbor, the butcher.

And then he was on the Quai de Montebello, standing beside a café named Panis, waiting for the light to change. Opposite him was the Pont au Double, the pedestrian-only bridge that took foot traffic to the Cathedral of Notre Dame, which he could see from where he stood.

At a break in the traffic he crossed the road and walked west, away from the bridge, soon pausing at a riverfront bookstall. These stalls were Parisian landmarks, each one made up of four metal boxes fixed to the stone wall overlooking the Seine. The boxes were green, and each was about six feet long and full of postcards, key chains, and other trinkets, as well as secondhand books. The seller, the *bouquiniste*, smiled a greeting, and Hugo practiced his French, asking whether they'd had snow and asking him how business had been. After a few minutes browsing, Hugo bought a postcard with Merlyn vaguely in mind, then continued along the sidewalk.

As he walked, he glanced over at the River Seine on his right. The water was high, confirming the bouquiniste's tale of no snow but plentiful rain, and Hugo stopped for a moment, leaning against the stone balustrade, watching the debris being swept along by the current. The river looked heavy, sluggish, rolling lazily past him, squeezed by its stone banks like charcoal paint being squeezed from a tube onto an artist's palette.

He straightened and checked his watch, then kept moving when he saw how little time had passed. As he approached the most historic of the bridges, Pont Neuf, he spotted another bouquiniste open for business and slowed. The seller was an older man with a large red nose and a shuffling gait. His head was topped with the traditional beret, and Hugo wondered if that was just for the tourists, like him.

"*Bonjour, monsieur,*" Hugo said. He stopped in front of the second of the metal boxes bolted to the wall.

"*Bonjour,*" said the old man. "*Américain?*"

"*Oui,*" Hugo said, continuing in French, "Is it that obvious?"

The man smiled and nodded downward, toward Hugo's cowboy boots, then went back to arranging his stall. Hugo looked over the books, surprised to see more than battered copies of the classics and mainstream thrillers. One book in particular caught his eye, partly because it was one of the few in English. It was a hardback, pocket-sized but thick, titled *Hidden Horror: The World's Most Evil and Least Known Serial Killers.* A subject close to his own heart. He picked up the book and started to flick through it.

He had, of course, heard of most of the men and women mentioned, but he was nonetheless impressed at the research that had gone into the book. Even a brief look told him new things about Texan Joe Ball, who fed his victims to his pet alligators, and about Elizabeth Bathory, who tortured and killed hundreds of girls in various castles in Hungary back in the 1500s.

And then his eye fell onto a picture of New Orleans, a drawing showing the French Quarter as it looked in 1916. He started to read the text and felt a rising excitement as several pieces of information reached out and grabbed, pulling him completely into the tale of the killer from the Big Easy.

He needed to buy this book, to stop himself from reading the whole thing here, but he skipped to the end of the passage to learn one fact: the New Orleans killer had never been identified.

Hugo held the book up. "*Combien?*" How much?

The old man shuffled over. "It's written on the back, *non?*"

Hugo looked. "Not this one."

"*Merde.*" The seller took the book. "I don't know, maybe five euros?"

Hugo thought he'd misheard. The book was in good shape, maybe not even secondhand, so he dug out a ten-euro note and handed it over. "Keep the change."

"You want something else for your money? Maybe something French," the old man winked, "you speak it well, I suppose you can read it?"

"With the help of a dictionary," Hugo said. He offered his hand. "Hugo Marston."

The old man seem surprised but took Hugo's hand. "Max." He winked again. "Just Max."

"*Enchanté.*"

"You live here, monsieur?"

"No. I'd like to, though. Maybe I can arrange it."

"If so, you will have to buy some real shoes, I think."

"Then maybe I won't," Hugo smiled. "These are very comfortable and I've worn cowboys boots for the last forty years. I'm not sure my feet would appreciate fancy French shoes at this point."

They talked about books for a couple of minutes, then the weather, until Hugo looked at his watch and said he had to go. They shook hands again, and Hugo started back the way he'd come, the Seine rolling along on his left, carrying a pair of tourist boats toward the Isle de la Cité ahead of him. He patted the book in his pocket, his mind wanting to toy with the possibilities that had leapt at him from its pages, whispers of a connection, just possibly, to the first murder that had captured his interest in England, a murder that was now a hundred years old.

But first, the Pendrith mystery.

CHAPTER TWENTY-TWO

Hugo waited at the café for thirty minutes. A sense of unease settled in long before that, almost as soon as he'd sat down and ordered coffee, a feeling that quickly grew into frustration and then annoyance.

He checked his watch every two minutes, resisting the urge to do it more often, his eyes locked on the front of Pendrith's building, breaking away only to scour the sidewalk. The obvious conclusion was that he'd been duped. Easily too, although at the time he'd not had much option other than to go along with Pendrith's arrangement. But duped nonetheless.

When it became clear that Pendrith wasn't showing, there was only one thing for Hugo to do. He paid his tab at the café for the second time and crossed the busy Rue Monge to Pendrith's apartment building. Two stone steps led up to the double front doors, and twelve buttons to the right of the doors connected the outside world with those inside. He noted that Pendrith's name was not listed and all the names were French. He started pressing buttons, and whoever lived behind the eighth one let him in without any questions.

A black-and-white-tiled entrance held mail slots for the residents, and another set of doors lay ahead of him. He pushed through and went straight up the stairs to the second floor. It was on the right at the top of the stairs, looking out over Rue Monge.

He paused by the door and listened, but heard nothing. He looked at the bottom of the door but saw no light, no moving shadows. Nothing. He stood to one side of the door, wishing he had his gun, and rapped his knuckles against the wood. When he got no response he knocked a second time, louder, and then a third. After a full minute of silence, he reached down and tried the handle.

It was unlocked, and his stomach tightened. Had Pendrith taken off and left his apartment open? *Unlikely*, Hugo thought. *Very unlikely*.

He pushed the door open, staying to the side, not eager to make himself a target. He waited for a moment, then ducked inside, eyes sweeping the room.

He saw Pendrith immediately, sitting opposite the front door in a large leather chair, feet propped on an ottoman as if waiting to receive guests. A single bullet hole dribbled blood over his right cheek and ear. Hugo moved closer and saw that the skin around the hole itself had been burned by a close-range shot. A gun lay on the floor beside the chair.

Hugo reached for his phone, then hesitated. He wasn't even sure who to call any more. He looked around and saw papers on a desk at one end of the sitting room. He'd call the local police, but he needed to look around first. He left his phone in his pocket and walked quickly through the apartment, making sure he was alone.

When he came back into the main room, he flicked on the lights. He pulled a handkerchief from his pocket and used it to methodically open drawers, check every surface, and scan every piece of paper. He wasn't sure what he was looking for—perhaps a link to the mayhem being wrought across the Channel, maybe just some indication that Pendrith's demise wasn't as it appeared.

The only thing out of the ordinary was Pendrith's desk. The top was covered with news articles and other papers, and Hugo sat down to study them, careful to keep his hands in his lap.

The majority featured the release of convicted criminals in England, mostly murderers, but a few rapists, who had been released and committed further crimes, the headlines screaming bloody murder. Two of the stories had been written by Harry Walton and, from their tone and judging by his choice of interviewees, Walton did not approve of the release of the prisoners, an I-told-you-so flavor to his writing.

Hugo saw, too, a recidivism study addressing all types of criminals, from burglars and drug dealers all the way up the ladder of crime to murderers. Beside it on the desk sat a draft of the bill Pendrith was championing, a bill that advocated for the release of England's aging convicts.

Hugo sat back and thought. So much of this didn't make sense. His eyes roamed over the desktop again, the sense that he was missing something nagging at him. He got up and went over to Pendrith. Gently, without moving him or touching anywhere that would hold a fingerprint, Hugo searched the dead man's pockets. The navy jacket contained a wallet in one pocket and passport in the other. Where was his phone? Hugo held his breath as he shifted the body enough to be able to be sure his pants pockets were empty, suddenly aware of the undignified whiff of urine that rose from Pendrith's body, an expulsion as natural and inevitable as his last breath.

Hugo searched his front and back pockets but they were all empty. He straightened and began to search the room again, knowing it was easier to find something when you knew what you were looking for. And yet, after ten minutes he still hadn't found it. He went back to Pendrith and stood looking at him, then knelt in front of the body and slid his hands down the sides of the seat cushion. As he worked his fingers toward the back of the seat, his left hand touched something cold, something wedged as deep as it could go. Pendrith's phone.

He tugged it out, suddenly aware that his prints were all over it. Too late to prevent that, he'd wipe it down later. Hugo hadn't moved over to this type of phone, one with a touchscreen. He still used a flip phone, didn't text, and had never even held one like this. He touched the screen and found himself looking at Pendrith's e-mail account and was about to open a message when his own phone buzzed in his pocket, vibrating against his leg. He fished it out and looked at the caller ID. Merlyn.

"Hey," Hugo said. "How are you?"

"Still pissed off. Where are you?"

"Paris."

"I know that, you arse. Where exactly, and doing what?"

Hugo looked down at Pendrith. Merlyn had been through a lot more than she deserved, and yet she didn't deserve to be lied to. "You sitting down?"

"Yes. And drinking. What's up?"

"I found Pendrith."

"What did that pompous arse have to say for himself?"

"Merlyn, hold up. Look, I'm sorry to tell you this, but Pendrith is dead."

A silence, then her voice came back, subdued now. "Oh, Hugo, no. Not him, too."

"I'm sorry, yes."

"How? Who did it?"

Hugo surveyed the scene. "It looks like suicide. One shot to the head, gun on the floor beside him. But . . ."

"But what?"

"Something's not right. He has papers lined up on his desk, neatly, like he wanted someone to see them. To find them when they found him."

"So?"

"So why not just leave a note?"

"There wasn't one?"

"No. And to be honest, if Pendrith was going to kill himself, I'd expect to see a note, a finished cigar, and an empty glass of something." Hugo looked at his left hand. "And I found his phone shoved down the side of his seat, which seems odd."

"Could it have fallen there if he shot himself?"

"I suppose," Hugo said doubtfully. And then it hit him. "The front door was unlocked. Shit, Merlyn, the front door was unlocked."

"Maybe he did that to make it easier for someone to find him, so they wouldn't have to break down the door."

"Nice idea, but I don't think so," Hugo said. He was scrolling through Pendrith's call log and seeing nothing in the two hours since they'd met at the café. "Because if he's dead, why would he care about a busted lock? And if he wanted to make sure that someone found him, he'd call the cops right before pulling the trigger. No, remember when we were staying at that pub? Every time he went in or out of his room, he locked the door—it was instinct for him. I don't think there's any way he'd leave his apartment unlocked, especially if he was leaving out important papers and planning to shoot himself. It might be consistent with some people, but not Pendrith."

"What are you saying, Hugo?"

"That someone else killed him. Someone else followed him and shot him here."

"Someone he knew?"

"Probably. I'm not sure Pendrith would have let a stranger into his apartment, given what's been going on. He told me he was planning to disappear, so I doubt he'd even answer the door."

"Wait, when did he tell you that?"

"I saw him. Today, barely an hour ago."

"Oh my God, Hugo, that's insane." She was quiet for a minute. "Wait, so that means either he knew the person or someone put a gun to the back of his head at the doorway."

"The former. I think he knew whoever it was." *Walton.* "Remember the phone?"

"What about it?" Merlyn asked.

"If someone had surprised him at his door, someone he didn't know, I don't see him pulling out his phone to stuff it down the side of the chair."

"But who even knew he was in Paris?" she asked. "Who the hell would want to hurt him?"

There was only one person, the only domino in this game that hadn't fallen or been knocked over. "I'm not sure yet," he told Merlyn, not having enough of an explanation to warrant giving her Walton's name. To be certain, he'd need to find out who died in the red Mini.

"This is all insane," she said. Hugo heard a faint beep, then Merlyn's voice again. "Someone's calling through, can I put you on hold?"

"No need, just call me back when you're done. I need to do a little more poking around here and I can't do that while I'm holding a phone." A sudden thought. "Who's calling?"

"I'll look." Her voice went quieter as she checked her caller ID and spoke. "Holy shit, it's that reporter, Harry Walton. What the hell does he want?"

"Merlyn, wait—"

"I know, I know. Tell you what he says. I will, don't worry—I'll call right back. Bye, Hugo."

"Merlyn, wait!" Hugo heard the desperation in his own voice, felt the fear clutching at his throat, and he fought the panic that surged in his chest as he saw that the connection with Merlyn was lost.

She was gone.

He tried calling her but was sent straight to voicemail. He tried two minutes later, then two minutes after that. He left three messages telling her to call him back, telling her to stay where she was, telling her not to go anywhere with anyone, no matter what. He didn't tell her that Walton was the killer, he wasn't even sure that he was right.

But nothing else made any sense.

CHAPTER TWENTY-THREE

DCI Upton sounded both relieved and irritated to hear from Hugo. But his professionalism kicked in when Hugo asked him, almost ordered him, to send officers to Merlyn's apartment.

"I'll do it, Hugo, but I want an explanation."

"Fine. Do that first, then call me back."

It took a minute, then Hugo's phone rang. "I've got uniforms on the way, lights and sirens, the works."

"Thanks. Let me know when she's safe."

"Will do. Look, the chief constable is looking to nail my hide to the wall. What's going on?"

"I wish I knew. I'm working on it, and when I find out, I promise you'll be the first to know."

"Somehow that's not very reassuring. Where are you now?"

"I'm in Paris. At Pendrith's apartment."

"He's with you?"

"Kind of. He's dead."

"Jesus, Hugo, what are you into? Have you called the locals?"

"Not yet, I don't fancy being caught up in a Parisian murder investigation right now."

"Murder? What the hell happened?"

"I think Walton is our man. I think there was more to his relationship with Pendrith than we knew. I think there was more to Pendrith than we knew."

190

"Walton's dead, Hugo. We found his body in his car, burned to a crisp. I told one of your guys about that, he didn't tell you?"

"He told me you found a charred body in Walton's car, one that matched Walton's height and frame. Did you confirm an ID yet?"

"No, but who else would it be?"

"No idea," said Hugo. "But I don't think it's him. And if I'm right, we're going to want to know more about his association with Pendrith."

"OK, until we get the body identified I can have some people look into that, but what are you thinking? What's your theory?"

"Pendrith had a bunch of papers on his desk, all to do with recidivism."

"So?"

"At the pub he told me about a bill he was trying to push through, to get more inmates released, older ones, even people who'd been convicted of murder." Hugo wandered over to Pendrith's desk. *What did any of this have to do with Walton?* "Can you get someone to pull all of Walton's articles for the last few years? Anything to do with prisons, criminal justice, stuff like that."

"Sure, what are we looking for?"

"I'm not sure yet. But look into his background a little more. I'm wondering what he did in his year off, where he was. We've missed something important about him. I'll have my people look, too, but you'll have more resources than I do."

"You really think Walton killed all those people? Harper, Ginny Ferro, Brian Drinker? And now Pendrith?"

"I know what you're thinking."

"I'm wondering what the hell's the connection, the motive."

"Me too. But I think if we look hard enough at Walton, we'll find it. Or find something that will lead us to it. Speaking of which, can you send some people to his house, or apartment, or wherever he lives?"

"You think we'll find something?"

"I do, but make sure you have enough for a proper warrant. I'd hate to find evidence and have it thrown out because we didn't paper the trail properly."

"I'll see if we can find a friendly magistrate. Are you coming straight back?"

"Yes. But I need to try Merlyn again, and I'll keep calling all the way to the Channel Tunnel."

"Our men should be at her place in about ten minutes. I'll ring and let you know when they have her, but you should call the locals in Paris, let them come take care of Pendrith. And don't touch anything, for crying out loud."

"I won't," said Hugo, slipping Pendrith's phone into his pocket. "And I'll call the police just as soon as I find a pay phone."

He strode to the Maubert-Mutualité metro station, his head down and his hands deep in his pockets, immune to the swell of the evening traffic starting to choke the Paris streets. Occasional spits of rain made him blink, but the warm glow of the sidewalk cafés went unnoticed as Hugo's mind worked against the tide of sleep that fogged his brain and drained him of the ability to find any pleasure in his favorite city.

It took less than ten minutes to reach the metro station, and he immediately looked for a phone, knowing that a public one would allow the cops to record the call but not trace it to him. He took a deep breath and dialed the police, grateful for the shuffle and scrape of busy feet around him that provided the mask of anonymity he needed.

The call made, he waited for his southbound train, sitting in one of the odd orange seats unique to the station, a whole row of them that looked more like discs than chairs. The train would take him south to Austerlitz station, where he'd change lines and head north to the Gard du Nord and get back on a train to London.

Trains rumbled around him and he sat lost in thought, then started as his phone buzzed again, surprised at getting reception underground. He recognized the number immediately.

"Upton, this is Hugo. Do you have her?"

"Hugo." *He sounds tired. I bet I do, too.* "No, I'm sorry, she wasn't there."

"Dammit."

"I know. Our uniforms got there and tried to make contact. She didn't come to the door so, after what you said, we were worried about a hostage situation. I'd sent a TAC team behind the uniforms, and when they went in, she was gone."

"Gone how, any idea?"

"Of her own accord, best we can tell. No signs of a struggle, nothing broken in the apartment."

"I wouldn't expect there to have been a struggle," Hugo said. "That's not what I'm worried about."

"What do you mean?"

"If Walton killed Pendrith, he's not even on English soil," he said, irritated at having to explain, more irritated at leaving Merlyn unprotected. "He told her to go somewhere, and she did."

"She's still not answering her phone?"

"No. He probably told her to turn it off, said she was in danger and could be tracked if her phone was on." Hugo shook his head. "If I wanted someone to disappear off the grid, that's what I'd do."

"Sneaky bastard."

"That he is," said Hugo. "He must have told her to meet him somewhere. We need to figure out where."

"Why would he hurt her? What's this about?"

"I don't know what this is about, but he might assume Pendrith told her. Maybe he knows they were both visitors to Braxton Hall, figures they were somehow in cahoots, that she knows something. Whatever happens, we have to find her." Hugo heard the desperate note in his own voice, and it shocked him a little.

"Wait, what does Braxton Hall have to do with this?"

"Little bits of this make sense, but I don't know exactly . . . and I still don't know why he's doing this. If you can get me anything and everything on Walton, from research and from his home, maybe that'll help. I have Pendrith's phone, maybe I can find something on it that will connect them." He felt the desperation creep back into his voice. "In the meantime, find Merlyn. She's an innocent in this."

Upton paused before speaking. "You're sure about that, Hugo? If we don't know what's going on, how can we know about her for sure?"

"I know it," Hugo said. But he'd not considered the alternative, it had never even crossed his mind.

"Well, I don't. She's as much in the middle of this as Pendrith and Walton, and remember, you told me that she's the one who showed up at Braxton Hall."

"She did, that's true. But I got her into this, Clive, I'm sure she's on our side." As he said the words, he knew he was partly wrong, he knew that he shouldn't rule Merlyn out of the mix on the basis of some gut instinct, and yet he was doing just that. "It's Walton, not Merlyn," Hugo said. "And we need to find her before he does. If I'm right, he's coming in from France. Can't you watch the border, the trains and ferries?"

"I'll do what I can," Upton said.

"He may be using a different name and, if so, there might be evidence of it at his house. Another reason to look, and look now."

"Like I said, I'll do what I can. But remember, borders aren't what they used to be."

CHAPTER TWENTY-FOUR

Hugo was the last to board the train back to London, hurrying on and barely seated when the platform outside his window began to slide away.

He wanted to rest, to close his eyes and give his mind and body a few moments to catch up and recharge. He'd not slept in two days, and the velvet cloak of darkness that slipped around the train as it left the bright lights of the city seemed to wrap around his exhausted body, too, its softness and the rocking of the train an irresistible lullaby singing his tired limbs and mind to sleep. It took a force of will for him to find his phone and call Merlyn, yet again. Still no answer.

There was little he could do. Bart and DCI Upton were both mining into Walton's life, trying to connect him to Pendrith, to find something they had in common, something that put Pendrith into Walton's sights, find whatever got the MP killed.

Hugo sat forward, mentally urging energy back into his body and fighting the desire to close his eyes. He pulled Pendrith's phone from his pocket and brought it to life, bleary eyes taking extra seconds to focus on the screen. He'd start with the man's e-mails.

Two minutes later, Hugo had been through all the correspondence, what little there was. A few messages to staffers, but nothing personal. It seemed clear that Pendrith wasn't big on e-mailing—no surprise for someone of his generation.

So why have a smartphone instead of a regular one? Hugo wondered. He turned to the other applications, opening the web browser to try and see where, if anywhere, Pendrith had been surfing the Internet. But Hugo's poor knowledge of technical things was a barrier, and he soon became frustrated, resigning himself to the fact that one of his tech guys would have to search it for any data.

He glanced through the other applications and one looked like a notebook, so he opened it and started reading. The very first words stung him, jolted adrenalin into his blood, and made his head swim.

> I need to start by saying that people were not meant to die. Not those people, anyway, and certainly not in the way they did. There was a greater purpose behind these events that I'm afraid will be overshadowed by the death of innocents; or relative innocents. That original purpose, perhaps ironically, is still alive, which is why I must remain vague.
>
> Is a half-apology worth anything? Who knows. Perhaps I shall delete this all and try to deal with the consequences, one way or another, the best way I can. But please know that I worked for the greater good, always, even in this horror that has unfolded. And should the full facts, every twist and turn in the story, become known, then you should know that I have seen, understood, and mourned for the deep irony at play.

It was a confession. At least, a kind of confession, though Hugo had no clue what Pendrith had meant to do with it. Send it to the media? His colleagues in Parliament? The police? Worse, it didn't answer any of the substantive questions rattling around in Hugo's head, although it did, possibly, change one of his conclusions. After all, a confession written by a man found with a gun by his side was usually called a suicide note. As he read and reread the words, Hugo wondered whether he'd been wrong, wondered whether Pendrith had taken his own life, after all.

But then he remembered where he'd found the phone and the wave of relief surprised him. The phone had been pushed down the side of the chair, hidden. Hidden from whomever killed him.

Hugo looked at the message again and tried to distance himself
from the situation, to pretend he'd found the note at another crime
scene, one where he didn't know the victims personally. What did the
words tell him? *Parse it*, he thought, *parse the message piece by piece.*

Before he could start, his phone rang. Bart.

"Hey Bart, I'm on my way home."

"Everything OK?"

"Not really. Merlyn is missing, Pendrith is dead, and Walton is on
the loose. It's only a matter of time before we get him, but in the meantime I think he's set his sights on Merlyn."

"Jesus, really? I only spoke to you a couple of hours ago, what the
hell happened?"

"Yeah, this is moving fast. Too fast. I saw Pendrith an hour before
he was killed. He told me he was planning to disappear, but I went
to his apartment and found him dead." Hugo described the scene and
could hear the scratch of Bart's pen as he took notes.

"You sure it wasn't suicide?" Bart asked.

Another thought struck Hugo, reinforcing his opinion that it
wasn't. "He had his passport on him. Now I think of it, I didn't check
to see the name but it's probably a fake. It means, though, that when he
told me he was planning to disappear, he meant it. Why would he carry
a passport then shoot himself?

"Good point. But why would someone shoot him, make it look
like a suicide, but not check his pockets?"

"Several reasons. Because the shooter's not a pro, or because he was
too busy looking for something else."

"Such as?"

"Pendrith's phone. Which I found, with something on it. I want
your opinion." He read the note to Bart, slowly so he could copy it
down word for word.

"Reads like a suicide note," Bart said. "I'm not saying you're wrong,
but it's definitely a . . ." He went quiet, searching for the right word.

"Confession?"

"Yeah, pretty much."

"I think there's more to it than that. Pendrith was working toward a goal, and he wasn't working alone."

"Walton?"

"Right. Has to be. It's confusing because Pendrith suggests that the wrong people died. Do you read it that way?"

A moment's silence. "I do. But what does he mean by 'the purpose is still alive'?"

"I think that's a direct reference to Walton, to whatever he's doing. And I think that's why the note is so vague, because he doesn't want to tip his hand, give away their grand scheme and have us stop it."

"It's like he's apologizing for Walton but still wants him to succeed."

"Exactly," said Hugo. "Smart guy, that's why I hired you."

"Thanks, but the ambassador hired me."

"Shut up, Bart, and help me figure out the last line, the key to this little mess: whatever the greater good is, that's what Walton is doing. If we can figure that out, maybe we can find him and Merlyn."

"Agreed, but you're the brains of this operation, so just tell me what to do."

"I already put DCI Upton on this, but I want to know everything possible about Pendrith and Walton. Maybe work with him so you don't duplicate, and call me when you know anything that I don't. I'm sitting here twiddling my thumbs, so if I get twenty calls with tiny pieces of info, I don't mind at all. Tell Upton that, too."

"Yes, sir. Talk to you soon, I hope."

Hugo sat back and exhaled. Good people were working hard on finding Merlyn, finding Walton, and figuring out what he and Pendrith were up to. For now, there was nothing more Hugo could do. He looked out the window as the French countryside passed by, its towns and villages invisible behind the veil of night that surrounded the train, its darkness pressing in again on Hugo and the occasional, piercing flashes of light from streetlamps and cars encouraged him to close his eyes, light and dark working together to pull him down into a welcoming sleep.

He woke to a metallic voice announcing their imminent arrival at Saint Pancras, the words echoing in his mind and not settling clearly, instead provoking a flash of panic and disorientation that the darkness outside and the stillness inside the train did nothing to dissolve.

He pulled himself upright in his seat, and the memories of the day came at him like arrows, each one a shot of alarm. He scrabbled for his phone on the little table in front of him but found only a piece of paper, folded in half. Dread rose in his throat like bile as he opened it.

I could have killed you but that's not what this is about. This no longer concerns you, and once I have made my point, I will end it. But you need to stop <u>now</u>.

It was unsigned, but there was no doubt that Harry Walton was on this train. Walton had stood right here beside him, maybe even ready to kill if Hugo had been awake.

Hugo pushed himself out of his seat, his legs stiff like boards, and he willed calmness into his body as he searched his pockets one more time for his phone, then for Pendrith's phone. He stooped and rummaged through his overnight bag, knowing he wouldn't find either there.

Not only was Walton on the train, but he'd taken away Hugo's ability to let anyone know.

Hugo looked up and down the aisles, deciding which way to go. But before he could move, a sleeve of light slipped over the train and the windows filled with the columns and ironwork of Saint Pancras station. In seconds the train was still, and Hugo abandoned any thought of searching its compartments for Walton. He hurried to the door and waited, stepping out as soon as they opened, scouring the walkway for any sign of the man. The platform slowly filled with stretching and gossiping travelers, and Hugo realized that he couldn't possibly see every compartment as it emptied, couldn't possibly catch Walton unless . . . He cursed. Walton would have gone to the front of the train to be nearest the exit. Hugo turned and ran that way. Heads turned as he flashed by, and Hugo found his way suddenly blocked by a team of rugby players who had fanned out across the platform, burly shoulders and tree-trunk legs making passage impossible for a few precious seconds. By the time he'd bundled through them, and earned himself a few choice words in the process, Hugo realized he had another problem.

Once he got to the exit, either he had to wait there for the platform to empty, in case Walton was lingering at the back of the line of passengers, or he could keep going, keep looking for Walton, and maybe find a pay phone to call in some backup. The second option seemed far preferable. Waiting wasn't Hugo's idea of taking control.

He ran into the main concourse, eyes on every face, drifting past people he'd already vetted without seeing them again, brushing shoulders and bags, apologizing under his breath as anger and desperation grew.

After five minutes he abandoned the hunt, like a fisherman finally letting go of the bucking fish, too slippery to grasp. He needed a net. He found a public phone and, with some patience, managed to have the operator connect him to the US Embassy, where he was put through to Bart.

"Hugo, where are you? I've been calling for an hour."

"I know, that bastard took my phone from under my nose while I slept."

"Jesus, he was on the same train?"

"Yes, he was. And I let him get away."

"We'll find him," Bart said. "You're at the station right now?"

"Saint Pancras, yes, and so is he."

"You want the cavalry? We can shut the place down, but it'll take a while, I'll have to ask the ambassador before we call the English police. I guess I could call Upton, go straight to him."

Hugo looked around him as the lone travelers and groups of people swirled and eddied through the station. "Forget it, Bart. He's gone by now, he has the subway, buses, other trains, taxis. All he needed was a minute's lead, and I gave him five times that." He ran a hand across his brow. "I'll find a cab and come in. I assume you've not located Merlyn?"

"No, we haven't. I tried calling to let you know that Upton's having trouble finding a friendly face to sign the search warrant. I was also calling to let you know that if you head out of the station and find the taxi rank, there's a police car waiting for you." His voice turned apologetic. "Sorry Hugo, no rest for you just yet. Maybe you can sleep in the car."

"To where?"

"Upton thought you'd want to be present when they finally get the warrant for Walton's house. He said they'd wait as long as they could."

"Where does the bastard live?"

"Some place called Walkern, just north of London."

"Never heard of it. I'll call you from the—dammit, my phone. Bart, track my phone. Maybe he forgot to turn it off. He has Pendrith's phone, too, so track them both."

"Will do. And I'll scrounge up a new one for you, in case you don't get yours back."

Hugo hung up and walked outside, glad for the cold night air that nipped away his tiredness, for a few seconds at least. He spotted a burgundy Vauxhall that sat alongside the line of taxis, like a sheepdog minding its herd, the nervous eyes of the cabbies looking back and forth between it and the station exit as they waited for fares.

Hugo smiled when the rear door of the car opened and DCI Upton stepped out. They shook hands.

"A little out of your jurisdiction, aren't you?" Hugo said.

Upton smiled. "I always thought you Yanks were more into that jurisdictional crap than we are. At least that's how the movies make it look."

"And God knows they show nothing but the truth."

Upton stood to one side and ushered Hugo into the comfort of the Vauxhall's leather seats. This was a police car for ferrying the brass, he saw, not criminals headed for lockup. "Nice wheels. Mind if I take a nap?"

"We have an hour's drive, so be my guest." He nodded to the driver, who turned in his seat and smiled at Hugo.

"Nice to see you again, sir. PC Agarwal, from the church in Weston." He turned back and flicked a switch, starting the overhead light on the car. "Sirens too, sir?"

"Not until someone gets in our way," said Upton. He fastened his seat belt and turned to Hugo. "Now, what the hell is going on? And why haven't you been answering your phone?"

Hugo told him about the note and his phone, and about Walton being on board the train.

"An eventful day," Upton said. "Something doesn't make sense, though."

"Several things don't make sense," Hugo said wearily. "Which one are you talking about?"

"If Walton is some murderous lunatic, why didn't he slit your throat while he had the chance? He left a bloody note, for heaven's sake. A note."

"I know, and I don't get it either. Although, even for him, killing someone on a moving train would be rash. He'd certainly get caught. On the other hand, maybe he didn't have a weapon? It's not like he could have throttled me, I'd have woken up and beat the crap out of him."

Upton smiled grimly. "True enough, but if we're right about him, the guy's killed several people in cold blood, and I can't imagine it's that hard to find something heavy or sharp enough to kill a sleeping man, even Hugo Marston."

"I agree. Maybe he knows that killing cops, or in my case ex-cops, will turn this from a manhunt into something he'll never get out of alive."

"Cop killers tend not to fair well once they are caught, that's true," Upton said. "You think that's it?"

Hugo just shook his head. He thought for a moment and asked, "What did you find on him?"

Upton opened a briefcase at his feet and pulled out a manila folder, then switched on the light above his head. "Most of it you know. Grew up in Weston, Hertfordshire, family religious, father—"

"Skip to the recent stuff if you don't mind, I'm still hoping for a nap," Hugo said with a gentle smile.

"OK, well, you remember how he took a year off, after winning his little bundle in the lottery? Turns out it wasn't to catch some rest and relaxation, at least not in the traditional sense. He went a little bananas and spent eight months in a mental-health facility."

"When was this?"

"Three years ago. No lasting damage, and he didn't hurt anyone. Sound relevant?"

"Hell yes. Was he committed or did he seek treatment himself?"

"He was committed. Found wandering the lanes, covered in mud, and when some local tried to help him, he started yelling and screaming about God and the church. Then, according to my reports, he just went kind of silent and brooding. For months."

"God and the church, eh?"

"The usual subject for lunatics," Upton said. "That and aliens."

"Anything else?" Hugo asked.

"Not really. He bought an apartment in London with his winnings, paid his taxes, then bought this place we're going to in Walkern, and soon after sold the family home in Weston."

"Are the two villages close?"

"Less than five miles, I'd say. Why?"

"Curious that he'd move from the family home to someplace close by. Any friends there? Is it a fancy new house?"

"No friends, or lady friends, that I know of. And his new house is pretty much the same as his old one, just in a different village."

"Why would he do that?"

"No idea," said Upton. "But before I forget, the vicar of the Weston Church confirmed that the grave you found wasn't intended for one of her parishioners or dug by her gravedigger."

"Must have been Walton again. What's the deal with the vicar, by the way? A woman, and one with tattoos, must be pretty unusual in the countryside."

Upton shrugged. "Not really. Not that close to London, and Weston is pretty much a suburb by now. Anyway, she was up front and doesn't have any connection to these people. Interesting background though, since you're wondering about her tattoos."

"Oh? Do tell."

"All rather tragic, actually. She was married to some fellow a few years ago, down in Dorset. He was abusive and one day she got fed up and put a stop to it, with a shotgun."

"Can't blame her for that."

"No, except some of the pellets went through an open doorway and killed their only son, he was a toddler, I think. She buried her husband in the back garden but when the police showed up she was cradling that little boy, catatonic. She did some time, not much, and when she got out she turned her life around and, as they say, gave herself to God."

"Prison tattoos on a vicar? Somehow that tickles me. But I'm glad it's not been a problem for her there."

"She's no-nonsense, takes care of people day or night, and gives interesting sermons."

"I bet." Hugo thought for a moment but had no immediate questions about Walton. He hoped the search of the man's house would turn up more. "Anything on Pendrith?"

"Even more of a blank than Walton, I'm afraid. Single, devoted to his work, fought passionately for the causes he believed in." Upton held up his hands in surrender. "Other than that, nothing."

"What were those causes?"

"He doesn't like Muslims much, I gather, not these days anyway." Upton referred to his notes. "But a few years back it was more domestic stuff, like compensation for victims of crime, especially children. He's toughened drunk-driving laws. Now he's on his kick to get inmates out of prison before the system has to take care of them."

"What do you think of that?"

"Me? Sounds like a bloody good idea to me, but apparently I'm in the minority. The idea comes across as soft on crime, and Pendrith was pilloried for it."

"In Parliament or the press?"

"Both. Mostly his colleagues and opponents in government, because some of the liberal press support the idea. But coming across as soft on crime doesn't get you far these days."

"Try it in Texas," Hugo said dryly.

Beside him, Upton looked at his watch and reached up to switch the reading light off. "By my reckoning, we have about thirty minutes."

Hugo settled back into his seat and closed his eyes. "That'll do for now."

CHAPTER TWENTY-FIVE

U pton woke him just as they passed through the village of Weston, offering him a cup of sweet, black coffee from a flask that the driver, Agarwal, kept on the front passenger seat. Hugo took the cup and held it in his hands while the shrouds of sleep slowly fell away, the aroma making his stomach feel at first queasy and then growl with hunger. He sipped at the liquid and relished the warmth and energy it gave him.

Beside Hugo, Upton reached inside his pocket when his phone rang. The policeman listened, shaking his head. "That's ridiculous. You're absolutely sure?" More listening. "Any pub or hotel in Walkern, I don't care. Just make it close to his house and get me that damn warrant first thing in the morning."

"Bad news?" Hugo asked as Upton tucked his phone away.

"No warrant tonight, we'll have to hole up until the morning. No judge or magistrate answers the door at this time of night on a weekend, apparently. No friendly one, anyway. My man promises it'll be early in the morning, when one of them walks his blasted dog or goes for a jog."

Hugo grunted, irritated at the delay but deeply grateful for the possibility of some proper rest. Outside, the clear night flashed by, brimming with tiny pinpricks of starlight that were never so visible from the city. At some point, Agarwal had turned off the police car's flashing light, maybe to let him sleep. As they swept past the rolling farmland, Hugo drained the cup and handed it back to the driver with his thanks. Agarwal almost dropped the cup as his phone rang and he hurried to answer it, listening for a moment and then saying simply, "Yes, sir." He reached back and handed the open phone to Hugo.

"It's for you, sir. Your embassy." When he saw a quizzical look on Hugo's face, he smiled. "We gave them my number, so as not to tie up DCI Upton's phone when they wanted you. My wife's the only one likely to be inconvenienced."

Hugo smiled. "Very sensible, and give her my apologies." He liked PC Agarwal, capable, intelligent, and possessing the kind of ever-present humor a good policeman needed. He took the phone, expecting to hear Bart Denum's voice, but it was the night message service.

"Mr. Marston?" The voice belonged to a young man, a little wary of speaking to his embassy's security chief.

"Yes, what's up?"

"Sir, a message was left for you ten minutes ago. When Mr. Denum went home he said that you were on important business, so I thought I'd call and let you know, in case it's significant."

"Who is it from?"

"She didn't say, sir, just left what sounds like a code name."

Hugo sat up straight. "Merlyn?"

"Yes, sir." The young man sounded surprised. "One second and I'll play it."

Hugo turned up the volume and held the phone between him and Upton, so the Englishman could hear. They waited for five seconds, then heard her voice. "Hugo, just wanted to let you know everything is OK. Harry said you'd called him and asked him to make sure I was safe. Thanks for doing that. Anyway, he suggested I leave a message for you here, rather than your phone. I'm keeping mine switched off so they can't track me. Anyway, I won't say where we are in case someone hears this message, but he said I could tell you it was the place you'd talked about. In Edinburgh."

There was a moment's silence before the young man came back online. "That's it, sir. Do you want to hear it again?"

"No, but I need you to type it word for word and e-mail to Bart Denum, then have him forward it to DCI Upton."

"Right away, sir."

"What's your name, son?"

"Chris Collings, sir."

"You did the right thing, Chris, good work."

Hugo closed the phone and handed it to Agarwal.

Upton pulled out his own phone and made a call, giving instructions to have officers watching every stop on the way to, and including, Edinburgh rail station. When he'd finished, he turned to Hugo. "Too many roads to watch, obviously, which is probably how they're traveling. So, what's in Edinburgh?"

"No idea. We never talked about anywhere like that."

"You sure? Not even in passing conversation?"

"We didn't have much of that." Hugo frowned, deep in thought, then shook his head. "What the hell is he playing at?"

"I don't know," Upton said, "but we're here."

Another small inn, much like the Rising Moon, but as long as it had beds Hugo was past caring about its other quirks, quaint or not.

Hugo slept with Agarwal's phone beside him, but it didn't ring, or if it did he didn't hear it. He was woken the next morning by Upton banging on his door, a mug of black coffee in his hand. The coffee was too sweet but welcome nonetheless.

"What time is it?" asked Hugo, forcing himself to sit up.

"Six. Get dressed—we're in business," Upton said on his way out the door.

Hugo climbed out of the bed, splashed water on his face in the small sink in his room, and quickly pulled on yesterday's clothes between sips of coffee.

He was downstairs in five minutes and they climbed wordlessly into Agarwal's car. The constable watched him buckle in, then peeled out of the parking lot and drove hard toward Walton's house, half a mile away, headlights cutting through the morning darkness. Hugo sat forward, looking through the windshield as they slowed, turning onto a smaller road and then nudging between two police cars that blocked off the street. Two more cars performed the same job at the other end, and a dozen officers in military-style fatigues moved like silhouettes in the dark, forming a ring around the house, Heckler & Koch G36 carbines slung across their chests. Agarwal brought the car to a halt in front of the house next to Walton's. Armed officers opened the car doors, and Upton and Hugo climbed out. One of the officers handed a piece of paper to Upton and said, "Warrant signed, sir."

Upton looked over at Hugo. "Ready?"

"Yes. No one inside, right?"

"Right." Upton smiled grimly. "Unless he's dead in there."

"Just for once, I think we're going to be corpse-free," Hugo said, returning the tight smile. "So let's go in slow, no need for the cavalry. I want to see the place the way he left it, not after your storm troopers have turned everything upside down."

"We need to let a couple of them take the lead, Hugo. If we're wrong about it being empty and you catch lead, then I'll be directing traffic for the rest of my career."

Hugo shook his head. "No, your boys can open it and shout loudly, but I want in first."

"Hugo." Upton turned and stood directly in front of him, his voice low but firm. "My op, Hugo, we do it my way. I'm helping you all I can, but don't push it, OK?"

They locked eyes for a second, Hugo realizing he was on thin ice. He nodded.

"Thank you," Upton said. "We'll breach with four men at the entry point, then I'll have just two men clear the place without touching anything. And then you can go in."

"That works," said Hugo. "And you know I appreciate your help, Clive. I guess I just need to work on showing it."

"Forget it, we're both tired." He looked over Hugo's shoulder at his men. "OK, let's get on with it."

They moved up the short path to the front door, the four-man breach team taking the lead, Upton behind them, Hugo taking up the rear. Walton's house was a stone-washed row house, probably built in the 1930s and touched little by time. Small cracks had been filled in with mortar over the years, but it had been a while since the window frames had seen paint. The front door looked solid enough, but the front two policemen and their designer battering ram made short work of it.

Hugo waited beside Upton and two cops in battledress, trying not to show his impatience, and in just three minutes the advance pair returned and assured Upton the house was clear.

Hugo entered first, Upton in his wake. They moved along the hallway, which ran the length of the house, a staircase to his left. Hugo started his search in the small sitting room, which held a desk and a two-drawer filing cabinet beside it.

"Take the desk, I'll look at his files," Hugo said. He pulled the top drawer open and ran his fingers over the row of hanging folders, starting at the front and working his way back. "Household stuff, phone and electric bills, tax stuff . . ." He got to the end of the drawer and slid it shut, opening the bottom one. Beside him, Upton was opening and closing desk drawers, leafing through stacks of papers on the desktop. "You got anything?" asked Hugo.

"I'm not entirely sure what I'm looking for," Upton said, "but nothing stands out."

"Me neither. Anything with Pendrith's name on it, any kind of diary, or ramblingly insane manifesto." He saw Upton's raised eyebrow. "Hey, it could happen. Just ask the Unabomber."

"Here." Upton pulled a slender laptop computer from the desk's bottom drawer. "This might tell us something."

"Great, have a look through it, if you can."

Upton pulled a chair to the desk and sat, opening the little computer. Hugo went back to the file cabinet. Walton had kept meticulous records of his freelance work, photocopies of checks, a ledger with dates and payments, and copies of everything of his that had been published, each article carefully pasted to a sheet of paper and inserted into a scrap book.

At the back of the drawer, Hugo found what looked like a manuscript, a ream of paper covered in type, held together with a red ribbon tied around the middle. *Like an old-fashioned legal brief,* Hugo thought. He pulled it out and ran his fingers over the front page. Typed, not printed from a computer.

"Anything else in that desk drawer?" Hugo asked Upton.

"No, not that I saw, except an old typewriter."

Hugo stood by the desk, the manuscript in his hands, and undid the ribbon. He began reading, laying the pages face down on the desk as he finished each one. Upton stopped what he was doing and looked up.

"The manifesto you'd hoped for?"

"Not exactly," Hugo said. "I'm not sure whether it's a biography, an autobiography, or fiction. But either way, it's about his father."

Upton picked up a page from the desk. "He typed it? On that typewriter?"

"Yes."

"Why would he do that when he has a computer?"

"I think it was very intentional. And I'm seeing a pattern."

"What pattern?"

"Our man Walton is a throwback. An anachronism." Hugo read another page. "It seems like . . . I think he's turning into his father."

"How's that possible?"

"Anything's possible if you have the right state of mind. Or the wrong one."

"Hugo, what the hell are you talking about?"

Before Hugo could answer, Upton's phone rang. He listened for a moment, then closed it. "The men are in place."

"Men?"

"Yeah, Edinburgh, remember?"

Hugo stroked his chin. "Call them off. They're wasting their time."

"Why?"

"Walton's not going to Edinburgh. Merlyn maybe, but she's by herself and he's not going to hurt her. He never planned to hurt her."

"Hugo, for heaven's sake, what are you talking about?"

"She was a distraction. A red herring. He wanted us to go charging up to Scotland to save the damsel in distress."

"Even though he was never planning to hurt her, according to you."

"Right. Precisely."

"OK, so he wanted us out of the way. Why?"

Hugo set the manuscript down on the desk. He looked up and met Upton's steel-gray eyes. "The book starts with a story about Walton's christening. About the role of the church in the lives of him and his father after his mother's death. It's not literature, but he's going somewhere with it, you can feel the anguish, anger even, bursting out from the page."

"Don't tell me he wrote the ending and is now carrying it out," Upton said. "That would be a little too much."

"No," said Hugo. "Not that, this diatribe looks unfinished. And I'd guess he knows enough to realize that he can't control the ending anyway, the way things turn out. Remember, too, this isn't about him, it's about his father."

"Then we should study the book, get some shrinks to look at it. And pronto."

"No time. If he's wanting us up in Scotland hunting Merlyn, then he's planning something." Hugo flipped through the manuscript with his thumb. "The church," he murmured. "The church . . . And it's Sunday." He grabbed Upton's arm, startling him. "We have to go, now."

"Where?"

"Weston Church." Hugo ran out of the room, down the hallway, and outside, where the sun had made no effort to shift the night. He stopped and turned to Upton, who was close behind. "Have your men keep an eye on this place, no one goes in or out. We can come back later." *If we need to.*

A surprised Agarwal trotted over to the car when he saw his charges making for it. "Sirs?"

"Weston Church," said Hugo. "Lights, sirens, the works."

When they'd settled into the car, Upton spoke. "What's going on? What's at the church?"

"Walton is acting out some kind of vendetta. It doesn't make complete sense yet, but the church is at the center of it. It was the start of his manuscript, it was central to his life growing up. And he moved from Weston to Walkern when Reverend Kinnison took up residence."

"He doesn't like women priests?"

"He doesn't like something about her, and every time he doesn't like someone, they die."

"That's insane. He'd kill her because she's a woman?"

"No, that doesn't fit for me."

"Then what?"

"I'm not sure." Hugo thought back to the typed manuscript. "If this is about his father, it could be about his father's work."

"As a soldier?"

"No. As an executioner."

"Jesus, what are you saying?"

"I'm not sure, but it makes sense. Several things happened at once, right? Walton won the lottery, had a mental breakdown, and Kristi Kinnison took over at Weston Church."

"OK, that's all true."

"When someone with psychotic tendencies starts acting on them, there is usually a trigger. Something that sets him off."

"And here we have several triggers. But none of them relate to his father."

"Actually, I think they all do, as does his obsession with going back in time, recreating history, so to speak."

"Explain."

"His father executed killers, murderers. But he was laid off when the death penalty was repealed. The war hero and public servant, the only parent Harry Walton had, was destroyed by that law. If the manuscript means anything, not long after that, the old man basically drank himself to death."

"So?"

"I would bet that when Harry Walton won the lottery, it was on or close to a significant date. Let's check." He took out Agarwal's phone and dialed Bart Denum. "You in the office, Bart?"

"Yes, sir. I've a few bits and pieces to do, plus I figured you might want some help. And the wife's spending the morning at church, this way I don't have to go."

Hugo smiled. "Good man. What do you have on Walton?"

"A timeline of his life, as well as—"

"The timeline's perfect," Hugo interrupted. "I'm looking for a connection between the date he won the lottery and his father."

"Let me look." Bart hummed gently as he looked. The car dipped and rose, Agarwal leaning forward as he concentrated hard on the road. "Well," said Bart, "here's something. But it's not just his father."

"What do you mean?"

"His winning lottery numbers were published soon after the fiftieth anniversary of his mother's death, which now that I look was the same date as his father's, just a couple of decades difference. Jeez, how did I not notice that before?"

"And there you have it. Thanks, Bart." He leaned forward and dropped Agarwal's phone onto the front passenger seat. "How far to the church?"

"Less than five minutes," Agarwal said.

Hugo sat back and turned to Upton. "His mother and father died on the same day and month. Walton won his little stash just after the fifty-year anniversary of her death. I'm guessing his father committed suicide by booze, literally, on her anniversary, too."

"That seems like a hard thing to plan."

"Not if you know your liver is already shot."

"Fair enough. And so that's an important date to him."

"And if he collected the money soon after the anniversary, my guess is he bought the ticket on that exact date."

"Now that would be something of a coincidence. Especially for him."

"Yeah," said Hugo. "Coincidences mean a lot to those looking for reason, and add to that, at about the same time, a woman takes over at his beloved church."

"I still don't get the gender connection."

Hugo didn't either, so he thought about Reverend Kinnison. What he knew about her, what Walton would know. The most interesting thing about her was . . . He looked up. "I was right. It's not that she's a woman. It's that she's an ex-con."

"You think?"

"And not just any ex-con. She killed two people, right?"

"Well, yes, but—"

"Look at all the people who have died," Hugo said. "Forget the Drinkers for now, the others. Name them."

"Well, Ginny Ferro, Dayton Harper, Pendrith."

"Right. And all of them have been responsible for the deaths of another."

"Not Pendrith."

"I'm not so sure," Hugo said. "If he was in league with Walton then we can't be sure what he's done. And maybe Walton knows something about Pendrith's days in MI5. Either way, I wouldn't cross him off the list. And if he does belong on it, in the old days, the past that Walton pines for, those people would probably have ended up on the scaffold."

"And if we don't forget Brian Drinker?"

"He's different." Hugo shook his head. "I think he was in the wrong place at the wrong time. Remember what he said to us?"

"He said that Harper was there, and that he apologized, said he was sorry. Which leaves Harper as the man who killed Drinker, but I have no damn idea why."

"Wait, though. Harper was there, yes. Drinker told us that, he said he wasn't going to let him in. But what if Walton was there, too? What if Walton was the one who apologized?"

"For shooting Drinker? Could be. Either accidently while going after Harper, or on purpose so he couldn't be identified."

"Exactly. Think, too, about the way Harper and Ferro died."

"Different ways," Upton said. "Don't serial killers have a methodology that they stick to?" He grimaced as Agarwal swung the car up onto the narrow Church Lane. "Puts a hole in your theory, no?"

"No, actually, it doesn't. Ferro was hanged, the way she'd have been executed for murder back in the fifties. And Harper was shot. Through the heart."

"Why the difference?"

"Because Ferro was born in England. Walton executed her consistent with history, and Harper with the way they'd have done it in Utah, where he was born." A thought occurred to him. "The paper. They found minuscule pieces of paper in his heart during the autopsy."

"Meaning?"

"Meaning it wasn't paper exactly. They used to pin a card over the heart, a little circle of a target for the firing squad to aim at. He did the same for Harper, put him against the stone wall of the church and shot him, just like they did it in the old days."

"He really is a psycho."

"Yes," Hugo said. "He really is. Ready for some more fun and games?"

The police car skidded to a halt in the church parking lot and all three men leapt out. Hugo led the way through the gate, Upton and Agarwal close behind. He ran straight up the path toward the front of the church. He stopped in the porch and leaned on the heavy wooden door. It swung open easily and they moved quickly into the nave. The place looked empty, and in the quiet Hugo was suddenly aware of the sound of their feet, his boots especially, on the black-and-red tiling of the floor. The space around them was lit but barely, patches of yellow seeping up the walls from low down, as if children's night lights had been placed every twenty feet or so along the side walls.

Hugo turned to Upton. "What time is the morning service?"

"No idea, why?"

"It's getting late, so it seems like Reverend Kinnison should be here already. Let's split up. And be careful—if Walton's here, he'll have a gun."

"We should wait, get some of the men from Walton's home here."

"No time," Hugo said. "If I'm right about him, he's not looking to hurt people who haven't, in his mind, committed murder."

"Tell that to Brian Drinker," Upton muttered, eyes scanning the dim interior of the church.

"Fair point," said Hugo, starting forward. "If he sees you, make sure he knows you're unarmed but have company. We want him to run, not shoot."

Agarwal nodded, then moved to the far side of the church, which was separated from the nave by thick stone pillars. Upton went to the right, leaving Hugo to move slowly between the pews toward the sanctuary. The air inside was still, the light in this part of the church flat, and a gentle smell of polish rose from the wooden pews. They progressed in a line, checking on each other as much as the church, and quickly came together in the sanctuary where an old, dark-wood lectern sat awaiting its minister.

Silently, they moved on between the choir stalls, their eyes fixed on a sliver of light that spilled out from under a plain wooden door to their right.

"The office?" Hugo whispered.

"That's my guess," Upton replied. "You sure you don't want to wait?"

"Could be bad for Kinnison if we do."

Upton nodded and Hugo looked over at Agarwal, his face ashen and taut. *Not an unreasonable response to one's first encounter with a serial killer*, Hugo thought.

They moved to the door, Hugo on one side and the English policemen on the other. They listened for three, four, five seconds, but heard no sounds. Hugo reached down and put his hand on the doorknob. He turned it a quarter inch.

Unlocked.

He steadied himself with a long, slow breath, then nodded to Upton and Agarwal. He turned the knob fully and swept the door open, plunging in behind it, the two officers behind him.

The small room was empty, the overhead light showing them only furniture, books, and papers, the vicar's chair swiveled to one side as if she'd got up in no hurry at all, just forgotten to push it back against the desk.

Hugo looked around the room once more. *Another door.*

Upton followed his gaze and said, "It goes outside."

Hugo started toward it, then stopped, his stomach lurching with a sickening realization.

"The shallow grave," he said. "It's for her. It's under a thick bough, and both are meant for Reverend Kinnison."

CHAPTER TWENTY-SIX

He ran toward the door, not waiting for a response. It had two bolts and both were open, as if someone had taken this route before him. How much before him was the question, and as he burst out of the church into the graveyard, he looked toward where he remembered the shallow grave to be.

The light was still poor outside, the weak winter sun struggling to assert itself against the darkness, and the shapes ahead of Hugo were just that, formless and shifting as he ran, unidentifiable. He heard the running feet of Upton and Agarwal behind him, and they all headed in the same direction, crossing the gravel path and dodging between gravestones, decorum lost to urgency. Once, to his left, Agarwal tripped and disappeared, then popped back up cursing.

Upton found her first. Hugo had gone too far to the left, Agarwal farther still. They heard him shout, and when they got to him he was straddling the grave, clear of brush now. He was holding her waist and trying to lift her, to take the strain off the rope, his head at her chest, his face drawn taut by the weight and his own distress.

"Agarwal, here, quick." Hugo stooped, his hands forming a stirrup that Agarwal stepped into. "On three." Hugo counted aloud and hoisted the constable high enough to loop his arms over the bough. Agarwal pulled himself up as Hugo went to help Upton, straining to hold up the limp form of the vicar. Agarwal shinned along the branch until he was directly over them and, as Hugo and Upton hoisted Kinnison as high as they could, he reached down and loosed the noose, then slipped it over her head. They laid her on the ground beside the grave that was meant for her, and Hugo put his fingertips against her neck.

"I think I feel something," he said, though with the adrenalin shooting through his body it was hard to be sure.

Agarwal was already on the phone for an ambulance and police backup, and Upton had sprinted to the parking lot in case Walton was still there. He came back minutes later, panting.

"No sign of him. That bastard, how evil can he be?"

"He doesn't see it that way," Hugo said, kneeling beside Kinnison. "In fact, he sees her as the bad one, the murderer who got away with it. He's just doing what he thinks his father would have done, should have been able to do."

"The executioner."

"Right."

"You sure that's what's going on?"

"I am."

"But why the grave for her? He didn't dig one for the others."

"Because she buried her dead husband in their garden. But forget that, we need to figure out who's next."

"You think there's more?"

Hugo touched Reverend Kinnison's throat again, sure this time he felt a pulse; her skin was certainly warm. He looked up. "I don't know. I also don't get Pendrith's involvement in this. It's like they should be on opposite sides, don't you think?"

"Right. Pendrith wanted to let convicted killers out of prison early, and Walton wanting them all hanged. They were on the opposite ends of the law-and-order scale."

"Unless they weren't." Hugo stood. "Walk with me. Agarwal, can you stay with her a moment?"

"Yes, sir, of course."

Hugo felt the burn of an idea in his mind, a flickering that he needed to nurture and coax into life, but not beside the wounded figure of Reverend Kinnison. Somehow, dealing with hypotheticals and theories, necessary though they were, seemed disrespectful within earshot of where she lay fighting for her life.

"What if their goal was the same, but they were just getting there different ways?"

"What do you mean?"

"Follow my logic, see what you think of this: for some reason, Pendrith was in league with Walton, and I can only think it was because he was doing something he didn't want people to know about."

"Sure, that makes sense."

"Now, when you make a deal with the devil, sometimes it doesn't go the way you want it to."

"The devil can be deceitful," Upton said. "It's kind of his shtick."

"Right. Walton's sins were prompted by some kind of psychotic break, something Pendrith couldn't necessarily know the extent of and certainly couldn't control."

"OK, keep going . . ."

"I don't think Pendrith foresaw any killing. He's an MP, for God's sake, an elected politician. No, I think he was running a sneaky little public relations campaign with Walton, almost an anti-public-relations campaign."

"Now you've lost me."

Hugo looked out over the fields as the distant wail of a siren cut through the murky morning. "Basically, I think they were both after the same thing. The return of the death penalty."

"Are you serious?"

"Yes. Before he became an MP, Pendrith was in favor of it but abandoned that position because it made him unelectable. It goes without saying that Walton wanted it restored, too."

"So how do you explain Pendrith's bill to get killers released?"

"Simple reverse psychology. He probably thought they'd come out and be a danger to society, maybe even hoped they would."

Upton nodded. "I'll admit that there's nothing gets the people stirred up as a killer released from prison who kills again. You can't buy that kind of publicity."

"Right. But I think Walton messed with that scheme, had his own vision of justice that got in the way."

"Those suicides. Sean Bywater hanged himself after being released."

"Right. Except I'm betting you Harry Walton had a hand in that. If I remember the story, Bywater supposedly carved the word *SORRY* into the wall."

"Seems appropriate given what he did to his victims," Upton said.

"True, but if you're Walton it's also a nice way to avoid having to forge a suicide note. And Bywater isn't the only one who died after being released."

Upton snapped his fingers, excited now. "Walton's car. Remember where it was found?"

"Church parking lot, or a parking lot owned by the church."

"Exactly. Not a church but a halfway house run by the Church of England."

"So to find out who burned up in the car, we just need to see who checked in to the halfway house in the last week or two and hasn't been seen for a few days."

The siren was loud now, and Hugo could hear several more close behind.

"Here comes the cavalry," Upton said. "Let's head back."

They wound their way between a dozen headstones to where Agarwal sat on the ground holding Kinnison's hand, talking softly to her, his voice reassuring, encouraging. Hugo knelt again, touched her throat, and shook his head. He stayed there for a moment, then stood and spoke quietly to Upton. "Weak pulse. We have to hope there's not too much structural damage or, God forbid, brain damage."

"God forbid. We also have to figure out what's next," Upton said in a low voice. "Is he just going to keep killing?"

Hugo watched Agarwal tuck his coat tightly around Reverend Kinnison as the ambulance pulled into the parking lot and its siren died. "I don't think so," he said to Upton. "Honestly, if I had to guess, I'd say he's going out with a bang. He knows the game is up and he'll want as much publicity, as much media coverage, as he can muster."

"So he's going to make one more kill?"

Hugo nodded. "But I can't imagine—"

The lawmen moved aside as two paramedics passed by and went to Kinnison, crouching over her as they went to work.

"You need to understand that even though we call profiling behavioral science, the truth is that much of it is guesswork based on experience."

"So give me your best guess."

"I think he's got one more kill in him. Someone that will bring the newspapers running and have the TV cameras close by to capture the aftermath." He held Upton's eye. "Maybe even capture the murder itself."

CHAPTER TWENTY-SEVEN

They made no promises, but the paramedics said she'd live, prompting Hugo and the two English policemen to exchange relieved looks. After Reverend Kinnison had been gently laid on a stretcher, the three followed slowly behind and decided to head back to their inn to discuss what to do next. And maybe get some coffee.

They made small talk in the dining room as their host, the stocky and smiling publican, poured fresh coffee and called back orders for breakfast to his wife in the kitchen. As his cup was refilled, Hugo wanted to get to the one question they needed to address: Who was next on Walton's list?

Before sitting down, he and Upton had called their respective offices and asked them to check for all convicted murderers on their way back into society in the previous and upcoming two weeks, information they might need before that question could be addressed.

Upton was wiping the last of the runny yolk from his plate with a piece of toast when his phone rang. He listened for almost a minute, pushing his plate aside to take notes in a small leather-backed pad. When he hung up, he looked at Hugo and Agarwal. "We've got just five names from the whole of England and Scotland that fit our criteria. Four men and one woman."

"Who's the woman?" Hugo asked, always inclined to examine the outlier.

Upton looked at his notes. "Stanton. June Michelle Stanton," he said.

"June Stanton." The name floated in a haze, familiar to Hugo, yet he wasn't immediately clear why. Then it came to him. "She killed a police officer, didn't she?" Now he could picture her face on the television, a face he'd seen the same day he met Harper.

"She got forty years," Upton nodded. "She served twenty-five years, now getting out. Used to be gorgeous but got hooked on drugs, lost her modeling contracts, and ended up robbing banks with her boyfriend. Quite a downward spiral, and it didn't turn out well for either of them. He got himself killed during a robbery, and she was arrested in the car outside."

"And the other four?" Hugo wanted to be thorough, not jump to conclusions because he recognized one person. Upton read them off, and Hugo said, "The names don't mean anything, but maybe their crimes . . . ?"

"One murderer, three rapists. None of them famous, their crimes not especially heinous. Relatively speaking, of course."

"Of course. So if you want to go out with a big splash, you go for Stanton."

"Yep," said Upton. "Which means we need to find her."

"Where was she released from, when, and do we know where she's going?"

"Yes." Upton looked at his notes. "From Houseblock Two, Her Majesty's Prison in Peterborough. Jesus—yesterday."

"Which is why Walton wanted us in Edinburgh, far away from what he has planned. Where is she going?"

"According to this, she was released last night to her daughter and sister, who live in Hendon."

"That's north London, isn't it?" asked Hugo, remembering his trip out of the city.

"Right. Not my area of operations, as it were."

"Seriously?" Hugo looked up. "I thought you guys weren't worried about jurisdictional crap."

Upton smiled. "I'm not. Some others might be."

"Well, until they speak up, it's you, me, and PC Agarwal." Hugo turned to the constable. "You have a first name, right?"

"No, sir." Agarwal stood and picked up his cap from the seat beside him, ready to go. "Not until I'm a sergeant."

"Shouldn't be long. Just tell me you know how to get to Hendon."

"That I do."

"Excellent," said Hugo. "Then you drive and I'll use your phone."

They moved quickly across the parking lot toward Upton's Vauxhall and had just opened the doors when two police cars turned in and headed toward them. The first stopped yards away and the rear door opened an instant before the car had even come to a stop. The solid figure of Upton's boss, the chief constable, stepped out and strode across toward them.

"Oh shit," murmured Upton. "This isn't good."

She got to where Hugo and Upton stood by the open rear doors of the car and stopped, her hands perched on wide hips. Hugo wanted to smile when Agarwal slid behind the wheel, as if taking shelter from the impending storm.

"Going somewhere, Detective Chief Inspector?"

"Chief Blazey, I didn't know you were coming."

"How could you know," she said, a thick eyebrow raised high, "you've been a little out of touch lately."

"Well, we've had some new information about—"

"I don't think this is a conversation we need to be having in front of our American cousin," Blazey said icily. "Why don't we go inside?" She turned to Hugo, "Please excuse us, Mr. Marston, we have police business to discuss."

"Chief Constable, if I may," Hugo began, "DCI Upton has been—"

"I'm well aware of what he's been and what he hasn't been," Blazey said. "And while I appreciate you Americans haven't intended to cause all this trouble, nonetheless several people are dead, and so far you've not done the most exacting job at finding out who or why, so you'll forgive me if the British police return to following orders from their British superiors. We may not have as many murders as you do, but we're quite good at solving those we do have. As I said, please excuse us while we discuss police business inside." She shot an icy look at

Agarwal as he climbed out of the car and stood to attention. "You too, Constable."

She turned on her heel and started toward the pub, and Upton looked quickly at Hugo before following, his blank expression saying plenty. Agarwal followed, too, rounding the front of the car and passing close to Hugo on the passenger side. Hugo started to move out of his way then saw the keys in his open palm, saw the look in Agarwal's eyes. He palmed the keys like a spy as the constable brushed by and fought the urge to smile at the man's whispered words.

"Remember," Agarwal said, "we drive on the left."

Chief Constable Blazey's driver and two other uniformed officers traipsed behind Agarwal into the pub, leaving Hugo alone in the parking lot. He moved around to the driver's side of the car and slipped behind the wheel. *First step, get on the road to London. Second step, call Bart Denum for the address and directions.* But when he started the engine he saw that Agarwal had gotten into the car for a reason: he'd programmed the GPS system with Stanton's address.

He pulled out of the lot and followed the calm and directing voice that drew him through the web of country lanes toward the A1 motorway and London. As he passed the first exit, he noticed his gas tank was near empty. He smiled. If he was borrowing a police car, the least he could do was fuel it up.

He left the highway at the next sign for a gas station, beating a blue Ford to the only open pump. He took a moment to locate the right buttons and the right fuel, then stood patiently as the machine beside him throbbed and the pleasant smell of gasoline drifted up from the tank. He looked over his shoulder to see if the Ford had found a pump, feeling slightly guilty about screeching to the head of the line. But the Ford was tucked between two SUVs in front of the station's convenience store, doing other business.

He turned his thoughts to what he was going to tell Stanton, aware that he was going into this situation with no authority, no proof, and no weapon. But at the very least he could warn her, let her disappear of her own accord until this thing was over.

As the pump clicked off automatically, Hugo felt a sudden pressure in the small of his back. Words spoken closely to his neck sounded like the hiss of a snake.

"It's loaded and you know I'm willing to use it. At this point, I have no reason not to."

"I believe you, Walton, don't worry. What do you want me to do?"

"Finish up here and get back in the car. And don't do anything stupid. Even if you do manage to get away from me, I see several other people I can shoot."

"Seems to me you don't shoot innocents." Hugo turned to face him and felt the nub of the gun in his stomach. "Am I right? Isn't that the point of this?"

"*Innocent* is a relative term," Walton snarled. "And right now, what I have planned is more important. The bigger picture, if you like."

Hugo held his eye and nodded slowly. "Fine. Where are we going?"

"Finish up and get in," Walton said. He tucked the gun back in his coat pocket. *Confident I'll obey. Which means he's desperate and dangerous.*

Hugo slid the nozzle back into its slot, collected his receipt from the pump, and moved to the driver's door. He looked over at the blue Ford, wondering where Walton had stolen it from, furious that he'd not noticed being followed. Walton walked to the front of the police car, a hard eye on Hugo, who got behind the wheel and put the key in the ignition. The journalist then walked to the rear door and slid in behind the passenger seat. He had a lightweight travel bag slung over his shoulder.

"You were watching us at the pub?" Hugo asked.

"Well, I couldn't very well go home, could I? You forget that watching is what I do for a living, and you people are operating on my turf," Walton said. "You better believe I was."

"And the Ford?"

Walton smiled thinly. "I borrow cars too, you know. If we do happen to pick up a tail, a quick squawk on the radio will redirect them here to it. A nice distraction for us all."

"Nicely done," Hugo said. "Where to now?"

"Just get back to the motorway, and leave your seatbelt off."

To stop me intentionally crashing, Hugo thought. *Again, smart move*. Hugo drove slowly out of the gas station and headed back onto the A1, merging carefully with the passing traffic, letting Walton know he was going to cooperate and not wanting to risk a bullet in the back, which would likely take out more than just him at these speeds.

The traffic thickened as they made their way south, trucks and vans clogging the slow lanes as the faster cars dodged by, tapping their brakes when they realized the Vauxhall was a police car. Twice they passed patrol units perched on the side of the road, but neither moved to intercept them. Hugo didn't expect them to, not really. Chief Constable Blazey would put out an APB if she knew Hugo was driving one of her cars, but Agarwal and Upton would do all they could to keep her from finding out—for their own sake as much as his.

"It's something of an irony, isn't it?" Walton said from behind Hugo's left ear.

"What is?"

"All these people slowing down around us, afraid we'll pounce. Yet it's you, in the seat of power as far as they are concerned, sitting there begging for a policeman to light us up."

"Begging?" Hugo said, raising an eyebrow. "Hardly."

"No?" Walton's voice was soft, but turned hard. "Then that's your mistake."

"I'm curious about one thing," Hugo said. He wanted to keep Walton talking, not with any specific goal in mind, but because he'd learn nothing sitting in silence. And silence also gave Walton more time to plan, to think. "What's Pendrith's role in all this?"

"In all what? You think you know what's going on?"

"I think you're living in the past, Harry. You really think there's a chance in hell that the death penalty will be reinstated?"

"That was Pendrith's thing, not mine."

"Bull. I've read some of your articles, or should I call them rants? You want to drag Britain back to the sixties, back to the good old days when guilty men and women were strung up for their crimes."

"Shut up, Marston. You don't know a damn thing."

"Then enlighten me, Harry. Fill me in." He risked a look over his shoulder, but Walton hadn't budged, sitting forward with his left shoulder against the passenger seat, his eyes drifting between Hugo's hands, the GPS device, and the road ahead. A thought occurred to Hugo, one he decided to try on Walton. "So did Pendrith double-cross you? Did he start believing in his new cause? Is that why you killed him?"

"Me, kill Pendrith?" In the mirror, Walton wore a smirk. "He committed suicide."

"Right, with a passport in his pocket and an hour after telling me he was fleeing the country. No one's going to buy that story, Harry."

"Like I said before, you don't know the first thing about Pendrith. He was a duplicitous bastard and cared about one thing: Lord Stopford-Pendrith. You know why he fought against reinstating the death penalty when he first ran for Parliament? Because he knew damn well it was the popular thing to do. No way he was going to win if he kept supporting it, and he'd be a flip-flopper if he just changed sides, so he had to publicly see the light, become a champion against hanging." Walton snorted. "Imagine that, a lying politician."

"Less original than a murderous journalist, I grant you," Hugo said.

"Murderous? Coming from an American that's pretty rich. The place with the highest murder rate in the world, where everyone gets to carry a gun and you dumb bastards wonder why you have more homicides per capita than fucking anywhere else. And you, you, coming from the state that happily executes . . . how many people a year? More than fucking China, that's how many. No, no, you don't get to call anyone else murderous." Walton leaned closer, spittle flying from his lips like venom from an angry cobra. "And it's not murder when you kill killers. It's justice."

"So Harper, Ferro, and Pendrith. They all deserved the death penalty?"

"Damn right." Walton sat back again, eyes on the road. "If I hadn't stepped in, you would have smuggled those spoiled, pampered Hollywood brats back to America where they would have been given a hero's reception, as if they were dissidents who'd made it home from the gulag instead of common criminals getting away with murder."

"I would have smuggled them? So what does that make me?"

"Now you are understanding your situation." Walton's voice was calm, matter of fact. "An accomplice to murder, of course."

"What about Drinker? You killed a grieving father, a man who'd done nothing except lose his only son. What does that make you, Harry?"

There was a pause, and when he spoke Walton's voice quavered. "That was unavoidable. And yet somehow . . . a perfect irony."

"An irony? That was a man's life you ended, not a goddamn irony."

"Shut up," Walton snapped. "You should be a little more afraid of me, Hugo Marston."

Hugo kept his tone flat. "You think this is the first time I've sat near a serial killer? I did that for a decade, Harry, and the one thing I learned was that in the daylight, when they're done sneaking around in the night, they're no different from other people. Crazy, sure, but flesh and blood."

"You think I'm a serial killer?" Walton laughed, a dry, cracking noise.

"You've killed a series of people, Harry. Wake up, you're not some vigilante imposing justice. You're a mentally ill man with a gun and a vendetta."

"Now I'm mentally ill? You know what I really am, Marston?"

"I just told you, Harry, though I can think of other words to use if you like."

"I'm a fucking executioner, that's what I am. It's what my dad was until those wet, cowardly do-gooders decided that murderers had the right to take other people's lives but hang onto their own. What fucking sense does that make? Huh?"

"Harry—"

"No, you shut up and listen, Marston. Because soon they might do it in your country too, stack a bunch of vicious, evil men in a cage and let them out, one by one, in the dead of night or the early morning. Cage them together so they can share their evil ways and be better prepared when they get out to kill again, and this time to do it without getting caught. That's where things are headed, my American friend, make no mistake. Headed to the place we were at in 1965, when they gave life back to cold-blooded killers and in the process took it away from my dad. Might as well have poured the drink down his throat themselves, and not so much as a pension. Took a career away from me, too. Luckily my dad had given interviews to someone at the *Hitchin Gazette*, so he got me a job there instead. Writing about murder instead of putting a stop to it." The derision in his voice was unmistakable, as if reporting on crime was tantamount to committing it.

"You? You were going to be an executioner?"

"I was. Like the Pierrepoints, keep it in the family. My father taught me everything I'd need to know, where to put the noose, the kind of rope, and the most important thing of all, the calculations for the drop."

"Which is why Ginny Ferro died immediately. You went to all that trouble, following her, getting the right-length rope, even the mask over her face." Hugo looked up to see Walton's grin in the mirror.

"I liked that touch. Most people think it's was black cloth they used over the face, but it wasn't. Now, it's true the judge put a piece of black cloth on his own head when he passed sentence, but for the executions it was a white, silk bag. Were you there for the autopsy? She died immediately, right?"

Hugo felt a knot of sickness in his stomach, the same one he'd felt every time a serial killer expressed pride in his handiwork. Yes, Ferro had died straight away, just like she was supposed to, but he wasn't about to give Walton the pleasure of knowing that.

"So Stanton is next?" Hugo said.

Walton patted his bag. "She is. And no doubt you think you can stop me, but remember how close to a death sentence you are. Any time I pull the trigger, it's justified."

"In your crazy world, Harry. But what do you think will happen afterward? They know it's you, so sooner rather than later you're going to end up in a prison cell."

"Watching TV and getting food, clothing, and medical care." Walton laughed. "And thanks to Pendrith, they'll let me out in a few years."

"Not you, Harry. I have a feeling you'll be inside until they carry you out in a wooden box."

"Which is how it should be!" Walton shouted. He banged his fist against the front seat and then flopped back. "You idiots have no fucking idea. By the time I'm done, people will see how it should be. You just see if they don't."

"You're doing society a favor, is that it?"

"You better believe it. Just like my dad, only I don't expect anyone to be grateful. We do the dirty work and get nothing for it, except in my case maybe a prison cell."

"Society's button man, is that it?"

"Oh yes, society's button man." Walton grinned mirthlessly. "I like that. And you just wait and see, wait and see what happens."

"Wait, you said 'maybe a prison cell.'" Something clicked in Hugo's mind but at first he couldn't find the words, the realization of Walton's insane scheme finally dawning. "It's your death, isn't it? You want to bring back hanging, and you want them to start with you." Behind him, Walton kept quiet. "That's it, isn't it? You really think that people are going to be so outraged by you killing Harper and Ferro that they'll call for hanging to be brought back? That's really what you think is going to happen."

Looking out the side window, Harry Walton just smiled.

CHAPTER TWENTY-EIGHT

June Stanton's home was small and painted white, a two-story detached house with no grass in the front, just a concrete square for parking cars—a space that was empty when Harry Walton steered the police car into it. Walton didn't like this part of London, the part that had no sights worth seeing and no countryside to temper the endless lines of houses, the wide roads lined with them, going on for miles. These drab boulevards used to be the suburbs of London, but now the houses were lived in by students, two to a room, or large families of Pakistanis, or other blue-collar workers who couldn't afford to live close to the city center and couldn't afford the prices in the new suburbs, where the houses were larger and the spaces between them greener.

The only saving grace for this particular stretch of anonymity was a patch of ragged grass taken up by a pond, right across the road from Stanton's house. A circle of gray water surrounded by as many trash cans as trees, a pond that Walton would put to good use in just a few minutes.

Parked in front of the house, Harry Walton sat quietly in the car for a moment before climbing slowly out and casting an eye over the neighbors' houses. Once satisfied, he went to Stanton's front door and knocked, then knocked again when he got no answer. He waited a full minute before walking along the front of the house to peer through the front windows, but the white net curtains obscured his view and made it impossible to see much of anything. But the lights were off, he could see that.

With no one home, his plan was to wait, so he went back to the police car and started it up, executing a quick one-eighty so the car faced the road and its rear bumper hung over the flower bed by the front window. He wanted enough room for a second car to park in the space and a good view of whoever came. He switched the engine off and relaxed, a peace and a calm settling about him as he watched the road.

It took just ten minutes. A white Renault nosed into the driveway, pausing when its driver saw the police car, then easing forward again to get its tail out of the main road. It stopped ten feet from the police car, Walton watching it all the way, pleased the driver was alone.

A woman stepped out and Walton recognized her at once, the face that was once beautiful, worn with age and hard living, eyes suspicious of the police car. Her hair was different—she'd dyed it black already—and a long, olive overcoat hung across her shoulders. She stopped short of the police car and Walton knew what she must be thinking, that somehow her release was a mistake, that her brief taste of freedom was over. *Damn right.*

When she got within six feet of the police car, Walton slid out to meet her.

"Who are you?" she asked. "Police?"

Walton smirked. "Not quite. Think of this as real justice."

"What do you want?"

"I just told you," said Walton. He pulled his hand out of his pocket and pointed the gun at her stomach. "Get inside the house, now."

Stanton put a hand to her mouth, her eyes wide. "Oh God, no, you don't understand, please, I'm—"

"Quiet!" It was the first time Walton had needed to raise his voice and it irked him. People should follow instructions when a gun is pointed at them. The American had known to do that at least. Funny thing, it seemed like the more people knew about guns, the more familiar they were with them, the more scared they were. Or maybe it was the other way around. Stanton was a killer, but she was too stupid to be afraid of a gun. What sense did that make?

As soon as they were indoors, Walton felt a warm rush of relief.

Imposing justice on the unwilling was never easy, and in several instances he'd gotten lucky with the circumstances, a thick enough tree branch, a nice stone wall. And again here, the staircase overlooking the hall with iron balusters half an inch thick.

"Go up the stairs," he said.

"Please, just tell me what you want."

Walton raised the gun. "Up the stairs." He watched as she started up, paused on the second step, then kept going. He wondered if her legs might give way, they were shaking so much. He waited until she was three-quarters of the way up. "That's far enough. Sit down, on your hands."

When she complied, he started up the stairs himself, slipping his bag off his shoulder as he climbed, eyes and gun trained on Stanton. Halfway up he stopped and kicked one of the iron balusters with his toe. Solid enough, for sure. He knelt and emptied the bag with his left hand as he watched Stanton, not because he wanted to see the horror on her face, but because he didn't want her to escape. He felt the white silk of the face mask under his fingers and almost smiled. His old mind wasn't as sharp as it used to be, but the occasional good idea came to him. He threw the hood to Stanton and she stared, wide-eyed, as it landed on her right knee.

"No, wait, you're making a mistake. I told you before, I'm not—"

"Quiet," he hissed. Irritated, he reached into the bag and pulled out a ball gag. A stupid sex toy but one, the description had assured him, that would keep a person submissive and silent. He'd hoped not to use it, but Stanton had neighbors and, clearly, no desire to go quietly. In seconds, the red ball had filled her mouth, the strap tight across the back of her head. He waved the gun at the silk hood. "Put it over your head," he said. "Do it."

Her eyes widened further, filled with fear, and without looking away from Walton she reached for the hood, her fingers recoiling at the touch of it.

"I said put it on, unless you want me to shoot you." He half rose and aimed the gun at her, watching as her trembling fingers reached again to touch the slippery material. Her nostrils flared as she breathed hard and fast, her eyes closing as the bag slid over her forehead, then down over her nose and mouth. Walton smiled to see the cloth puffing in and out, little breaths of fear that were long overdue.

He went to work with the rope, threading one end into the eyelet that he'd already secured to the other end, pulling it through to form a noose. With practiced fingers he hitched the free end to the baluster, pulling back on it with all his weight to make sure it wouldn't give. It didn't. All was ready.

Stanton flinched when he reached the step she was on, pulled away when he forced her to stand, and sobbed when she felt the hard steel of the gun pressing into her stomach. Walton knew he had more time to take care of Stanton than he did Ferro, not much but enough, and he felt a stirring down below, a rush of warmth and a sudden shortness of breath that he'd not felt in several years. He stood beside her for a moment, his eyes running down her body, lingering on her breasts that heaved and shook as she sobbed, noticing the flatness of her stomach that he'd felt under the gun. He wanted to touch her, to have her.

But he wasn't here for that. He was here to do what should have been done decades ago. He took a deep breath and put a hand on her shoulder, turning her away from him, holding her as she gasped and staggered, losing her balance for a fleeting second, righting her so she wouldn't fall. Yet. He put the gun between her shoulder blades.

"Put your hands behind your back." He was surprised to hear a thickness in his voice, annoyed at himself for noticing her as a woman, for thinking that she'd been without *that* kind of companionship for even longer than he had. Her body and his power were aphrodisiacs, yes, but ones he needed to ignore.

Stanton complied, arms quivering, fingers flicking at each other as if for comfort, and he silently bent and placed the gun on the stair, swapping it for a zip tie that he'd already made into a loop, a miniature plastic noose. He gripped her wrists and held them together, slipping the loop over her hands and letting his fingers linger on her skin, letting them brush against the tightness of her jeans, provoking that rush again. She shuddered and he remembered why he was there, why she was there, and that flash of excitement angered him this time. He tugged the zip tie downward, hard, the plastic cutting into her skin as she moaned in pain.

That's OK, it won't hurt for long.

Her moans turned into whimpers and she began to mumble into the gag, indecipherable words caught by the cloth that now showed three patches of damp from her breath and her tears, gray blurs marring the perfection of the white silk, making Walton glad he didn't have to reuse it. But he didn't like the way she sounded, he worried she might be about to hyperventilate or, worse, collapse.

He couldn't have her unconscious before the sentence was carried out.

He took hold of her arms just below her shoulders, half pulling and half steering her down four steps to where the noose waited. He positioned her carefully, with her back to the banister, her feet tight together on one step.

She shuddered as the noose slid over her head and fell onto her shoulders, and a low whine escaped the hood as he knelt in front of her. A prayer ran across his lips and he put his arms around her body.

When he held her tighter, she gave another whine, starting low in her throat and rising in pitch, one final exhortation for mercy that ended when Harry Walton, son of Britain's last executioner, scooped up the trembling figure of his victim and rolled her over the banister. He watched her fall the five feet three inches of her body length, and the extra two feet recommended by the Home Office's *Official Table of Drops*, 1913 edition.

Walton stood quietly for a moment, as if to let her spirit depart in peace. He took a deep breath and repacked his bag. As he moved down the stairs, he heard a thumping sound from below. He looked down and to his left, noticing movement in the rope. His blood froze when he heard a moaning sound. He moved quickly to the ground floor, swearing at the realization that something had gone wrong. *The weight estimation?* he wondered. *My drop calculations?*

He rounded the end of the staircase and saw Stanton kicking for a floor she was never going to reach, her feet scrabbling at the only possible purchase, the smooth wall behind her. Walton calmed himself, then put his arms around the bucking woman's legs and hugged them tightly. His mind blocked out the choking noises coming from the silk bag, and he closed his eyes as he took her weight, straining to lift her up six inches, then six more. When he'd lifted her as high as he could, he fell to his knees, using his weight and hers to complete the job. Her last, muffled scream ended with the soft click of her spinal cord as it snapped, and they stayed like that for a moment in the silence of her house, locked together, one sinner dead and another on his knees.

Walton did not believe in God, not much, not anymore, but the Bible that Stanton had kicked onto the floor, and the side table it lay under, needed righting. It was, as much as anything, an aesthetic correction. Maybe even an evidentiary one. When the police arrived they should see one thing, focus on one thing, not be distracted by a mess and wonder if there'd been a struggle. Because there hadn't been one. In fact, now that he thought about it, she'd not even realized what was happing until the end. But then again, the end, done that way, wasn't just for her.

He picked up the table first, squared it away against the wall, then put the Bible on it. As his fingers stroked its cardboard cover, he wondered if he ought to turn to a specific page, find a passage or a verse with meaning. Highlight or underline it, even. But this wasn't about biblical vengeance either, and hadn't he just told himself he didn't want to leave behind distractions, irrelevancies?

This desire was new to him, a growing urge that he'd not felt before today to leave more behind than was his original intent. A need born, perhaps, from what was to come next, but most certainly an urge he had to fight if he was to remain on course.

And "on course" meant a long walk to Hendon tube station, right after dealing with the police car and the man lying in its trunk. Walton smiled sadly. A shame to end the life of someone outside the intended circle, but it wasn't the first time. He was pretty sure the American had taken lives, too, and justified doing so in much the same way: For justice. To end evil. Whatever. How lucky, though, to find two convenient ponds, just when he needed them.

He turned suddenly as he heard a key scratch the lock of the front door. Instinctively, his hand dipped into his coat pocket but the gun wasn't there, it was in the bag at his feet.

He stood there, stock-still, eyes on the door, his insides burning with fear. Not the fear of being caught but of facing the disintegration of his plans, and with only his old, weak hands to fight back.

He caught his breath as the door opened and a woman stepped into the hallway. He couldn't believe his eyes at first, confused at the blonde hair that fell about a face that was once beautiful but that now wore the gray pallor of decades in prison, her eyes hardened from years of watching her back.

She looked at Walton calmly, appraisingly, then her eyes drifted over his shoulder to where her sister, Anna, hung by her neck, no longer moving. She looked back at him once more, for just a second, and then June Stanton turned and ran.

CHAPTER TWENTY-NINE

Hugo awoke in darkness. The air around him was close, stuffy, and the back of his head ached. He was on his left side in some kind of container that smelled of oil, leather, and dirt. His chief sensation was a stinging in his wrists, which felt glued together. When he wiggled his hands, that pain got worse.

He lay still, not willing to risk exertion until he knew where he was, who might be nearby or even watching. His mind looped back to the last thing he could remember, which was driving Walton to London, coming off the A1, and driving through Hendon.

A lay-by in Hendon, a quiet place, that was next. Hugo pulling over in Upton's car and following Walton's instructions to get out, waiting for a chance to get close to the old man, to take the gun away, and end this.

Now Hugo remembered the look in Walton's eye, how the journalist watched him like a hawk and never came closer than ten feet, the gun always pointed at Hugo as they stood at the back of the car. The zip ties. Walton had fished one from his bag and thrown it to Hugo.

"Put it on," Walton had said. "Hands behind your back."

"I can't," Hugo told him. "If you want me to tighten it, I need to use my teeth. It's either in front, or you have to do it."

Walton paused, the first hint of doubt creeping across his face. "In front then," Walton decided. "Tight, so I can see."

Hugo had done as he was told, relieved that Walton was relying on zip ties and not handcuffs. The former were relatively easy to get out of, the latter all but impossible without a key. They cut like a knife when too tight, so he adjusted his position, now sure he was in the trunk of Upton's car, until he felt the pressure ease and the blood flow back into his hands. But as that pain subsided, his head throbbed harder, especially when he moved it. Walton must have hit him, maybe with the gun, but when? He'd put the zip tie on to Walton's satisfaction, then . . .

The trunk, he'd been facing it with Walton behind him. He'd not even heard the old man move forward, certainly didn't remember being hit. And Hugo had no idea how long he'd been unconscious. He thought he'd heard voices at one point, but the memory was foggy and maybe not real.

The car rocked suddenly as one of its doors thumped closed and Hugo's stomach lurched at the sound of the engine starting. The floor under him began to vibrate and the car moved forward.

Whatever Walton had wanted to do, he'd done. And Hugo knew that now it might be his turn. He started to feel around for the emergency release tab that he knew was there, somewhere. Every car had them, though it flashed across his mind that a police car, modified in some ways, might not. But he had to look.

It took several seconds to work his way onto his back, and his methodical search was thrown off for a second when the front of the car bumped up over an object, and seconds later he was knocked onto his side again as the rear tires hit that same solid object. A curb?

Beneath him the smooth road had turned to something bumpier, and Hugo had trouble holding himself still to search for the latch, the car rocking and jerking, but at least it was moving slowly.

Then it stopped again. Hugo held his breath, wondering whether he was about to see Walton's face, his gun. Instead he heard a light tap, as if someone had laid hands on the trunk above him and the car started moving once more, an inch at a time, gradually picking up speed until it suddenly slowed, as if it had run into something soft, rolling Hugo onto his right side as the nose of the car tipped downward.

In an instant, the gurgle of rushing water told him exactly where he was and what was happening.

Pressed into the back seat by the angle, Hugo had more room. He knew he had a minute, maybe less, to find the latch and get out. He had no idea how deep the water was, but just three feet would be enough to seep in and drown him.

The latch. In a new car it should glow in the dark, and from where he lay with his back to the rear seats of the car, he should be able to see it. He calmed himself, tried to ignore the sounds of the water pressing in on the car, his eyes scanning the blackness in front of his face. Why couldn't he see it?

There. A spec of something luminous, but not big enough to be the latch. He started to shuffle toward it but his hands brushed against something small and hard in the way. He worked his fingers around the object, testing its shape and feel. A roll of tape. Walton had wrapped tape around the release latch so he wouldn't see it. The spec that glowed was his escape.

He wriggled his way toward it, hope growing within him. He closed his hands around it and then shut his eyes and mouth tight as he tugged. The trunk popped an inch and water gushed over him. Hugo held his breath and positioned himself to push the lid up, bracing his back against the floor. His pinioned hands pressed upward, and immediately water filled his nostrils, threatening to suffocate him, yet the lid barely moved. He pushed harder, panic starting to fill his chest as he wondered whether he'd made the wrong decision, whether Walton had somehow tied down the trunk . . .

And then the lid was up, and he felt hands on the front of his coat, tugging him up, not strong enough to lift him but strong enough to help. He blinked, but the water stung his eyes and he couldn't see who it was. Gasping, Hugo rolled himself from the trunk into the pond, the stranger still pulling at him, and together they fought their way to the bank where they collapsed in parallel heaps, panting and sodden.

His face pressed to the wet grass, Hugo turned his head to see his rescuer, and when he recognized her, his breath caught in his throat. She looked at him, too, her face set, wet strands of hair streaking across her cheeks.

"June Stanton," he panted. "He didn't . . . find you?"

She rolled onto her back and let an arm fall over her eyes. "He found my sister. Whoever that was, he killed her instead of me."

Hugo closed his eyes tightly. Another death he'd failed to stop, and Walton was still on the loose. "You saw him? Where? When?"

"I walked into the house . . . I saw what he did and ran. He came after me but he's old, he didn't run far. I hid between two cars and watched him get into this one, drive it to the pond. I thought he was just trying to hide it."

"How did you know I was in there?" Hugo sat up, soaking wet with the cold beginning to feed on his skin.

"Just before he pushed it into the pond he made the sign of the cross. I could tell it was a cop car and I thought maybe the policeman he'd taken it from was inside."

"Close enough," Hugo said. "And thanks."

They cut down the body of Anna Stanton and laid her on the hallway floor before calling the police. There was no crime scene to preserve, not really, just the dignity of an innocent woman to restore. June sat on the floor with her sister's head in her lap, rocking gently back and forth as they waited to hear sirens. She didn't speak and her eyes stayed dry, but Hugo knew her heart was forever broken and that she blamed herself for this. They'd shared everything growing up, a home, food, their very genes, but the one thing that June had been responsible for, all alone, had killed her twin sister.

Hugo wanted to leave her there and go after Walton immediately, but she just shook her head and looked around the house. For June, her sister came first, and Hugo owed her this, these few moments to say good-bye to her twin unmolested by cops and crime-scene specialists.

But Walton was on foot now, an elderly man with no way to travel far or fast, and Hugo couldn't wait any longer.

"June. Which way did he go? After pushing the car into the pond, which way did he go?"

She looked at him, her face blank, eyes taking him in as if for the first time. "Hendon Central. Toward Hendon Central."

"The center of town?"

"No. The tube station. He went down Wykeham Road to the station."

"Which line is that on?"

"The Northern."

"Any others?"

"Any other what?"

"Is it on any other rail lines? I need to be sure which way he's going."

"No, the Northern Line is the only one that comes out this far. He must be going into London. Either that or north to Edgware. But there's nothing there, why would he do that?"

"He wouldn't." He laid a hand on her back. "I have to go, try and catch him. I don't know if he has more names on his list, but if he does, I have to stop him."

"Wait, you're soaking. Let the police find him."

"Oh, I will," said Hugo. In truth, he didn't want to be here when the police arrived, didn't want to explain a submerged and stolen police car from another county. "But he keeps getting away from me, and that makes me mad."

She nodded toward the stairs. "Anna has a boyfriend about your size. He keeps clothes up there, you should take some."

He'd almost forgotten about being wet, but he didn't want to endure the stares of fellow tube passengers and, quite possibly, the attentions of a curious cop. "Thanks, I will." He took the stairs two at a time and found Anna's room, reappearing in three minutes wearing borrowed jeans, a shirt, and a wool sweater. His boots stayed; they'd been through worse and would be dry in an hour. He fished his wallet from his sodden coat and turned to June Stanton. "Do you have a cell phone I can take with me?"

She looked at the coat stand by the door. "Take Anna's, it's probably in her jacket."

Hugo frisked the jacket with practiced hands and pulled out a flip phone. "Thanks," he said. The sound of sirens drifted through the open door with the cold November air. "I'm sorry, but I have to go."

"It should have been me," she said from the floor, stroking Anna's hair. "This, so many dead, just because of me."

"Not true, June." Hugo paused in the doorway. "This one was all him."

CHAPTER THIRTY

He dialed Upton as he ran, slowing to a walk when the detective chief inspector answered, his tone brisk.

"Upton here, who is this?"

"Clive, it's Hugo."

"Hugo, Jesus, are you—"

"I'm fine." Hugo stood to one side as two elderly women with their miniature pooches, sporting matching doggie sweaters, waddled past him. Once they'd passed, without a word of thanks, he started up again at a brisk walk. "Listen and do what you can, as fast as you can. He's killed again and right now is on, or headed to, the Northern Line at Hendon Central. He has to be going into London. You have to stop the trains, have them searched."

"Hugo, it's not that simple."

"Make it simple, Clive. I don't know where he's going, but he just hanged an innocent woman."

"He did what?"

"Stanton's sister. He killed her by mistake, executed her. The point is—"

"Hugo, stop. I'm off the case. They think I gave you my car and . . . how did you get my car by the way?"

"I took it, Clive, you didn't give it to me. What do you mean you're off the case?"

"The chief constable. She didn't like the way things were going."

245

"Clive, come on, we don't have time for this bullshit. Walton just killed someone and is less than a mile from me. And once he's in London, God knows what he'll do."

"I'll try Hugo, but I don't have the power to stop trains. And right now, I'm not in good with anyone who does. But I'll try."

"OK. Save this number and call me if you have any luck or hear anything. Should I talk to your boss?"

"No, no, I appreciate the offer but that wouldn't help, believe me. What are you going to do?"

"What choice do I have?" Hugo spotted the entrance to the metro station and made a beeline for it. "I'm heading back into London and on the way I'll try and figure out what he's up to. I'll call you later."

"Hugo, wait. We heard from Merlyn. Our colleagues from across the border picked her up at Edinburgh station."

"How is she?"

"She's pretty pissed off. But otherwise she's OK. Want me to give her this number?"

Hugo thought about it for a second, knowing he didn't need more distractions even though it'd be good to hear from her. "Better not. Just get her home safely, I'll talk to her then."

"OK. Do you have any idea what he's doing? Walton, I mean."

Hugo paused before speaking. "I thought that Stanton was going to be his swan song, but I was wrong about that. It was done in secret, as far as I can tell. And that means he has one more trick up his sleeve."

"Another victim. Who?"

"That's what I plan to figure out while on the train."

"It's a quick ride in, old chap. Think fast."

Hugo bought a ticket into the center of London and then quickly scoured the station for Walton. He'd already seen one train pull away from the platform toward central London, and he was pretty sure Walton was on it. A digital sign told him the next train would leave in seven minutes, so he moved out of the flow of foot traffic. He found a free bench, planning to make a phone call, but sat staring at the grimy floor of the tube station, assembling and reassembling the pieces, taking out ones that didn't fit and trying pieces of evidence that he'd ignored until now or forgotten about.

He believed that Walton would, eventually, turn himself in or let himself be caught. It would be a supreme irony, one Walton would love to paint large for his reading public, the perfect way to get his insane message across: *Look at all the people I killed . . . And your taxes will now pay for me to live!* But he'd fled after killing Stanton. Because he'd killed the wrong sister?

Hugo pulled out Anna Stanton's phone and dialed Bart Denum. "It's Hugo."

"Hey, what's up? You've been quiet, everything OK? I was just going to call you."

"Why?"

"Got your number from Upton, he's in deep doo-doo but still doing what he can."

"He's a good guy. We'll see if we can pull some strings to help him out when this is over. He really has been a good cop, despite what his boss thinks."

"Agreed," said Denum. "Anyway, the Brits processed Walton's laptop and found a blog."

"Walton? A blog?" Hugo sat up. "Why didn't we find this before? We shouldn't need his computer to do that."

"We don't, you're right. But it just got published. I'm guessing he wrote it some time ago and set it to publish on a particular date. Which was today. Want me to e-mail it to you?"

Hugo held Stanton's phone away from his face. A basic model with a small screen and probably no e-mail capacity. "No, I don't think you can. Right now, I'm between Hampstead and Belsize Park. Can you print a copy and then meet me at King's Cross, out by the taxis, in about fifteen minutes?"

"Sure. Which reminds me, Upton's had no luck stopping trains. He made a few initial inquiries but saw it wouldn't fly."

"I gathered," said Hugo. His travel had been smooth and uninterrupted, and not a uniform in sight. "Did you ever get a list of the people being released from prison, the little group that included Stanton?"

"Sure did, you had someone e-mail it to me."

"OK, I need you to go over it in more detail, try and figure out if there is someone else on there Walton might go after."

"Any parameters?"

"Well, the first one is that the victim might be in or heading to London. Of course, Walton may just be heading into the city to find a way out. Planes, trains, motorways... So don't get stuck on that. Think like Walton; ask yourself whether he'd see one of the four being released as a particular injustice. You know what I mean, Bart, right?"

"Sure, I'll do it right now and call if anything leaps out at me."

"No, assign it to someone else, I want you to meet me at King's Cross. But first, tell me what his blog says."

"It's just one entry."

"OK. Read it."

Time alters everything, and not always for the better. Why do we assume that societal changes automatically mean progress? Are we so arrogant to think that we can't, collectively, make mistakes? That we shouldn't reexamine policy shifts, no matter what?

I have done all I can do to show you what should have happened. Those who died at my hand should have died by the State. You may look at me with spite, even fear, but I did the work for you, just as my father did, as I should have been able to do with him. He was your executioner back then, and I have been today. I don't expect your thanks. My father never even got a pension.

If you revile me, so be it. But think about paying for my food, my shelter, my television, my medical care. Instead of a length of rope for my neck costing just a few pounds, you'd be stumping up a couple million.

It's not a moral issue, or shouldn't be. Every day our weak and timid politicians make decisions that consign people to the grave. Those stuck on NHS waiting lists get sicker and die because money is being funneled to defense contractors. Soldiers are sent to fight other people's wars, and die. We can't pretend that life is precious, that we value human life so greatly that executing murderers is out of the question. Sick people and soldiers can die, but not serial killers? Explain that to the parents of those who die in Afghanistan, or the little girl who dies waiting for treatment in a Newcastle hospital.

Don't mourn for me or those I killed. Mourn for the death of justice in this country.

❧

When Hugo emerged from King's Cross station, a wash of cold air greeted him, and his ears were filled by the sound of the rain that pounded the street, drumming off the roofs of the black cabs waiting for business, filling the gutters.

Hugo spotted the US Embassy vehicle, another black Cadillac Escalade, as it pressed its way under the station's canopy. Once it was out of the rain, Hugo trotted over and slid into the front passenger seat of the familiar vehicle, and it felt like coming home. Hugo and Bart shook hands, an expression of relief as much as anything.

"Just for the record," Bart said, "Your boss approved your request for leave, effective immediately."

Hugo closed the door and the beat of the rain disappeared almost entirely, a leather-enforced hush taking over. "My request for . . . ?"

"Precisely. Some ruffled English feathers, plus we have no official interest in any of this right now."

"Except the bastard tried to kill me."

"Which is still a matter for the Brits, you know that."

Hugo looked at the square head of the former marine, his large hands on the wheel. A reassuring presence in any situation. "Yeah, I know," said Hugo. "Did you bring the printout of his blog?"

"Yep, just that one article, as I said. Find any hidden meaning?"

A taxi honked behind them, unimpressed by the diplomatic plates, only concerned with its place in line.

"Not yet," said Hugo. "You drive, and I'll read it again. Maybe something will jump out."

"Will do. Anywhere in particular?"

"Nope." Hugo already had the article in front of him. He read it once more for the overall impression, then started to take it line by line, letting everything he knew about Walton filter through the prism of this missive, like water running through coffee grounds. "I was right about his father," Hugo murmured.

Denum looked across. "What do you mean?"

"He feels very close to him, he wanted to be like him, and when his father was robbed of his career, and ultimately his life, Harry Walton felt like he, too, had been robbed of everything."

"I thought serial killers were all about their mothers?"

Hugo allowed himself a smile. "Technically, I don't think he'd qualify as a serial killer." *Even though I called him one to his face.*

"Why not?"

"He has the required number of bodies, but the FBI also mandates a cooling-off period between kills. And there's usually a sexual element to the crimes, manifested in a way most people wouldn't see as sexual."

"So you don't think he gets off on what he does?"

"He gets satisfaction, sure, but not the way Ted Bundy or David Berkowitz did. His is almost a professional satisfaction. And his motives seem political, not sexually perverse."

"Maybe time to rethink the FBI definition," Denum said. "After all, I'm not sure the victims give a crap why he kills them, do they?"

"Good point. But the question is, what's he going to do next?"

"He must know the net is closing."

"Definitely." Hugo stared at the piece of paper in his hand. "He's readying himself for prison. For him, it's the soft option. He's railed for so long about killers getting prison instead of hanging, he really sees it as a decent ending for him. And yet . . ."

"And yet what?"

"I don't know. The guy's a journalist. He's been planning this for years."

"Yet he couldn't know Ferro and Harper would be involved."

"Oh, no, he didn't know the details," Hugo said. "But he'd been waiting for something like this to set him off; he may not even have known it. And as a journalist, one who's not afraid of what's going to happen to him, why would he go out with a whimper?"

"I have a couple of people working on that list, but when I looked at it no one stood out. And I checked before I left—none are from or planning to head into London, at least according to their parole files."

"You got a look at their parole files?"

Denum smiled sheepishly. "Friends in high places."

"Always helpful," Hugo nodded. "This line bugs me: 'Instead of a length of rope for my neck for just a few pounds, you'd be stumping up a couple million.'"

"Bugs you?"

"He uses the conditional tense." Hugo tapped the paper and sat back, thinking. "Where the hell is he going?"

"His apartment isn't safe. His face will be all over the news and Internet by now. He has to go somewhere he won't be known."

Hugo sat bolt upright. "Yet somewhere he knows."

"And from your tone of voice, you've thought of that place."

"It's about his father, he feels a responsibility to his father, and I was right, he does want to end this with a bang."

"He's going to kill again?"

"No," said Hugo. "His father is."

CHAPTER THIRTY-ONE

The rain had stopped by the time they splashed onto Marylebone
Road, the sidewalks refilling with window-shoppers and those
out for an afternoon stroll, the adults relieved at the break in the rain
and the kids jumping delightedly, two-footed, into the shallow puddles.

Bart Denum steered the car skillfully, taking them as directly as
he could to their destination where, when they abandoned the car out
front, the tourists were already back in line, shaking out umbrellas and
looking hopefully toward the brightening sky.

"How do we get in?" Denum asked as he rounded the front of the
car.

"Shiny badges and attitude," Hugo said grimly. "If that doesn't
work, we push and let them call the cops—we'll need them anyway."
Hugo chose the door designated for groups to enter the museum, figuring it would be easier to deal with people already in sheep mode than
dozens of irritated singles and couples.

Their badges got them the initial attention, but it was Hugo's brusque
and urgent tone that got them inside. Two guards gave him their full
attention as he dropped his voice to a conspiratorial whisper, relaying the
threat of a danger much greater than merely letting two American offi-
cials in without paying. After radioing for their chief, the two anxious
guards started turning guests away and steered those nearby back into
the street. Hugo and Denum moved to a map of the interior.

"I've never been here before, which way?" asked Hugo.

"I was here with the wife and kids, it should be . . ." Denum quickly traced a path from where they stood to where they were going. "Here."

"Not exactly direct. And God knows how long he's been here already."

"If he's here at all." Denum looked around. "Wouldn't there be a commotion?"

"That's the beauty of it, from his perspective. He's worked here and knows the place, which includes the shortcuts. He can go through his entire weird setup and no one will bat an eyelid."

"OK, then I'm going to have security clear that area. I know, I know." Denum held up a hand. "Quietly and without alerting him."

"Fine, but the security people may not know who they're looking for, so have them close off that part of the museum subtly. People will leave of their own volition, so we just need to stop people going in."

"You don't think any of the tourists are in danger?" Denum asked.

"Do you?"

"No, but you seem to know him better than I do. I just want to be sure of that if we're not going to hit the panic button and clear the whole place."

"We do that and he disappears with the crowds. Bad idea, Bart, very bad."

"OK, I hope you're right." He nodded at a broad-shouldered man in his midfifties, tall and lean, headed their way. "Here's the cavalry leader. I'll start giving orders."

"Good, but I'm not going to wait."

Denum patted Hugo's shoulder. "I never thought you would."

Hugo took another look at the map, drilling the route into his mind. *Dammit, gotta go up before I can go down.* He nodded to Denum and started up the stairs to the first exhibit, his eyes automatically drawn to the people around him. He passed plenty he didn't recognize but several he did and had to resist the temptation to slow down; he wasn't there to stare into Nicole Kidman's sparkling eyes or check out the tone of Brad Pitt's skin. A pink light tinted the whole room, and he brushed past the tourists who laughed and pointed at the stars, many going nose to nose with their favorites. He followed directions to the next space, where red and gold dominated, except for the looming green figure of Shrek and the even greener and larger Incredible Hulk. Hugo looked for the way through, stepping around the gawkers who lingered in the spaces between Marilyn Monroe and Spiderman, all the while the buzz of voices around him giving the colorful room the air of a Hollywood after-party. He spotted the way out and moved quickly down some stairs into the Sports Zone, where a Formula 1 motor-racing exhibit seemed to be drawing most of the spectators, the waxen Pele almost ignored, save for a small boy who stood gazing upward, his head tilted to one side as if trying to place the soccer legend.

As Hugo pressed on, a sense of surreality wrapped itself around him, a many-layered blanket woven from the lifelike images of the Tussauds exhibits, the blissful ignorance of the tourists who admired them, the bizarre nature of the man he was looking for, and the horror of what that man had planned. Hugo had already noted that cameras were allowed in the museum—not just allowed, but being held in almost every hand, a fact that Walton was no doubt counting on.

In the next exhibit, Hugo bumped into a German couple as he passed several members of British royalty, almost tripped over a little girl taking some kind of interactive test with Albert Einstein, and wanted to block his ears at the music as he sped through the Music Megastars Zone. Finally, adrenaline pumping and barely able to think amid the crowds and visual stimulation, Hugo moved to the last door, the exit out of the World Leaders Room. Two men stood in front of the closed door, calmly steering customers to an alternate exit to their left, their buzz haircuts and cold eyes persuasive enough for most, their bulk and stony silence adequate deterrents to at least one irate tourist, an Eastern European who'd paid to see the Chamber of Horrors and was going to either see it or get his money back.

Hugo caught the eye of the security guard farthest from the now-crowded exit, a rock of a man whose narrow eyes told of an Asian lineage, and showed him his US security badge, hoping these guys had been told he was coming.

The man looked at him, unblinking, then took Hugo's ID in a

meaty paw. He handed it back with the merest of nods. "You want some company down there?"

"No, I'll be fine." *If I'm right about what he's doing.*

"I hear you screaming, I'll be down." The man nodded again and stepped aside, opening the door with the flat of his hand. Hugo started down the stone steps.

The door to the bustling exhibition room closed behind him, darkening the stairwell and bringing a quiet that had been sorely missing for the last five minutes. Hugo took a calming breath and moved slowly downward, aware of the cold air that pressed up to meet him.

The stairs were wide and made of stone, the walls slick blocks of granite like those of a medieval, Thames-side dungeon. The realism of his descent into the museum's most gruesome display extended his earlier surreal feeling, the garish colors of the entertainment world supplanted by indistinct black-and-white images that flickered in the back of his mind, creating a schizoid and dichotomous eeriness that put him as either a soon-to-be victim in a Béla Lugosi horror flick or a doomed explorer in the real world.

He touched the cold wall to bring himself back into reality, sure that tiredness was helping play tricks with his mind. *It's a museum, just a museum.*

His feet echoed softly on the steps and he tried not to scuff them. Halfway down, he paused, listening, glad to hear silence because it meant that the exhibit had emptied. Almost emptied, anyway. As he started forward, he heard a shuffling sound from the foot of the stairs, then the squeak of something metallic opening or closing. He kept going, now able to see the cobbled floor of the chamber, eerie glow from recessed lighting casting shadows in front of him.

As he reached the last step, he looked around for Walton, but his eyes were drawn to the men and woman who lay, or hung, dead and dying around him. A pair of ragged figures were strapped to suspended wheels, their frail bodies broken by the executioners' rods. Gaunt figures, hard to discern whether men or women, hung around the little anteroom, imprisoned in rusting gibbets for the feasting eyes of the curious. Under his feet, Hugo noticed that the cobblestones had been laid in concentric circles, in rings that grew smaller and smaller, the last one encircling a grate in the floor that looked like it would welcome the blood of the tortured hanging from the walls.

The only figure not dressed in rags was the wax statue of a man, standing in a deep stone recess and wearing a dark suit and tie, his collar cinched high and tight in the style of the forties. A perfect mustache gave character to an otherwise weak face, a nose that was small and thin, an insignificant chin. Black eyes bored out from under a bowler hat, glaring at Hugo, as if daring him to inspect the rope that he held in his right hand, his thumb and forefinger gripping it just below the noose. In his left hand, the man carried what looked, to Hugo, to be a white silken bag. The man had been placed between two oak beams that stood erect, a crossbeam joining them, and a square hole in the ground was visible behind him. The trapdoor.

A gentle voice floated down from above Hugo's head. "It's my father. Do you see a resemblance?"

Hugo stepped back to the foot of the stairs and looked up. "Harry. Yes, I do. You look a lot like him."

Walton sat on the cross beam, a rope looped around his own neck. "How did you know?"

"Lucky guess," said Hugo. "How about you come down and we talk about this?"

Walton smirked. "I'll be down in a minute, don't worry."

Hugo looked around and saw the step ladder lying on its side, kicked over after Walton had pulled himself up to his drop spot. Beside it was Walton's tote bag. Hugo sat on the lowest of the stone steps and stretched out his legs. "I'm not going to stop you Harry. You murdered a lot of people."

"No!" Walton shouted the word. "I executed criminals. They are the murderers."

"You're full of crap, Harry. If you're the great executioner, then what are you doing up there? If you were only carrying out justice, then you're a hero, and no one hangs heroes. Not even in Texas."

Walton shifted position and Hugo felt his gut tighten. But the old man just sat there, chewing his lip, watching Hugo with his coal-black eyes.

"Oh, I get it," said Hugo. "Brian Drinker and Pendrith. They didn't deserve to die, so you're going to atone for killing them?"

"That's right."

"You even killed the wrong Stanton, didn't you?"

"That wasn't my fault," Walton spat. "How was I even to know? She could have said something, told me."

"You put a gag in her mouth, Harry," Hugo said, his voice cold. "She *couldn't* tell you. And what would you have done if she'd insisted she wasn't June Stanton? You'd have hanged her anyway, just to be sure."

"The price of justice is high. Are you telling me Texas never killed an innocent man?"

"No idea, Harry, but when we take someone's life, we sure as hell know who it is we're killing." Hugo pointed to his father. "You think the old man would be proud of what you've been doing?"

"Of course he would. It's what he did for a living. It's what he wanted me to do."

"Not exactly," Hugo said. "So how would he feel, then, seeing his son hanging by his neck? Think that's what the old man wants?"

"He knew about justice. And anyway this isn't just about me, or him."

"Sure it is. It's why you came here, to be with him at the end. Come on, Harry, it's pretty obvious even for a dumb Yank."

Walton suddenly grinned. "Yeah, you figured me out, didn't you?"

"I also figured out that you want the publicity. But look around, there's no one here but you and me."

A look of concern flitted across Walton's face, and the old man turned his head to look through the high archway on his right, into the next part of the exhibit. "Where . . . where is everyone?"

"We couldn't let people be around you, Harry. Too many end up dying that way. You know, in the cause of justice."

Walton's eyes flashed. "I didn't come here to hurt anyone else, you know that. But I need them in here."

"I know. But against all my instincts I'm supposed to persuade you not to do this thing, Harry. And it seems to me, without anyone here to watch, there's no point."

"Get them back in here!"

"No."

"I have my gun—do what I say."

"First of all, if you shoot me there'll be no one to get your adoring crowds back in here. Second of all, I'm guessing your gun is in your bag, not on you. Your father would never let an armed man onto the gallows, would he?"

Walton laughed. "You called my bluff, very nice. The problem is, and I know this to be true, it'll get out. Within minutes of me being executed, someone will tell the media and then you can bet there'll be reporters crawling all over the place. An executioner's son hanged in Madame Tussauds. It's a beautiful story, one that will serve my purpose wonderfully."

Hugo softened his tone. "We don't do public executions anymore. They're not coming back and, if you die today, I promise that I'll just cut you down and say you tripped on the stairs. An old journalist falling down some stairs, even at Madame Tussauds, isn't much of a story, is it?"

"You'd lie, Marston?" His voice had changed again and was lighter now, almost mocking. "You'd lie to the media, to the police? You'd lie under oath at an official inquest? Somehow I don't think you would."

Hugo returned the smile. "Calling my bluff now?"

"You're a rule follower, you do it all by the book. You don't get that sometimes to get to justice you have to tread on a few toes. Crack a few heads. Or necks."

"It's not going to happen, Harry. You're not going to change anything, especially with this little stunt. Better you go to jail, preach from there. I'm betting you'd get more followers that way."

"But that wouldn't be justice, would it? That'd make me a hypocrite, that's all."

Hugo shrugged. "I'll say it again. Hanging yourself isn't justice and it won't change anything out there."

"Well," said Walton quietly. "I'll just do the best I can, and leave the rest to God."

Hugo opened his mouth to speak but stopped when Walton shifted position again, putting both hands flat on the cross beam and looking down at his father below. Without another word Walton eased his weight forward and slid from his high perch on the beam, his body stiff and his arms by his sides, as if he were jumping into a lake on a hot summer day. Hugo started forward but didn't get there in time, couldn't have crossed the fifteen feet of cobbled ground in the second it took Walton to drop to the end of his rope, for the noose under the left side of his chin to jerk tight and snap his head back, severing his cervical cord as cleanly as if a surgeon's knife had made the cut.

Harry Walton swung gently on the end of his own rope, his legs brushing against the waxen image of his father, the smartly dressed man who stared defiantly at Hugo as if daring him to cut his son down.

Hugo stood in front of them both for a moment, resisting the urge to speak to them. He shook his head and passed through the rest of the Chamber of Horrors, following the path a million tourists had taken before him to the exit where Bart Denum, four members of museum security, and a dozen armed police officers had no trouble reading the look on his face.

CHAPTER THIRTY-TWO

T hey watched the press conference at the Coachman pub on a television Al had recently installed so his customers could watch the weekend football games.

Chief Constable Dayna Blazey stood at the podium and spoke without breaking eye contact with the assorted journalists, telling them about her force's role in tracking and cornering Harry Walton. Hugo sat beside Ambassador Cooper, glad for Blazey to take the credit if it meant the heat was turned down on everyone who had rubbed her the wrong way, including Upton and himself.

"Working in close proximity with agents from the American embassy," she was saying, "and with officers from Scotland Yard and the Metropolitan police, as well as French authorities in Paris, we were able to discover . . ."

Cooper took a long drink from his early-evening beer. "Looks like Walton got his publicity after all."

"I never doubted it," Hugo said. His own beer was untouched—he was too intent on what Blazey was saying, hoping that his boss wouldn't be maligned, that the memories of those killed would be properly recognized. For Hugo, that was the trouble with these operations; the exploits of the captured or dead murderer stole most of the show, and whatever was left got soaked up by those taking credit for the capture or kill. Which left nothing for those who'd suffered the most: the dead, and those who survived them.

The pub door opened and Hugo glanced over, then stood as the familiar face of Clive Upton peered in.

"I meant to tell you," Cooper said, smiling wickedly, "a couple of friends are on their way."

Upton, dressed in a tweed jacket and corduroy pants, stepped into the pub and Hugo grinned when he saw who was behind him. Merlyn stood in the doorway, her hands on her hips, shooting him her dirtiest look. Then she smiled and skipped past Upton, ignoring Hugo's outstretched hand to give him a bear hug. When she finally released him, Merlyn stood on tiptoe and whispered into his ear. "Didn't bother chasing me up to Edinburgh, huh? I'll get you for that."

Hugo smiled and directed her to the chair next to him. "I knew you were safe," he said. "But I'll buy you a drink to make up for it."

"My round," said a voice behind him. Hugo turned and saw Constable Agarwal in a pair of jeans and a sweatshirt, but still wearing the erect posture of the policeman on duty. Agarwal shook his hand. "Mr. Marston, how are you, sir?"

"It's Hugo. And I'm fine, how're you, Constable Agarwal?"

"You can call me Sandy now, sir."

"Oh?" Hugo turned to Upton. "Someone get promoted to sergeant?"

Upton shook Hugo's hand and grinned. "The chief constable couldn't very well take all the credit for snagging Walton, she had to share a little."

"Which means you're now a superintendent?" Hugo asked.

"It means I got a pat on the back and wasn't fired for letting you steal my car."

Hugo and Agarwal swapped quick looks, then Agarwal excused himself and headed for the bar.

Hugo took his seat beside Merlyn, who reached into her bag and handed him a book. "I believe this is yours," she said. "Clive told me you left it at the pub the other day when you were off chasing Walton. And not me." She flashed her teeth to show she wasn't really mad, and Hugo took the book. It was *Hidden Horror*, the book he'd bought from the bouquiniste named Max, in Paris.

"Thanks," Hugo said, tapping the book with his fingertips. "I'd almost forgotten."

"You don't get enough of that in the real world?" Upton asked.

Cooper raised his glass. "Amen to that. The man is obsessive. Tell them about your little lady in the alley, off Gable Street."

Hugo smiled and picked up the book. "I bought this because it may help me with that."

"You have a new case?" Merlyn chipped in.

"No, an old one," Hugo said. "Very old. A woman killed in that alley a hundred years ago, right about the time of the Ripper. But," he held up a finger, "not killed by the Ripper. You know, in the back of my mind I wondered if there was a connection between her death, the Ripper, and a serial killer who stalked my hometown, Austin, at about the same time. Not that I was the first to theorize a connection, of course; other people have written about those deaths and how the killer might be one and the same."

"The Servant Girl Annihilator, isn't that what they called him?" asked Upton.

"Yes, you know about that case?" Hugo was surprised. "Anyway, over the years I've wondered about that connection and even looked to see if there was any evidence. I never found any, so I looked for other transatlantic possibilities but never came up with any of those, either. But I was always looking for serial killers, cases where there was some kind of overt sexual motive. Then Harry Walton came along and that made me wonder. Motives differ and some killers don't get classified as serial killers, or didn't in years gone by, if their motives were more concrete."

"Like politics?" Upton asked.

"Right." Hugo paused as Agarwal arrived with a tray of beers, apparently noticing the rapt expressions on the faces of Upton, Cooper, and Merlyn. He laid the tray on a neighboring table, sat down, and quietly passed out the pints. "Revenge, too," Hugo said. He waved the book. "And then I was flicking through this and read about a mysterious killer known as the Axeman of New Orleans."

"I'm from there," Cooper said. "And I hate to dash your theory, but the Axeman used to sneak into people's houses and attack them in bed. Your gal was found in an alley and you, of all people, should respect the MO of a serial killer."

"Fair point," said Hugo. "But remember, my victim was found half-naked and without shoes. Her house was nearby, unlocked, and blood was found on her bed. It's possible that the killer got into her house, attacked her without killing her, and when she fled, he chased her into the alleyway and finished her off. That would explain the blood and her attire—and it's consistent with the way he killed and the time period."

"But what is the New Orleans–to–London connection?" Cooper asked. "Any evidence of that?"

Hugo smiled. "Not yet. It's just a theory, and now that this little bit of fun is over, it's one I can explore."

"Where was this woman killed?" asked Merlyn. "You said Gable Street?"

"Right," said Hugo. "You know it? It's close to where Ginny Ferro died, near the Whitechapel cemetery."

"Can we go look?" Merlyn asked. "That case sounds interesting, but I'd also like to pay my respects to Ginny, in the place she died."

Hugo looked up at Chief Constable Blazey. She was wrapping up the press conference, taking a few last questions, her face serious as she told the BBC reporter that she had no idea if there was going to be a Harry Walton exhibit at Madame Tussauds—he'd have to ask the museum that question.

"Sure," Hugo said. "It's a nice afternoon for a walk. Would you gents excuse us?"

Agarwal, Upton, and Cooper all stood as Merlyn worked herself out from behind the table. Hugo nodded his thanks and turned to Cooper. "Need me back at work this week, or am I still on vacation?"

Cooper grinned. "In exchange for your untouched beer, you may return to work."

"Deal," said Hugo. He shook hands with Agarwal and Upton, then waved to Al and the girls behind the bar before following Merlyn out the door into the bright, and warm, afternoon sun.

The traffic was starting to build around them, coughing up its gray exhaust into the atmosphere, so Hugo led them on a less-direct route though the quieter, narrower streets. They walked in silence for a while, a comfortable silence, Merlyn with her head down, apparently deep in thought. As they turned the corner onto Gable Street, she looked up.

"Do you think it will come out? The stuff they were into?" she asked.

"Ginny and Dayton?" Hugo frowned. "I honestly don't know. The press here are pretty relentless, but the focus of their story is Walton. He's their bad guy, and once they start painting Ginny and Dayton as victims, well, let's hope they don't want to make themselves look dumb by then portraying them as perverts."

"You don't think they're perverts, do you?"

"Me?" Hugo stopped and looked at her. "No. As far as I'm concerned, people can do what they want with each other, as long as both parties consent. Why should I care?"

She shrugged. "People do, though. People like to judge."

"I have plenty of other people to judge," Hugo smiled. "Real bad guys. I don't have time to be puritanical."

When they started walking again, Merlyn wrapped her arm around Hugo's. "Do you mind?" she asked, her voice soft.

"No, of course not. You doing OK?"

"I think so. Pretty tired. I was thinking about writing a book about all that's happened."

"Is this an interview then?"

Merlyn laughed. "No, we'll do that in a more appropriate location, not wandering the streets of London."

"Such as?"

"My apartment?" Her eyes were wide, hopeful and teasing at the same time.

"Still married, Merlyn. And still a few years older than you."

"I don't care about the age thing," she said. "And your marriage sucks."

"Says who?"

"Am I wrong?"

Hugo ignored the question. "Apart from the book, what's next for you?"

"Couple of things. I'm thinking of going pro."

"Pro? As in . . . ?"

"Pro domming. Being a dominatrix. Good money, and fun. Only part-time, though and, on the vanilla side, I've always been interested in history, so I may try and get a degree in that. I've always wanted to look into genealogy. It's fascinating, don't you think?"

"Sure. Lots of people in the States like to trace their family histories."

"That's what I'd heard. I could help them, maybe make some money while I'm at it."

"You should do that. Start a business like that." He slowed and pointed with his free arm to the alley's entrance. They started down it and stopped where Meg Prescott had taken her last breath. "Here," Hugo said. "This is where they found her."

They stood quietly for a minute but, as ever, there was nothing to see. The menace that lurked in the alley on dark nights when the clouds hung low or when fog clung to this part of the city was absent today, and with no atmosphere to hold them, Hugo and Merlyn turned to leave.

They walked alongside the brick wall of the cemetery as Hugo described where he'd found Ginny Ferro. At the gates, Merlyn stopped.

"Can I tell you a secret, Hugo?"

"Sure." He smiled. "I think I know most of them though."

"You do." A slight smile played on her lips. "But this one will blow your mind."

"Fire away."

"OK then." She cocked her head, appraising him. "So, all that stuff that goes on at Braxton Hall. Do you feel like you understand it?"

Hugo sighed. "Merlyn, I don't judge you. How many times do I have to say that? I don't know why it matters what I think, but I don't care what you do. I don't care how you or anyone else get their kicks."

She surprised him by smiling. "I just wanted you to know," she said, "that I'm a virgin. That's all."

Hugo felt his mouth fall open and saw Merlyn's grin as he quickly closed it. Her green eyes sparkled and she squeezed his arm.

She looked over her shoulder into the cemetery. "Do you mind if I go in alone?" she said. "Ginny was the only other person I told that to. And I've got some other things I want to tell her, stuff that you don't get to hear about. Not yet, anyway."

"Sure, take your time, I'll be right here."

"Thanks." She flashed another smile, turned, and leaned on the iron gate. It stuck for a second, then swung open with a welcoming squeal.

Hugo watched as she strolled up the gravel path before angling off between the crooked gravestones, her fingertips casually brushing the tops of a few older stones. Her slim figure moved with an easy grace, a natural sway of the hips and a lightness that defied the horrors she'd lived through, flouted the solemnity and gloom that lay over the grave-yard like a fog. She seemed, Hugo thought, almost childlike from this distance.

He turned his back to the cemetery, giving Merlyn her privacy, and smiled to himself as he perched on the low stone wall to wait.

ACKNOWLEDGMENTS

As ever, I send my thanks to the kind people who took time to read the manuscript and point out its flaws and flourishes: Jennifer Schubert and Theresa Holland, your feedback was invaluable. I thank you.

I should also thank the real-world people who were so excited about becoming characters: Dayna Blazey, Chris Collings, James Booher, Jeremy Sylestine, and Bart Denum. I kept you safe in this book, but who knows what'll happen in the next!

Also my thanks go to Inspector Peter Knight of the Hertfordshire Constabulary, who provided quick and helpful responses about police weapons and vehicles, and Liz Edwards at Madame Tussauds for her help on matters waxy. Also to Simon and Margaret Armitage for their input with regard to Weston Church.

Again and ever to Scott Montgomery and the fine people at Book-People here in Austin, who continue to press my books into the hands of eager readers with faith that my stories will entertain. In fact, to booksellers everywhere: you rock.

Penultimately, to the professionals in my life: Dan, Jill, Meghan, and everyone else at Seventh Street Books, and my agents, Ann Collette and Taryn Fagerness, thank you for all you do!

Finally, to the precious ones in my life: Sarah, Natalie, Henry, and Nicola (this one's for you!), I love you all so much and couldn't do this without you.

ABOUT THE AUTHOR

Mark Pryor is the author of *The Bookseller, The Crypt Thief,* and *The Blood Promise,* the first three Hugo Marston novels, as well as the true-crime book *As She Lay Sleeping.* An assistant district attorney with the Travis County District Attorney's Office in Austin, Texas, he is the creator of the true-crime blog *D.A. Confidential.* He has appeared on CBS News's *48 Hours* and Discovery Channel's *Discovery ID: Cold Blood.* Visit him online at www.markpryorbooks.com, www.facebook.com/pages/Mark-Pryor-Author, and http://DAConfidential.com.

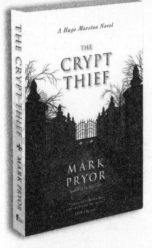
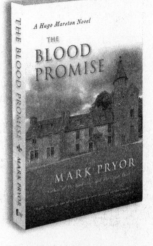